The Fall
of the Year

Books by Howard Frank Mosher

Disappearances

Where the Rivers Flow North

Marie Blythe

A Stranger in the Kingdom

Northern Borders

North Country

The Fall of the Year

The Fall
of the Year

HOWARD FRANK MOSHER

Houghton Mifflin Company

BOSTON   NEW YORK

Library of Congress Cataloging-in-Publication Data

Mosher, Howard Frank
The fall of the year / Howard Frank Mosher.
p.   cm.
ISBN 0-395-98416-5
I. Title
PS3563.O8844F3   1999
813'.54—dc21   99-28502   CIP

The Introduction appeared, in somewhat different form,
in the September 1999 issue of *Vermont Magazine*. A version of
Chapter 2, "The Journey," appeared in the July 1999 issue of *Yankee*.

Book design by Anne Chalmers
Typefaces: Sabon, Cheltenham

Printed in the United States of America

QUM 10 9 8 7 6 5 4 3 2

For

PHILLIS,

the Fortuneteller's Daughter

The Fall
of the Year

Introduction

THE BATTERED wooden sign shaped vaguely like a pointing finger read KINGDOM COMMON 1 MILE, though in fact the village was probably half that distance from where I stood. Weathered nearly illegible by twenty or more northern Vermont winters, the sign was set so far back in the constantly encroaching puckerbrush that from May to October it was barely visible. For most of the rest of the year it was buried under several feet of snow. And as Father George liked to tell me on our way home from a hunting or fishing expedition or an away ball game, it was as if we didn't really want anyone from beyond the county line visiting our town in the first place. And as I grew older and wiser in the ways of Kingdom Common, I came to believe he was right.

This much was certain: coming up into the remote and rugged mountains of Kingdom County by highway in the late 1950s, unless you'd been there before and knew exactly where you were going, you were far more apt to miss my hometown than to find it.

I listened to the Greyhound that had brought me through the dense woods from St. Johnsbury in the darkness before dawn as it shifted gears on the grade north of the cutoff to the village. A few moments later the bus passed out of earshot, headed toward the Canadian border. Except for the murmur of the nearby Kingdom River, invisible in the thick fog, everything was still.

I picked up my bag and started walking, a little uncertain about what lay ahead of me but glad to be home.

❦

Fifteen minutes later I was sitting on the unpainted bleachers beside the baseball diamond at the south end of the village green, the site of some of my fondest boyhood memories. Just two days before this morning in early May, on my twenty-first birthday, I had graduated from the state university. I had returned home to spend the summer with Father George Lecoeur, who for nearly forty years had been the priest of our local Catholic church, Saint Mary's of the Green Mountains.

Like Kingdom County itself, Father George, my great-uncle by marriage and my adoptive father, was something of a paradox. A big, ruggedly built man, well over six feet tall, with bright blue eyes and snowy hair parted in the middle, at sixty-eight Father George looked like a judge in the old photographs in the courthouse hallway. Like the village's real judge, Forrest Allen, he was courteous in an old-fashioned way — until he got mad, at which times his face became very red and he took the name of the Lord in vain and threatened any and all who dared oppose him with a "good old-fashioned public horsewhipping." But most of the time, the priest was a man of notable sympathy and common sense, who made himself available twenty-four hours a day to everyone who needed advice or assistance. For many years he had been compiling a chronicle of life in the village entitled "A Short History of Kingdom Common"—which had grown to nearly three thousand pages!

The son of French Canadian immigrants, Father George had an unusual history of his own. He had been born and raised on a farm in Lost Nation Hollow, ten miles northeast of the Common, and at fifteen had become the teacher of the local one-room school. Two years later he had walked into the Common barefoot, with his one pair of shoes in a paper bag, and started working at the furniture mill at night and attending the Kingdom Academy by day. He had put himself through college by playing minor league baseball in Canada in the summers and boxing in the northern New England semipro circuit in the winters, then had returned to the Common to teach and coach at the Academy. Soon afterward he bought the old Anderson house, known locally as the Big House, with money he'd made smuggling Canadian whiskey into Vermont using a float plane with homemade pontoons.

In 1917, at twenty-seven, Father George joined the Royal Canadian Air Force and flew more than eighty sorties over Germany and France before being shot down near Château Thierry. He was found unconscious, deep in the forest, by a party of Benedictine woodcutters, who hid him in their monastery and nursed him back to health, an experience that transformed his life. Back in the States, he enrolled in St. Paul's Seminary in Burlington, and three years later he was installed as the priest of St. Mary's, where he soon became known as "the unorthodox priest and greatest scholar and third baseman in the history of Kingdom County."

To conform, at least nominally, to his poverty vows, the unorthodox priest leased the Big House to the diocese for a dollar a year. He continued to coach at the Academy, play baseball for the powerful Kingdom Common Outlaws, fly his float plane, and fish and hunt with his neighbors.

When my Canadian parents, both teachers, were killed in a highway accident in Montreal just before I turned two, Father George took me in, and within a year he formally adopted me. I grew up with him in the Big House, and for as long as I could remember, I had wanted to follow in his footsteps. In fact I planned to enter St. Paul's myself in the fall.

As I sat on the bleachers watching the village come slowly awake in the rising mist, a faint breeze drifted across the green, bringing with it the distinctive scents of Kingdom Common. Whenever I returned to the village after being away for two weeks, or two days, or even two hours, I knew immediately, with that first whiff, that I was home again: the woodsy aroma of a million feet of hardwood boards, curing in the yard of the American Heritage furniture factory; the heady fragrance of the orange shellac that the maple office chairs and desks were dipped in before being varnished; the sharper odors of diesel fumes and hot tar from the railroad switching yard; and the blended pungencies of cattle, hay, and manure from the com-mission-sales auction barn next to the hotel. In Kingdom Com-mon the distinction between village and country often blurred to no distinction at all.

I knew, of course, that throughout the Kingdom, family dairy farms were going under at an alarming rate and the county's outlying four-corner hamlets, with their ramshackle stores and one-man sawmills and one-room schools, were vanishing like the once-cleared fields around them. Yet change, like spring, came very slowly to Kingdom Common, which still resembled a rural New England town of, say, the Great Depression era far more than a typical American community poised on the brink of the Space Age.

Although the Common was both the county seat and a railway junction, with a courthouse, a high school, two churches, the furniture mill, and a hotel, it had no motels, no resorts, no fancy restaurants or gift shops for tourists to browse in, and, for weeks on end, especially in the winter, no tourists. The ski complex at Jay Peak, twenty-five miles to the west, was still in the planning stages. Jay was just another wild granite crag a few miles south of an isolated and mountainous stretch of the Quebec border. And, truth to tell, few of the three hundred or so Commoners who lived in the village proper had the slightest interest in downhill skiing anyway. Our principal recreations were still trout fishing and deer hunting, and they were both very good indeed.

As a boy growing up in the Big House, I could sometimes see, from my bedroom in the cupola atop the second story, a faint suffusion of coral-colored light in the night sky far off to the northwest beyond the mountains. Father George had told me that this mysterious illumination, which was especially noticeable on hazy evenings in the fall, was probably caused by the lights of Montreal reflecting off thin clouds high above the city. But Montreal was one hundred miles away over bad mountain roads, and to me, as to most Commoners, that hundred miles might as well have been a thousand.

In my early years, the village and the surrounding hills,

woods, and streams made up my universe—a universe that now seems to have vanished almost entirely. But the summer I came home from college, it had changed scarcely at all.

Frank Bennett
Kingdom Common, 1999

❖ 1 ❖
The Savant of
Kingdom Common

Like most small towns in those years, the village of Kingdom
Common could be a remarkably tolerant place to live and
work and raise a family. Or it could be as cruel as any place
on the face of the earth.

—Father George Lecoeur,
"A Short History of Kingdom Common"

For starters, Frank," Father George was saying to me,
"I'd like you to see what you can do to help Foster Boy
Dufresne. Lately he's been getting out of the traces pretty frequently—looking into people's windows after dark, lying down
in the road to get people to stop and give him a ride, that kind
of thing. I think he needs a big brother to look out for him for a
while."

Father G got up and put another stick of wood in the kitchen
stove. On the way back to the table he got two more beers out
of the refrigerator and opened one for each of us, though at
sixty-eight, with chronic angina, he was under strict doctor's orders not to touch a drop of alcohol.

"So I've arranged for you to take him trout fishing in the
morning," he said as he handed me my beer.

Take Foster Boy Dufresne trout fishing! It was the evening of my second day back in the Common, and we'd finished supper an hour before. We had been engrossed in our two favorite topics, baseball and trout fishing, when Father G had abruptly brought up his proposal, leaving me totally astounded. But when I finally found my tongue and said something to the effect that if I didn't watch him every second, Foster would no doubt fall in the brook and drown, Father George just laughed.

"The falling in the brook part's true enough, son. But if you're serious about entering St. Paul's in the fall, helping people like Foster is a big part of a priest's job. And much as I hate to admit it, at this point I can't do it all myself."

"There aren't any other people like Foster," I groaned. "He's unique."

Father G's eyes snapped, and I could see him beginning to lose patience. "Damn it all, Frank, what difference does that make? I told him you'd be at his place at eight tomorrow morning."

Then he looked at me seriously with his shrewd blue eyes and said, "Everyone needs a friend, son. Maybe that's all you can be to Foster. But at least that would be something. What do you say?"

In fact, when it came to Foster Boy Dufresne and his antics, no one in Kingdom Common knew what to say. Not Father George or Doc Harrison or Judge Allen or Editor Charles Kinneson, not even Foster Boy's parents, Ti Donat and Silent Jeannine Dufresne, who lived across the river in a row house in Little Quebec and did piecework at the furniture factory.

But Foster Boy was no idiot. Before he was three he could recite the alphabet forward and backward, as well as the capitals of all the states in the union. At four, he'd astonished Father George by reading aloud, with perfect inflection, stories from the Book of Genesis. By the time he started first grade at the Academy he could multiply three-digit numbers in his head at the speed of lightning.

A reporter for the *Boston Globe* caught wind of the child wonder and made the long trek north to see for himself if the rumors were true. His article, "The Savant of Kingdom Common," was the talk of the town for weeks afterward. An authentic prodigy in the wilds of northern Vermont — astonishing!

But for all his precocity, Foster Boy never made the least headway in school. If John had two apples and Will traded him two more, John didn't necessarily wind up with four pieces of fruit. Not in Foster's scheme of reckoning, anyway. Maybe, the savant would suggest with a wild laugh, maybe old Johnny-boy gobbled his apples all down on the spot and had nothing to show for his pains but a bellyache. Foster's yellow eyes gleamed like a billy goat's. "Hoo hoo hoo" — you could hear him roaring all the way down the Academy corridor to Prof Chadburn's office.

About the time Foster turned twelve, Bumper Stevens, our local cattle auctioneer, conferred another title on him, that of village idiot. You might think that the savant would be offended, but Foster was proud of his new role and played it to the hilt. Yet as Foster Boy himself often remarked, being the official town fool wasn't always a bed of roses, even if you happened to be a savant.

Looking back later on, I was ashamed of myself for the tricks I played on him when I was a kid.

"Foster Boy! I'll give you a quarter to lick all the frost off the iron hitching rail in front of the hotel."

"Foster, my friend. Here's a brand-new dollar bill, goes to the first fella to pee on the electric fence behind the auction barn."

The worst was when I told Foster to stick his hand into Old Man Quimby's thatch-roofed beehive, and the bees would give him all the honey he could eat. Out they came in a great furious swarm and stung Foster so badly he had to be rushed to Doc Harrison's for a shot to save his life. When word of my prank got back to Father George, he told me that the next time he'd give me an "old-fashioned public horsewhipping I'd remember for weeks afterwards."

You'd think even Foster Boy would learn better, but he didn't. All he ever seemed to learn was how to grow, and this he accomplished at a truly amazing rate. At fourteen, when he left the Academy for good, he was pushing two hundred and fifty pounds and stood well over six feet tall, with a head as big around as a schoolhouse jack-o'-lantern. That was the year he began walking the roads with a Blue Seal feed sack slung over his shoulder, scavenging the countryside for empty bottles and other discards for the local junk dealer, always with a saying on the tip of his tongue.

"What goes around comes around," he liked to shout out. "And Foster Boy Dufresne goes around."

As everyone in the Common knew, Foster had at least one strike against him from the start. For several years after getting married, Ti Donat and Silent Jeannine had no children. At last, however, with the assistance of Father George and, it was rumored, Louvia DeBanville, the local fortuneteller, who had all kinds of unlikely connections on both sides of the border, they managed to adopt a baby boy from Quebec. But for reasons known only to themselves, the Dufresnes took it into their heads to bless their new son with a name that, of all those they might have selected, seemed the least propitious. A name that could only remind the child forever that he was not his parents' true flesh and blood and was therefore different from other children: Foster. Foster Boy Dufresne.

🍁

"Frank!" Foster shouted at the top of his lungs as he came barreling down the dirt path from his parents' house the next morning, waving his homemade fishing pole over his gigantic head. "Frank Bennett. Father G said you'd be coming by to take me fishing this morning. Like a big brother. What's it like being big brother to the village idiot, Frank?"

Foster's laughter pealed out over Little Quebec like loon laughter on a still Canadian lake. What a great hulking fellow he was at eighteen, in a filthy T-shirt, bib overalls fastened over his shoulders with baling twine, and a pair of castoff shoes from the town dump on his feet, his bare ankles riddled with black-fly bites. It was easy to see why the town made fun of him, shameful though it was.

With Foster Boy running his mouth a mile a minute, we started up the trail beside Little Quebec Brook, on the ridge above Louvia DeBanville's shanty. Did I know that he had been studying the Bible again recently? To learn why God had created village idiots and bottle pickers in the first place? Hoo hoo! Nearby, a nesting Cooper's hawk shrieked at us with displeasure. Foster shrieked back and laughed louder than ever.

Higher on the ridge the hardwoods were just budding out. Crimson flowerlets from tall sugar maples lay strewn over the logging trace near the brook. Painted trillium with raspberry-stained throats were in bloom. Warblers—green, blue, black, yellow—flashed through the treetops. The woods rang with their mating calls. I tried to call Foster's attention to the songbirds and wildflowers, but he was preoccupied with weightier considerations. He confided to me that he expected to find the answers to his questions in the Book of Job, which he was currently reexamining.

Soon we were fishing our way down the brook. Foster Boy plunged through the pools and riffles, his wake spreading out twenty feet behind him. The elegant dark shapes of panicked trout darted away for cover. Catching any of them was out of the question. Foster wondered, Did a trout have a soul? Did a village idiot?

Louvia the Fortuneteller was out behind her shack, knee-deep in the brook, netting the big flopping suckers that she smoked over a smoldering fire of green ash sticks and hawked from door to door in Little Quebec as delicacies. "Aiee!" she cried out in her harsh voice as the monstrous Foster Boy crashed through her sucker pool. She held her crossed index fingers high over her head and shook them first at Foster, then at me. I knew very well that the old gypsy's hexes were nothing but foolishness, but a chill went up my back even so.

Foster whirled around in the water, made the hex sign back at

Louvia, and went laughing down the brook to Little Quebec, leaving me to face the fortuneteller's wrath alone.

❦

Town-team baseball was still a going concern in Kingdom Common in those days. The Kingdom Common Outlaws played their home games on the village green, where on a sunny Saturday afternoon during the season it wasn't unusual for two or three hundred fans to turn out for a contest with a cross-county rival like Memphremagog or Pond in the Sky. I'd played shortstop for the Academy and my college team; and a few days after my fishing excursion with Foster, Father George, who still managed the Outlaws, recruited me for the team's opening game.

In the bottom of the first inning we jumped out to a 2–0 lead. Then who should show up but Foster Boy, apparently with the express intention of rooting for me, his new friend and fishing partner. What a spectacle he made of himself, hollering, "Yay, Bennett!" like a madman, clanking a great tin cowbell, throwing his extra-large baseball cap, made for him by our town tailor, Abel Feinstein, high into the air whenever I made a routine play, and exchanging taunts with Sal the Berry Picker, who for decades had led the cheering by parading up and down in front of the bleachers waving her long apple-gathering crook and chanting "Go Outlaws!"

"Dummy!" Sal yelled at Foster Boy when he chimed in with his cowbell. "Turd head!"

"Jezebel! Hag of Endor!" Foster shouted back, clanging his bell in Sal's wizened brown face.

In their contention for ascendancy in the cheerleading department, it was a wonder they didn't tear each other to pieces. "Hey, college boy!" Sal shouted when I allowed myself to be distracted by Foster's antics and booted a grounder. "Take your dogface friend and go home. We might as well have him out there as you."

"You're right about that, Sal," shouted Father George, who brooked no nonsense and tolerated no mental lapses on the part of his ballplayers. "What the hell is the matter with you, Bennett?"

This unpriestly outburst broke up the hometown crowd; but at twenty-one I found no fun in being shouted at by my father in front of half the village. Finally Father George called me over to the bench and advised me to bribe Foster Boy into toning down by inviting him to the weekly bingo game in the basement social hall of the church the following Tuesday. After that Foster contented himself with bellowing a play-by-play account of the game from the top row of the bleachers while the Outlaws rolled to a lopsided 18–2 victory.

❧

What an eye opener the bingo game turned out to be! For starters, Foster Boy insisted on playing eighteen cards simultaneously. Although he deposited his colored wooden markers on the faded cardboard squares at a furious pace, eventually he fell behind the caller, Father George. Then Foster kept track of his boards in his head—an astonishing feat, even for an ex-savant.

The scowls in his direction each time he thundered out "Bingo!" were something to see. Worse yet, he exulted in his victories by hooting like a great horned owl, croaking like a raven, producing an uncanny imitation of a swamp bittern's gulping cry.

"Under the N, forty-five!" Foster boomed out after Father G. "Under the B, twelve."

Louvia the Fortuneteller, herself a fanatical bingo addict with her own counters and good luck charms, stalked up to our table and threatened to put a twelve-month hoodoo on both of us if we didn't leave immediately. Foster reared back in his chair and bayed like a Canada lynx. When he strolled off with the fifty-dollar jackpot at the end of the evening, an outraged moan went up from the entire hall.

On our way back to the rectory together, I asked Father George why God *had* created village idiots, and he flew off the handle. "Well, Jesus Christ, Frank," he shouted, "how the hell would I know? You'll just have to ask God. I'm not God, you know."

"Maybe not, but the older you get, the more you act like Him around here," I said. "I thought that, being a priest, you might ask Him for me."

"He'd probably tell me to mind my own business," Father George said. Then he put his arm around my shoulder and laughed. "You're asking an age-old question, son. No one but God knows the answer. As for Foster, you know what I think he really needs?"

"No," I said. "But I'm afraid you're going to tell me."

"I am. I think Foster needs a regular paying job to keep himself out of trouble. Why don't you see if you can get him a job sweeping up over at the mill? He ought to be able to handle that."

❧

Despite my great faith in Father George's judgment, I had all kinds of misgivings about trying to wangle a job for Foster Boy at the mill. If the village of Kingdom Common was a world unto itself, containing the several smaller worlds of the railroad yard, commission-sales barn, courthouse, Academy, and furniture mill, the mill contained several distinct realms of its own. One of these was the exceedingly dangerous machine floor, where Foster was assigned a sweeping job on the graveyard shift. The floor was two hundred feet long and nearly a hundred feet wide, a tintinnabulation of shrieking saws, planers, lathes, sanders, and drills, badly lighted and poorly ventilated, with a choking mist of sawdust suspended in the air at all times. Over the previous sixty years it had claimed the lives of half a dozen French Canadians from Little Quebec, and the fingers, hands, or eyes of a hundred more.

Foster's job was to collect the discarded end pieces of lumber from around the saws and wheel them down to the waste disposal pit known as the Hog. At the bottom of the Hog, ten long, whirling knives reduced the wood scraps to chips, which were then fed through a blower pipe to the furnace that fired the steam boiler powering the woodworking machines. Some years ago a sweeper had tumbled into the Hog and helped fire the boiler himself, but this accident had not inspired the mill management to put any safety guards around the pit. So I was actually relieved when, on the second night of his new job, Foster Boy was summarily fired for a prank that could easily have resulted in a calamity.

Father George and I heard about the episode from Doc Harrison, over coffee at the Common Hotel the next morning. At the instigation of a few of the graveyard-shift bullies, Foster Boy had smeared his face and hands red with ketchup from the ketchup sandwiches Silent Jeannine had put up for him to eat during his break, then pretended to have fallen into the Hog. He was still playing dead when Doc arrived in his bathrobe and slippers; then just as Doc rushed onto the machine floor, Foster Boy leaped up, all bloody-faced, and trumpeted out in a demonic voice that he'd been resurrected.

Father George shook his head. "I guess my idea to put Foster to work at the mill wasn't such a good one after all, Frank. But if the boy's really serious about studying scripture, our ecumenical Bible study group meets tonight. I'll wager dollars to doughnuts that Foster would be tickled pink if you went by his place after supper and invited him to attend."

❧

Tricked out in his overalls, gunboat brogans, and beloved baseball cap, fresh from his triumphal performance on the machine floor, Foster Boy not only monopolized the Bible discussion that evening, he insisted on raising racy scriptural issues. Precisely what, he demanded to know in the middle of a solemn paper on the Sermon on the Mount being delivered by Miss Lily Broom, the young Sunday School superintendent of the United Church, did Delilah do to Samson in bed to get him under her thumb? What did she know that the Hebrew girls didn't?

Miss Lily gasped. But Foster Boy, whose impulsiveness knew no bounds, shouted out, "Here's an easier one. What, if anything besides her birthday suit, was Bathsheba wearing when King David gawked over at her sunbathing on her rooftop?"

Father George suppressed a snicker. But the dozen or so other ecumenical scholars stared at Foster in consternation.

Deacon Roy Quinn, head of the United Church board of trustees, grabbed the savant's shoulders and shook him. "For heaven's sake, Foster!"

"Exactly," Foster Boy shot back. "What, for heaven's sake, were the pleasures of the flesh Satan used to tempt Our Lord in the wilderness? Did the old red devil conjure up a troupe of hootchy-kootchy girls? Like the tent-show strippers at Kingdom Fair?"

Reverend Miles Johnstone sprang to his feet. He pointed a finger at Foster and then at the door.

"Be seated, Lot! Back to your daughters," Foster commanded Rev. Johnstone, and he laughed like a hyena as I hustled him out of the room.

"That sanctimonious outfit of hypocrites could all benefit from an old-fashioned horsewhipping," Father George told me on our way for coffee at the hotel the next morning. "Even so, I'm concerned that Foster may—my God, Frank! Look at that, will you."

Reeling blindly around the statue of Ethan Allen on the north end of the green was a full-grown moose. The animal, which seemed to be in the final stages of brain distemper, had evidently staggered into town in the night. A dozen or so Commoners had gathered on the sidewalk in front of the hotel to watch it, and not a minute later, who should heave into sight, feed sack and all, but Foster Boy Dufresne.

"Foster, my man," Bumper Stevens called out. "Here's a bill of the realm with Honest Abe Lincoln's picture on her, belongs to the first fella to march up to that Christly overgrown deer and plant a big kiss on its snout."

Bumper waved the five-dollar bill over his head. "Hey, hey, hey," he chanted in his raspy auctioneer's voice. "Going once, going twice, going three times to the one, the only, Savant of Kingdom Common."

This was all the encouragement Foster needed. Emitting his crazy laugh, he struck off straight toward the sick moose, which lowered its head and began to paw up great divots of grass around the base of the statue. Whereupon Foster promptly lowered his own head and scuffed at the grass with his broken old shoes.

"Jesus Christ!" shouted our unorthodox priest, to the great delight of the crowd, and started across the street to rescue Foster.

By then I'd seen enough myself. I raced past Father G, grabbed Foster by the back of his overalls, and dragged him, still whooping and laughing, off the green. The moose, in the meantime, gave an anguished bellow, broke into a wobbling charge, crashed head-on into the statue and, mercifully, collapsed dead at its base.

Later that morning Judge Allen signed papers authorizing the local sheriff to pick Foster Boy up and cart him off to be evaluated at the state mental hospital. Not that the judge, as he confided to Father George and me over beers at the hotel that evening, expected the hospital doctors to be of the slightest help to Foster. But if nothing else, the savant's "sabbatical" would give him a much-needed breather from the village and the village a much-needed breather from him.

🍂

In the first of more than twenty notes and letters that Foster Boy bombarded me with from the state hospital during the next two weeks, he spoke of his doubts concerning divine providence, suggesting that his own existence might contradict such a concept. He called his letters "Epistles to the Ephesians." In fact, most of them dealt with his ongoing metaphysical concerns and biblical studies, which seemed to have taken a radical new turn. Instead of scriptural passages dealing with intimacies between the sexes, Foster was now preoccupied by those that revealed what he deemed to be instances of God's injustice to man.

I had no idea how to respond to Foster Boy's theological concerns. Father George undoubtedly could have helped me, but he was laid up with another bout of angina. Not knowing what else to do, I wrote back to Foster with tidbits of village gossip that I thought might amuse him. After winning the hundred-dollar monthly bingo jackpot, Sal the Berry Picker had ordered the first television set in Kingdom Common. Unfortunately, her hemlock-bark shack overlooking the town dump had no electricity, and there was no TV reception in the village in those days anyway. At the same time a rumor had been noised abroad that Louvia the Fortuneteller had been observed driving a black potash kettle fast through the twilit sky above Little Quebec just before the worst thunderstorm to hit the Common in years. And on the day after the storm, Alf Quimby's honey bees had emerged from their hive, swarmed with a squadron of their wild brethren on the courthouse tower, and flown off toward Canada.

One morning toward the end of May I received six letters from Foster. "If God had really wanted to test Job's mettle, He'd have arranged for the old boy to be a bottle picker in Kingdom Common," one note concluded. "Don't you agree, Friend Frank?"

Friend Frank. This was how Foster had begun addressing me. "You're my closest friend, Frank," he wrote. "And I guess I'm yours. Like David and Jonathan."

"No girlfriend yet, though," he wrote the following day. "Maybe I ought to come back and set my cap for a hometown girl. Say a long-legged Sunday School teacher, like Miss Lily Broom. Or a plump juicy widow woman like Julia Hefner. Or should I throw in the towel when it comes to the girls and live on a pillar like St. Simeon Stylites? Or change my name, like Saul on the road to Damascus? Or to Job? Job Boy Dufresne? What do you think, Friend Frank?"

Memorial Day was just around the corner. The backyard apple trees were dropping their pink and white petals. From Little Quebec to the big houses on Anderson Hill, peas and lettuce were up and flourishing. Commoners had cut their lawns several times, the ratchety *click click click* of the hand-pushed mowers in the early evening after supper reminding me of so many miniature trains as I practiced with the Outlaws for our upcoming holiday double-header with Magog.

Father George was keeping me busy doing yard work and cutting wood for elderly parishioners, but then, two days before the start of the long weekend, the village woke to half a foot of new snow. The north wind out of Canada, known locally as the Arctic Express, had brought the Common its usual late-spring blizzard even later than usual, burying the young peas in Father George's garden and the yellow and blue pansies Judge Allen had set out around the base of his great-great-great-grandfather Ethan's statue, and transforming the pitcher's mound at the opposite end of the common into a miniature white ski jump. I spent most of the morning shoveling snow for shut-ins.

Around noon the village lost its electricity. When I returned to the rectory I found a note from Father George saying he'd gone down the hill to the church. As I lighted a kerosene lamp and set it on the kitchen table, a silence akin to the deep stillness of a winter night seemed to settle over the entire town.

Just then there was a loud rapping on the window by the table. A moment later the door flew open, revealing a towering figure completely encased in white. "Hello, Friend Frank," the snowman said. "What goes around comes around, you know. I've come around to find that hometown girl."

Foster Boy stepped inside, shaking off snow like a Saint Bernard, already hooting his wild laugh.

His storm gear consisted only of his Outlaws cap, a thin spring jacket, and a gigantic pair of galoshes with all the buckles missing. His gloveless hands were chapped red as the glowing stove. Yet what seemed to concern Foster most today was not his own plight but that of the songbirds on the ridge where he and I had gone fishing earlier that month. Wouldn't they freeze or starve in the blizzard? "Why would God do this to them, Frank? Would a truly loving father kill off his own creatures like flies?"

"I don't know that God personally manages the weather, Foster."

"Why not? Doesn't He know about every sparrow that falls?"

Foster grinned at his lamp-lit reflection in the window. "Hoo! God would need a savant to keep track of the fallen sparrows today. But let's get down to brass tacks, Frank. The question on the docket this morning is why God doesn't see fit to bring me a girlfriend. Say a young widow, all tanned from the Holy Land sunshine. Like Queen Bathsheba after King David knocked off her husband."

"Foster, when it comes to God's motivations, no one—"

Foster brushed aside my equivocations with an impatient gesture, repeated in mime by his distorted replica in the window. "Don't you think it was unfair that God rubbed out David's best friend, Jonathan? After all, what did Jonathan have to do with King David's transgressions?"

Foster shut one yellow eye and gave me a canny look with the other. He tucked his index finger under his middle finger and tapped me on the arm. "Frank Bennett and Foster Boy Dufresne," he said. "David and Jonathan."

He smiled. "Which one of us is going to wind up like Jonathan, Frank?"

"Foster—"

"So why doesn't God bring me a woman?" Foster Boy demanded again. Now he seemed to be speaking directly to his reflection.

"Maybe God has better things to do with His time right now."

"Like what? Killing off robin redbreasts in the spring storm of the century?"

Suddenly I realized that Foster Boy had undergone a transformation. There was a new intensity about him, a hardness in his saffron eyes and in the set of his mouth when he spoke of his on-going dialogue with the God he had never doubted. Today Foster Boy was not pleading. He was insisting, insisting that God let him know what was what. With a jolt of astonishment—astonishment with myself, mainly, for not having understood this before—I realized that my friend the bottle picker was suscepti-ble to all of the uncertainties and desires and frustrations of any other eighteen-year-old. And he was no longer willing to let God off the hook lightly.

"Let's level with each other," Foster Boy was saying. "We're all God's children, right?" But instead of looking at me, he turned for confirmation to the dim, bloated image of himself in the window.

"Right," the reflection replied.

"Well, then, my boy," Foster said to his reflection, "what could be more important to a loving father than making his son happy?"

"No one knows how God works," I protested.

"In ways wondrous to behold," Foster Boy's image informed me with an ironical bow. Then it broke into such a fit of laugh-ter that I was afraid that it or, rather, Foster, might have a seizure.

An inspired expression came across Foster's face. "Friend Frank. God helps those who help themselves, right? So what if I were to wander off in the bush up by the border? Like Our Lord in the wilderness. Would the Evil One vouchsafe me a vision of young dancing girls?"

"What in the hell are you talking about, Foster Boy?"

Foster jerked his head toward his reflection. "Ask him."

"He means would the Author of All Evil tempt him with the pleasures of the flesh," the image boomed out in a demonic voice.

The reflection nodded in solemn agreement with itself. Then it seemed to address both Foster and me. "Life is still good when everything's said and done. Wouldn't you gentlemen concur?"

"Certainly," Foster said in his own voice. "But—"

"But me no but's," interrupted the flickering image. "We have to believe that, for all its tribulations, life is good. Friendships are good."

My head was swimming. But the grotesquerie in the window roared out, "David and Jonathan!"

"Never mind him, Frank," Foster said. "Listen to me. This is important. Our Lord wasn't the only one to strike into the bush alone. Remember Prophet Elijah?"

I nodded vaguely.

"What became of Prophet Elijah after he wandered off?"

I had to think for a minute. "Supposedly he ascended directly to heaven."

"Supposedly is right. Don't you think it more likely that the old boy just hit the road for Beersheba or Stowe or some other resort town and went into retirement?"

Abruptly, Foster stood up. "What if I took a page out of Elijah's book? What if I lit out without telling anybody? To Niagara Falls, say, the Honeymoon Capital of the U.S.A.? Or Florida, the Sunshine State? What if I hooked up with a bathing beauty from California and put this hellhole they call a village behind me forever? Who'd have the last laugh then?"

Foster held out his slab of a hand and shook hands with me. He doffed his cap to the reflection in the window. "He who laughs last laughs best," he said.

And he vanished into the blizzard.

&

Overnight the storm clouds lifted, and the weather turned warm again in Kingdom Common. By six o'clock the next morning, when Father George and I arrived at the hotel dining room for our coffee, sunlight was pouring through the wavy old plate-glass window. In the palest of pale blue sheets, water from the melting snow ran down the gutter from Anderson Hill. At the far end of the green, a bluebird appeared on the backstop behind home plate, just as Doc Harrison showed up with the news of Foster's latest misadventure.

Sometime around midnight the night before, Doc said, Foster had burst in on Bumper Stevens's weekly all-night poker game at the commission-sales barn, full of crazy talk about God bringing him a mature older woman. Harlan Kittredge had promised he'd have just such a seasoned beauty waiting for Foster half an hour later in the auction barn's hayloft. Someone who'd had her eye on him for a long time and was dying to show him the ropes. Then Harlan had dispatched Little Shad Shadow, Bumper's softheaded ring man, up to the dump to roust out Sal the Berry Picker. At Harlan's instructions, Little Shad had told Sal that Foster Boy had designs on her and had offered her five dollars to lie in ambush for him in Bumper's loft.

"After she was ensconced there," Doc told us, "the good-for-nothings sent Foster up the ladder. When he got to the top, old

Sal jumped up out of the hay and lambasted him with her apple crook and knocked him down into the straw and filth below. Foster Boy picked himself up and ran out of the barn, and that's the last anyone's seen of him."

✿

I spent that day and all the next day and the day after that searching for Foster Boy, with no results. As each day went by and my friend did not turn up, I found myself seething every time I thought of the joke the commission-sales rowdies had played on him. I was tempted to file a formal complaint with the sheriff. But what could the sheriff have done about it even if he'd been inclined to? As Father George pointed out to me, a prank can be criminal without being against the law. The important thing now was to locate Foster before he came to any harm.

On the second day after he went missing, I had an unsettling experience. In the melting snow in the woods above Louvia the Fortuneteller's place, I came across an indistinct set of what appeared to be large overshoe tracks. The boot prints, if that is what they were, headed up the trail along the brook where Foster Boy and I had fished earlier that spring. But by then the snow from the freak blizzard was going off quickly, and the tracks simply ended near the top of the ridge in a clear-cut grown up to wild raspberry bushes. Whether they were Foster's was impossible to say.

That evening Father George and I sat up late in the rectory kitchen while I thought out loud about Foster. Might he be posting hard for Florida in search of a girlfriend? Or en route to

Utah to examine the tenets of Mormonism on the shores of the Great Salt Lake, his laughter ringing out over the desert? Father George shook his head. He was afraid not.

All right, I conceded. Maybe, even as we spoke, Foster was putting some hard questions to God Himself. Demanding, absolutely demanding, that, as promised in scripture, the heretofore ineluctable mysteries of the universe and his place in it be disclosed to him at last. Might not Foster be posing to God the questions mankind had asked of Him since the tribulations of Job, the questions at the heart of human existence? If so, what would God say?

Father George hesitated. Then he shook his head again. "It's hard enough to guess at what people will do, Frank. As for God, I have no idea. Neither does anyone else."

❦

Well. As Foster Boy himself had often said, life must go on. One morning in early June I lifted my eyes to the ridges rising in serried ranks to the mountains west of the Common and saw that the last of the spring snow was gone from the summit of Jay Peak.

I decided to go trout fishing. It was black-fly time; in the dooryards of Little Quebec, the smokers had been started up, rusty steel barrels in which damp chunks of black spruce were kept smoldering night and day to discourage the black flies and mosquitoes. The roadside ditches that Foster Boy had combed for bottles were pink and purple with wild lupines. High on the ridge above Louvia DeBanville's, the new leaves of the hardwoods were still more yellow than green, and the sunlight fell through the foliage in a rich golden haze. Drifting down the trail above my head at intervals of about thirty seconds came a progression of brilliant yellow-and-black tiger swallowtail butterflies. The brook trout rose readily to whatever flies I tossed into the stream, splashing right up to my feet to get at them.

Not far from the clear-cut where I'd lost the overshoe tracks ten days before, I set down my fly rod and fish basket and struck into the woods to check once again for any sign of Foster Boy. Of course I found nothing; but I spent an hour or so searching anyway, looking for something I knew I would not find, shrouded by the dense Vermont woods and the mysteries and sorrows of mankind, which no priest or prophet, no scholar or savant, not the wisest men and women in small villages or great cities the world over, can ever truly fathom.

❧2❧
The Journey

When Sylvie and Marie Bonhomme were quite young, maybe eight and seven, they were caught out on Little Quebec Mountain in a blizzard. They were in the gravest danger of freezing to death when a little blue Madonna appeared to them, illuminated like a Christmas tree angel, and led them straight as a string through the storm to their house in Little Quebec.

—Father George, "A Short History"

ONE SUNDAY AFTERNOON, a week or so after Foster Boy vanished, Father George dispatched me in his Roadmaster to visit Louvia DeBanville, who had sent word to the Big House that she wanted a ride into town immediately, if not sooner. Louvia's shanty was perched on a low wooded knoll overlooking the Boston and Montreal railroad tracks, the American Heritage mill, and the straggling French Canadian enclave of Little Quebec, where the clairvoyant was widely respected, especially by the older generation, not only as a perceptive seer but as an herbalist and matchmaker. Most of the rest of the village regarded her as something of a crank but took care not to cross her for fear of her sharp tongue. Yet despite Father George's own frequent disagreements with the fortuneteller—she was forever giving his parishioners advice that was contrary to his—from my early boyhood he had sent me to her place to stack firewood, clear a path through the snow, and take her presents of venison and trout.

Louvia's place was as gloomy as the village graveyard at midnight. Dark, looming hemlocks crowded up to her shack on all sides. On the banks of the stream that seeped out of the woods in back grew the fortuneteller's herb garden, rank with dogbane, ragwort, tansy, love-lies-bleeding, and all kinds of other plants with dubious medicinal properties. From dawn until dusk a pair of Toulouse geese and a lame mallard duck with a gleaming emerald head patrolled her precincts. As I climbed the path through the woods to her house, I had to watch where I put my foot at every step.

If you didn't know Louvia, her appearance alone was enough to give you a start. She stood an inch or two under five feet and wore long, bright-colored housedresses of the old-fashioned kind called dusters, which reached nearly to her ankles. Her hair was coal black, not a strand of gray in it anywhere. Her cheeks were rouged like a cheaply embalmed corpse's, with a compound she prepared herself from a vein of red hematite high on Little Quebec Mountain. About her at all times hung the sourish whiff of wood smoke, from the uncured hardwood slabs she scavenged from the furniture mill and burned in her kitchen range.

When it came to fortunetelling, most of Louvia's methods were conventional enough. She deciphered tea leaves, seized your hand and stared at it indignantly while muttering to herself in French, or squinted into a chunk of rose quartz she'd found years ago on the mountain, which she used as a gazing ball and referred to as her "Daughter." Her specialties were love, money, careers, matters of health, and the locating of lost items—so as she and I walked back down to where I'd left Father George's Buick, I asked her about the missing savant.

"Items, not people," Louvia snapped, as she climbed into the front seat. She reached into her reticule and drew out first her red high-heeled shoes, then her homemade sealing-wax bridgework, which she carefully inserted into her mouth. "The day before Foster disappeared he came up to consult me to see if I saw 'an attractive young wife' in his future, if you can imagine such a thing. You're the one who needs a wife, Frank, and I don't mean those wild young Frenchies from Little Quebec that you've been running with since you've come home from college."

"Good God, Louvia, what the hell are you talking about? I'll be starting at St. Paul's in September."

"Never mind St. Paul's. Drive down to Letourneau's Bakery. It isn't every day of the week that a backwoods fortuneteller has a chance to get her hands on a magic potion."

As we drove, Louvia told me that the night before she'd had a visitation from "the other side." Two elderly deceased sisters from Little Quebec, Sylvie and Marie Bonhomme, had manifested themselves to her and instructed her to go to the bakery they'd owned there, where a secret recipe known only to them, and once used to bake bread for the Last Supper, would be revealed to her.

It was all I could do not to laugh out loud. I vaguely remembered the old Bonhomme sisters myself. They had baked bread in an ancient stone oven in a flower garden behind their patisserie. The loaves had had a wonderful fragrance and flavor. Even Father George, a born skeptic, had told me the bread was said to have restorative properties, though this was the first I'd heard of a magic potion. As far as I was concerned, the search for Sylvie and Marie's miraculous recipe had all the earmarks of one of Louvia's many wild goose chases.

As we drove into Little Quebec, we seemed to enter a different country altogether. The mill workers' row houses were painted in a dozen different gaudy pastel colors, like the houses across the border in Canada. Many had bright orange metal roofs, which sparkled in the afternoon sunshine. Dooryards were ablaze with irises, poppies, and other spring flowers. Vivid patchwork quilts flopped from clotheslines, and sky-blue plaster Madonnas gazed placidly out into the dirt street from upended bathtub shrines.

Even in this hamlet of blossoms, Letourneau's bakery stood out. Behind a black iron railing, its front lawn was aglow with violets. Early-blossoming peonies, as crimson as Louvia's home-made rouge, lined the slate flagstones leading up to the porch. Bright blue morning glories clambered up the iron posts and handrails along the steps. A bathtub Madonna surveyed us from the flower beds.

The patisserie was bright and clean and fragrant with the aromas of baking bread and fresh coffee. Along one wall ran a spotless glass case crammed with golden loaves, some long, some as round as river stones. Another case displayed glazed buns. There were tortes and pies, cream-filled shells, pastries topped with glazed peaches and candied apricots. A wedding cake with white and pink frosting sat at the end of a short counter with several stools, where customers could enjoy a cup of coffee and a pastry.

Behind the counter, removing a tray of piping hot loaves from a wall oven, was a tall young woman with long black hair and eyes the color of the morning glories on the railing. Louvia spoke to her in French, and the girl replied rapidly in a clear voice. Though I couldn't make out a word, I could hear the constant suggestion of laughter in her voice, and wondered why.

The tall girl flashed me a smile, her blue eyes dancing, and I felt something I could not put a name to. It was as if, with that one glance, she had seen deep inside me and been both amused and delighted with what she had seen. And though I was positive we had never met before, something about her was familiar.

Louvia and the girl continued to converse volubly. Finally Louvia turned to me. "This young woman speaks excellent French. She claims to have lived in Montreal and Paris. She's working here this weekend for the Letourneaus, who've gone to visit relatives in Canada. She doesn't know a thing about the old sisters or their magic potion. She wants to know why you keep looking at her."

"I was going to have you ask her the same thing," I said. "Ask her what's so funny, while you're at it."

The girl, who wore a white, lacy apron over a dark blue dress that brought out the brighter blue of her eyes, looked at me and laughed out loud. Behind dark lashes her lovely eyes were constantly laughing.

Louvia went over to the display case and ordered a raspberry tart. The girl put the tart on a white plate and poured a cup of coffee.

"I've instructed her to show you the old stone baking oven

out back," Louvia told me. "Watch her carefully. She has a look in those saucy blue eyes that I don't at all care for."

Hoping that the laughing bakery girl didn't understand any English, I followed her outside and around behind the patisserie. She walked as lightly as a dancer. Once she looked back over her shoulder, her eyes dancing. In the back yard sat the disused stone oven, its brick chimney overrun with morning glories. The girl said something in French. Her teeth were as white as the frosting on the wedding cake inside.

"I'm sorry," I said. "I don't understand much French."

"That's quite evident," the girl said to me in perfect English, laughing. "This, at any rate, is the fabled baking oven your grandmother wanted you to see. As you can plainly observe, it's no longer in use. Rather like her, I should imagine. Is she always this disagreeable?"

"She isn't my grandmother and she isn't really disagreeable," I said, still recovering from my surprise. "That's just her way."

The girl looked me straight in the eyes, with her oval face very close to mine. "Her way is to be disagreeable then. Why are you making excuses for her? If she isn't your grandmother, what is she?"

"She's a friend."

"Indeed? I have heard of such friendships."

At close range, the girl's eyes seemed a slightly darker aqua color. And while they were perpetually laughing, like her voice, her wide-set blue eyes seemed serious as well.

"Why do you keep staring at me like that?" she said.

"I think you're the most beautiful girl I've ever seen," I said, astonishing myself.

She blew out her breath between compressed lips, like a person blowing out a candle. "That and a quarter will purchase you a cup of hot coffee in the patisserie, nothing else. Have you seen enough of this wonder of an oven? I have a great deal of work to do inside. University tuition to pay back. Travel money to save. I'm not slaving here for my health, you know."

"Where are you going on your travels?"

"That's for me to know. Has anyone ever told you you ask a great many questions?"

"Yes, as a matter of fact, Louvia has. The friend I came here with."

"Louvia! I knew she was a gypsy. We have to get back inside before she robs the shop blind."

The girl made no move to leave. Her face, framed by hair as jet black as her small polished shoes, was inches from mine. Her breath smelled like cloves, like the sweet Williams growing nearby. Her frilled white apron nearly brushed my legs. "Look," she said, tilting her head toward the shop. "The curtain's moving at the window. Just as I suspected, the crone's spying on us. Let's give her something to be outraged over."

Before I knew it, the bakery girl had thrown her slender arms around my neck and kissed me hard on the mouth. Then she grabbed my hand and led me back around the corner of the shop, where we met Louvia coming down the steps.

The little blue Madonna in the bathtub seemed to follow the fortuneteller with her painted eyes. Louvia spat in the direction of the plaster statuette and crossed herself in reverse. The girl laughed, rattled off something in French, gave my hand a squeeze, and ran lightly up the steps. At the top she looked back once more.

"Hurry up and get in the car," Louvia said to me. "We didn't travel down here for a box social. I intend to locate that recipe if it's the last thing I do."

"Au revoir, Frank," the girl with the morning-glory eyes called out, and disappeared inside.

❧

"What did the little tart do to you out back?" Louvia said as we drove back down the street between the bright houses. "I had time to eat a ten-course dinner while you were dallying with her. Did she make any untoward advances?"

I laughed. "What I want to know is how she knew my name?"

"Obviously she overheard me say it."

"I'm positive you never mentioned it in her presence."

"Don't contradict me. Inside, while she and I were talking, I threw in your name. You didn't catch it, it sounds different in French."

"Evidently."

"Did she expose her breasts for you out by the oven? They didn't look like much to me, I can tell you."

"For God's sake, Louvia."

"These college women are the worst kind, Frank. In and out of the sheets with a different young fellow every night. Pull up in front of the hotel. We'll go in and get a cold drink and reconnoiter."

Inside the dining room, we sat at a table overlooking the Common. I ordered a beer and Louvia sipped a tall glass of iced tea through a colored glass straw from her reticule.

"What happened to the Bonhomme sisters, Louvia? After they sold the bakery to the Letourneaus?"

The fortuneteller shrugged. "It was said that they returned to Canada, where they were born. The last I remember of them was during the big strike at the furniture factory. You would have been a small boy, ten or eleven, it was just before they unloaded the patisserie. Sylvie and Marie baked bread for the families of the men on the picket line. The stone oven behind their place was smoking night and day. They even marched with the strikers, if you can believe it. Two old women who didn't know a dozen words of English between them, hobbling along with the Trotskyites!"

"For God's sake, Louvia, Father George supported the workers, too. With the monsignor's permission. They eventually got a raise and shorter hours."

"We fortunetellers and matchmakers should be so lucky."

I laughed, but Louvia narrowed her eyes as an idea occurred to her. "Sylvie and Marie were great churchgoers, Frank. It may be that your senile old priest-father could help us run down that recipe."

"Father G isn't senile, and this is his afternoon off. He was going to play bocce on the back lawn and have a few beers. He hasn't been feeling up to par lately."

"He'll be glad for some company," Louvia said. "Much as I detest trafficking with a priest."

"What's wrong with priests? I'll be one myself in three years."

"Why?" Louvia said.

"Why?" As Father George, who frequently used baseball expressions in his homilies, liked to say, I felt like a picked-off base runner caught leaning the wrong way. "I don't know exactly why. It's something you feel more than you know. Living with Father G—"

"An excellent reason not to be one," Louvia said. "George Lecoeur is an overbearing meddler, no more cut out to be a priest at heart than you are, Frank. I hope you'll change your mind."

"We'll agree to disagree," I said. "I feel what I feel. What makes you think I'd ever change my mind?"

"That's for me to know."

I laughed. "The baker's girl told me the same thing."

"The baker's girl again. Why don't you run back and invite her out to the tall grass for another romp? Well, never mind. I was young and romantic once myself."

"Tell me a story about when you were young and romantic."

The fortuneteller frowned and tapped her dime-store rings, one for each finger, on the table top. "I'll tell you one story. Then we'll get on with our business."

Louvia took another sip of her tea.

"Now, Frank. Kingdom Common wasn't always just a failing little mill town. When I first came here from Canada and went to work in the mill myself, there was a beautiful white pavilion on the common with a hardwood floor and colored lanterns strung around the outside. Half a dozen times a summer big bands from Boston and Montreal came here on the train. We danced to all of them, the best times of my life."

"We?"

"I didn't dance with a broomstick. I had a boy who brought me. We met at the pavilion every Saturday night. As I told you,

I was very romantic, and even more foolish than romantic. Foolish enough to fall in love with my good-looking boy, bewitched by the big bands and the colored lights."

"But he wasn't in love with you?"

Louvia smiled. "I think he was."

"And?"

She shrugged. "The Great War broke out. He went for a soldier. I ran away to tell fortunes with a carnival. A summer romance. Nothing more."

❦

Just as I'd suspected, Father George was out on the spacious side lawn of the Big House, playing bocce alone. On a nearby iron bench sat an open bottle of beer.

Father G retrieved the four bright balls — red, yellow, green, and blue — from a sandy circle in the middle of the lawn and brought them back to the bench, where he dumped them clacking on the ground at his feet like four colored eggs in the same nest. Though baseball had always been his favorite sport, he'd learned to play a form of bocce in France, and he was exceedingly fond of the game.

Sunday afternoon was Father George's one time off. When I was a boy, we'd spend Sunday afternoons fishing or hunting, playing ball on the common, riding out into the country in Father George's Buick, or playing bocce. He'd used the four balls to explain all kinds of doctrinal matters to me. "Look, Frank. The red ball's the Father, blue is the Son, yellow's the Holy Ghost. The green one that doesn't know what the hell it's doing half the time is me!"

Or, when getting ready to bowl the red ball at the three others: "Here comes old Pharaoh in his chariot, hot on the trail of the Children of Israel. Look out, Moses!"

I'd roar with laughter, fall right down on the grass. But later on, in my early teens, when I began to pose hard questions to Father George about such matters as the Trinity, the Sacraments, and our ultimate origin and destination, he'd get frustrated with me and with metaphysical matters as well. To my delight his face would get red, and he'd shout, "All I know, goddamn it, is that God's creation is good and we're put here to celebrate it and the best way to celebrate it is to help other people, not bedevil the Lord and His aging representatives on earth with smart-aleck questions." By then, Father G was usually so worked up he was easy to beat, which made him even madder. He'd have to go into the house for more beer, and I'd laugh harder than ever.

Today, though, with Father George's health failing, I was reluctant to bother him. Today he was just an old man playing bocce on a warm spring afternoon, and here I was with his nemesis the fortuneteller. Not surprisingly, when he first saw me approaching with Louvia, Father G shot me a baleful look.

"Who are you playing against—God?" Louvia said.

"Yes," Father George said. "He's ahead, as usual."

"That swill you're pouring down your gullet isn't at all good for you, George. It'll take twenty years off your life."

"In September I'll be sixty-nine. I'll take my chances, damn it."

"The only reason you've gotten away with your shenanigans all these years, guzzling beer, swearing like a horse marine, adopting brats, and God alone knows what else, is that Kingdom Common's so far removed from the rest of the diocese no one knows what you're up to."

"Or cares, more likely," Father G said. But when he found out what Louvia wanted, he nodded and smiled. "Of course I remember Sylvie and Marie Bonhomme. They were faithful members of the parish, generous to everyone. A pair of saints, if you ask me. They departed about ten years ago."

"Where exactly did they depart to, these two saints on earth? That's the question."

Father George picked up the red ball and hefted it thoughtfully. "Unfortunately, Louvia, there I can't assist you. There I'm afraid that all Kingdom Common couldn't assist you."

"To hell in a handbasket with all Kingdom Common," Louvia said. "I want that recipe!"

Without rising from the bench, Father G rolled the red ball out over the grass. It stopped a few inches short of the circle.

Louvia made as if to stand up. "This palaver isn't getting us anywhere."

Father G picked up the blue ball, the Son, and lofted it out over the lawn. It nudged past God and wormed its way into the circle. He smiled at me.

"Are the two old birds dead or not?" Louvia interrupted. "If so, what became of their effects?"

Father George picked up the green ball and flipped it from hand to hand between his knees. "This one has always seemed to have a mind of its own," he said. "It's apt to behave in unpredictable and interesting ways." He looked roguishly at Louvia. Then he rolled the ball toward the others. At the last moment it wobbled off course and ran a foot past the circle. "See?" Father George said. "Its own master."

Louvia heaved a great sigh. "Are you going to tell us what became of the sisters and their recipe?"

Father George picked up the yellow ball, made two short false casts, then launched it out over the greensward. It rolled straight and true into the sandy circle and stopped beside the blue ball. "Behold," he said. "Just so the Holy Ghost conducted Sylvie and Marie safely to paradise. Snug as two bugs in a rug."

"I won't debate the point," Louvia said. "As long as you can tell me what became of the recipe."

"Well, there's the rub, Louvia. I can't."

"What do you mean you can't? Did they sprout wings and flap up to heaven with it like two old herons?"

Father George pushed himself to his feet. "Let's walk down to the church," he said. "There's something there I want you to see."

"I haven't set foot in a church in twenty years."

"You can see this from the entryway."

As we headed down the hill through a corner of the cemetery, the pink granite of St. Mary's glowed in the rays of the lowering sun. Inside, banks of candles burned for the dead. Stained-glass windows illuminated with biblical scenes lined both walls. Radiant in his multicolored coat, Joseph stood apart from his brothers. Jacob grappled with a muscular angel. Moses and Aaron were beseeching a haughty Pharaoh. These were the images I had grown up with as an altar boy, a choir boy, an acolyte in Father George's beautiful Church of St. Mary's of the Green Mountains, where I hoped to preside over masses myself someday. Despite herself, Louvia came inside for a closer look.

Father George led us down the west aisle and halted beneath a window depicting an ancient figure in a flowing white beard, rising into the sky high above a hillside of olive trees and attended by two angels. "'The translation of Elijah, directly from earth to heaven,'" he read from the brass plaque under the window.

"I imagine he got there as fast that way as any other," Louvia said. "Look! The two old Bonhomme busybodies are already up there, baking a loaf of bread in honor of his arrival."

Father G laughed. "I'm a skeptic myself when it comes to the Old Testament stories. Still, Louvia, the world is full of mysteries."

"More than you could ever dream of, George," Louvia said.

"What the hell is that supposed to mean?" Father G said.

"That's for me to know," Louvia told him.

Father George sighed, sat down in the pew below ascending Elijah, and slid over to make room for us. The beams of the setting sun streamed in on our heads and shoulders. "That feels good," he said.

Louvia nodded. "At last we agree."

For a few moments no one spoke. The interior of the big church was perfectly still.

"This was Sylvie and Marie's pew," Father George said. Inside the empty church his voice resonated. "They never missed a mass. But during the big strike Marie got sick. No doubt the excitement was too much for her. After that she claimed that their bread alone was keeping her alive."

"Enough about this wonderful manna," Louvia said. "Did Marie give up the ghost?"

"Not immediately. But when the strike finally ended, the sisters weren't able to bake any longer. They were worn out. Then they all but stopped eating. Finally, Sylvie asked if I'd arrange a special communion here in the church at sunset, just for them. She informed me—I don't know why I'm telling this now, I wouldn't expect anyone to believe it—that the little blue Madonna from their lawn had appeared to her and suggested the idea. That Mary had said if they'd come here one last time, a 'great event' awaited them.

"Well," Father George said, "how could I deny her request? In they tottered, arm in arm, at the appointed time. They sat right here, under our old friend the white-beard. When I started down the aisle with the communion service, I had the strangest sensation, as though the sunlight were streaming straight through them. As though they'd become translucent. It was just an illusion, enhanced by their dreadful thinness. But when we celebrated the sacrament and they reached for the wine, the sunlight seemed to shine through their hands onto the silver chalice. I supposed this must be the great event that Sylvie had mentioned."

Father George looked at Louvia, as if anticipating one of her comebacks. But she sat stock-still, listening attentively for once.

"After they'd taken communion, Sylvie asked if they could sit on a bit longer," Father George said. "I returned to the front of the church to put up the service. By then the sun had set, and to tell you the truth I wanted a cold beer in the worst way. Still, I intended to escort the sisters home first. But when I started back down the aisle toward their pew, this pew, it was empty."

Reliving his puzzlement, Father G shook his head. "I hadn't heard them get up to go. And at their rate of speed, so elderly, they certainly hadn't had time to reach the door. They'd vanished—there was nothing here but the faint scent of freshly baked bread. Or maybe it was the burning candles. Who knows?"

I looked at Louvia, who remained silent. During Father George's narrative the sun had set. Louvia's face in the afterglow was abstracted, as though she were thinking of something long ago.

"I rushed outside, but they were nowhere to be seen," Father George said. "In short, no trace of them was ever found."

"Wasn't there a search?" I said.

"What would the point have been?"

"They had to have gone somewhere. You're the skeptic, Father G."

My father rose slowly, reaching out to steady himself on the back of a pew. He shook his head. "Sixty-eight isn't twenty-six. My bocce days may be drawing to a close, though I hope not. I'm finally beginning to figure out the green ball."

"For God's sake, the recipe!" Louvia cried.

"I'm afraid it was in their heads and they meant to write it down but never got around to it," Father George said. "Still, I want to show you one more thing. Two things, actually."

We followed Father G down the aisle of the church and outside into the evening. Below us, at the foot of the hill, the lights of our little village were coming on. Across town, the furniture mill was lit up like a village itself. Father George led us up a path through a double row of cedar trees and into the cemetery.

He stopped on a knoll beside two oblong granite memorials about three feet long and two feet tall. There was just enough light beneath the cedars to read the names of Sylvie and Marie Bonhomme on the stones. In the dusk, the memorials bore an uncanny resemblance to bread loaves. Etched into the polished granite beneath Marie's name was an engraving of an outdoor baking oven with a wisp of smoke curling out of the chimney. On Sylvie's was a small Madonna in a bathtub shrine.

"Who paid for these?" Louvia said.

Father George shrugged. "It was a small enough gesture after all they'd done for the parish."

He rested his hand on Marie's stone. "Sometimes when I pass near here I'm sure I can smell the scent of baking bread. Very faint, but inexpressibly fragrant. Like the tiny white violets that come up in the grass all over my bocce court in May. I think I can smell it now."

I, too, thought I caught a whiff of bread baking. But true to form, Louvia scoffed at such a notion. "It's the cedar trees," she said. "Falling dew always brings out the aroma of arborvitae."

After leaving Father George at the Big House, Louvia and I drove back down the hill past the church toward the lighted town. Neither of us spoke until we reached the common.

"Bring your wife here someday, Frank," Louvia said suddenly. "Tell her the story of how you and Louvia the Fortuneteller journeyed up to the church and the cemetery and whiled away the afternoon listening to fairy tales."

I laughed. "Should I tell this wife of mine about the baker's assistant?"

Louvia reached into her reticule. "I'll consult my Daughter."

Under the street lamps, Louvia's rose quartz gazing stone glowed softly. "Yes, tell her. She'll be amused," Louvia said. Then: "Oh! I thought I caught a glimpse of the old dance pavilion on the common. Another vision from the other side, no doubt."

But thinking of the open dance hall with the colored lights where Louvia and her young man had danced to the Montreal bands made me suddenly angry. "That guy you fell in love with? He should have married you, Louvia, war or no war."

Louvia looked at me intently. "Would you have?"

"If I weren't going into the priesthood? Yes. If I loved a girl I'd marry her in a minute."

"Well, well. Never mind the priesthood. With the right girl, you might amount to something after all. And remember — who knows how the future can turn on a single day in our lives. Now step on it. I have to get home and pee!"

A few days later I returned to the patisserie in Little Quebec, looking for the tall laughing girl with raven hair and morning-glory eyes. But to my great disappointment the bakery was closed. The property had been sold again, the Letourneaus had moved, and I could find no one in the neighborhood who could tell me anything at all about the baker's assistant. I didn't even know her name.

What was I left with from my afternoon with Louvia De-Banville, in search of a recipe that probably never existed? A good day with a friend. Some questions about my vocation.

Mysteries. And stories. Stories of Louvia, young and beautiful, gliding across the hardwood floor of the pavilion with the colored lanterns shimmering to the trombone runs of the big bands. Of two elderly sisters, feeding the families of the striking mill workers. Of the scent of fresh-baked bread. And of Louvia's belief that our fortunes often turn on a single event in ways I could not have begun to imagine.

•3•
Enemies

Only in the Kingdom, Commoners said of the feud between the Lacourses and the Gambinis. Only in this forgotten enclave of the Appalachian Mountain chain stretching all the way north to Vermont from Georgia and Tennessee could such an anachronism as a full-blown multigenerational family feud be sustained and tolerated and, yes, even nurtured, well into the middle of the twentieth century.

—Father George, "A Short History"

FOR AS LONG as anyone could remember, the Lacourses and the Gambinis had hated each other with an implacable hostility, though they were otherwise hard-working, respected members of the community, with successful businesses and large families of bright children.

Emile Lacourse owned a productive lumbering operation, leasing tracts of timberland that he logged with the most modern methods and equipment, but carefully and responsibly, never scalping the mountainsides of every last stick of wood but instead cutting selectively and staying away from the banks of brooks and rivers. On the higher elevations he still used horses, as his Québecois ancestors had, to preserve the steep and delicate terrain from the deep ruts of gasoline-powered skidders.

For all his business acumen, Emile was a conservationist before his time.

Pietro Gambini's Italian ancestors were stonecutters. They had come from Milano to work the pink granite on the ridge above the Kinneson family farm, where the lovely sunset-colored building stones used for the Academy, St. Mary's, the courthouse, the railroad station, the big houses on Anderson Hill, and the monuments in the village cemetery had been quarried. Over the decades, as the granite pit had deepened, icy water from springs deep in the heart of the ridge made working the mine beyond a certain depth impracticable. The Gambinis had then turned to dairy farming and cheesemaking. Their cheese factory on the edge of the village manufactured a smooth and tangy cheddar that won awards at dairy festivals as far away as Wisconsin and Minnesota.

Apart from the feud, it was astonishing how much alike the families were. Both the Lacourses and the Gambinis maintained close ties with relatives in their homelands. Both families kept up ancestral traditions. The Gambinis concocted flavorful wines from wild blue grapes, blackberries, chokecherries, even dandelion blossoms. The Lacourses celebrated New Year's Day even more enthusiastically than Christmas, carting maple sugar pies and glazed cakes in the shape of logs to all their neighbors except, pointedly, the Gambinis. Both families owned expensive cars. When Emile Lacourse bought a new Pontiac, Pietro Gambini rushed to the same Burlington dealership to purchase a Super 88 Oldsmobile just off the assembly line. The following spring Emile traded his low-mileage Bonneville for a Chrysler. Soon neither family drove to mass at Father George's Church of

St. Mary's in anything other than an El Dorado, never more than a year old.

If Emile Lacourse bought his wife, Mimi, a mink stole in Montreal, Pietro Gambini drove hell-for-leather over the White Mountains to purchase his wife, Rosa, a full-length otter coat from the finest Boston furrier. Nor was the rivalry confined to the adults. Their children competed fiercely in school for academic and athletic distinctions. Father George's basketball team at the Academy once lost a state championship game by four points because Etienne Lacourse, a wizardly ball handler, refused to pass to Rodolfo Gambini, a high-scoring forward. In the locker room after the game, fists flew. Instead of celebrating an undefeated season with a three-foot-high trophy and a torchlight parade led by their El Dorados, the two quarreling families got into a brawl in the parking lot outside the gymnasium.

Even so, both the Gambinis and the Lacourses continued to be highly regarded in the village. As for the feud, vengeance had become its own sweet excuse. No one in Kingdom Common seemed able to do a thing to stop the trouble — which brings me back to Father George.

🍂

One bitterly cold November evening when I was about eight, two heavy cars roared up the drive of the Big House and skidded to a halt under the portico. Out of the automobiles poured Lacourses and Gambinis of all ages, screaming murder. From the trunk of his Cadillac, Emile Lacourse dragged an enormous buck, which he lugged up to the porch and dumped on the glider by the front door. The two families swarmed up behind him and stood around the dead deer, gesticulating wildly and shrieking at each other in Québecois and Milanese dialects that they otherwise spoke only rarely, even at home. Pietro Gambini was waving his deer rifle. Emile Lacourse ran to his El Dorado, opened the trunk, and pulled out a red chainsaw with a blade a yard long. Rushing back up onto the porch, he started the saw with a great coughing roar and brandished it over his head toward Pietro. Both men were bellowing for Father George.

I'd been sitting at the bird's-eye maple kitchen table listening to Father George read aloud the wonderful story from his "Short History" of his chance discovery of a stand of bird's-eye maples, high in Lord Hollow, from which he had personally made much of the furniture for the Big House. I was startled by the commotion; but Father George grinned and told me to sit on the woodbox near the stove and be as quiet as a church mouse, and I'd see and hear something I could write my own story about someday.

He hurried out onto the porch and said, "People, good people. For heaven's sake. This isn't Chicago in the twenties. Go lock your weapons in your cars. Then come back and we'll thrash this out together."

Muttering more threats and exchanging hateful glances, the two families convened in the Big House kitchen, but refused the hot coffee that Father George offered them. This was not, pardon us, Father, a social visit. Oh, no.

I watched, wide-eyed, from the woodbox as the litigants faced each other across the maple table, with their finely clad wives, both great beauties, and their handsome children to bear witness. At Father George's request, Pietro, a stocky man with dark hair and flashing eyes, told his story first.

It seemed that when he was out hunting, Pietro had jumped

the buck in question in a beech grove bordering the brook dividing his property from the Lacourses' and had shot it in the chest. The fatally wounded animal had sprinted a few yards, leaped the brook in one bound, and dropped in a heap at the feet of Emile Lacourse, out clearing brush from his sugar maple orchard. Emile instantly cut the throat of the dying buck with his chainsaw. But when Pietro started across the stream to claim his trophy, Emile drove him back onto his own land with the thundering saw. Pietro had then fired a round from his deer rifle into the steam vent of Emile's nearby sugarhouse. Pietro concluded his statement with an eloquent peroration, delivered at the top of his lungs and containing an explicit threat on his neighbor's life if he did not relinquish all claim to the deer immediately. "Excuse me, Signora," he added in a much lower voice, with a short bow toward Mimi Lacourse.

Emile did not dispute any of the facts of the case as presented by Pietro. On the contrary, he responded that he would be greatly interested to see his bosom friend and dear neighbor carry out his threat after his head had been severed from his shoulders with a thirty-horse gasoline felling saw.

Father George smiled at the two families, his bright blue eyes amused. Then he said, "Bring in the deer, Emile."

The buck was brought inside and laid out on an oilcloth on the bird's-eye table. It was a lovely animal, dark as a moose. Its heavy rack of horns was darker yet, with eight points on one side and nine on the other. After dispatching it with his saw and chasing Pietro back across the brook, Emile had dressed it out. Even so, Father George, a lifelong hunter, estimated its weight at two hundred and fifty pounds.

"Of course. It fattened itself on my apples all fall," Emile said.

"It spent the summer grazing like a prize heifer on my high upper mowing," Pietro responded.

"Well, gentlemen, a man doesn't need to be another Solomon to know what to do in this situation," Father George said. "If you'll give me your word to agree to my decision and make every effort to abide by it, I'll help you out."

What choice did the combatants have? With many intransigent looks across the table, Pietro and Emile agreed to abide by Father George's finding, whatever it was. To the letter and in the spirit? Well, yes. To the letter and in the spirit.

Father George spread a layer of *Kingdom County Monitor*s on the yellow linoleum tiles under the table. He rolled up the sleeves of his white dress shirt, exposing forearms as thick and powerful as Pietro's and Emile's. From the woodshed off the kitchen he fetched a meat saw and his hunting knife, with which he expertly cut off the head and hide of the great buck. Then he began to quarter the carcass like a beef. As he worked he told the story of the bird's-eye table, just as he'd written it in his "Short History." How for a hundred and fifty years the maple trees hidden on the ridge north of Lord's Bog had not been considered worth lumbering because of the mysterious dark oval imperfections riddling their wood. Then Father George, who had a hunting camp nearby, had recognized the bird's-eyes, in a pile of firewood, for what they truly were and decided to fell one tree for stock to make furniture for the Big House. By degrees, as Father George described skidding the logs down over the frozen bog, putting the cured lumber through the mill's shrieking ripsaw, planer, and sander, then shaping the dowels for chair and table legs, gluing the pieces, and sanding and varnishing the furniture, everyone's attention became focused on the story.

Suddenly Emile Lacourse spoke up. "Father G. What makes the little bird's-eyes in the wood?"

"Ah," Father George said, sawing through the last hindquarter of the deer. "That's the question, Emile. No one knows."

"The bird's-eye is a separate species of maple?" Pietro said.

"No, it's regular rock maple. But whether it's minerals in the soil where the trees grow or the way the wind blows or some virus that causes the eyes, I don't know. It's a mystery. Like how your quarrel began."

No doubt my adoptive father hoped, with this exemplum, to drive home the ultimate futility and madness of the feud. Even at eight, I could see that. But now it was time for his decision. Everyone's eyes moved from Father George to the deer and back to Father George.

"Well?" Emile said.

The head, with its trophy rack and dark cape, went to Pietro to have mounted, along with one forequarter and one hindquarter. The rest of the hide and the two other quarters went to Emile for dispatching the animal. It was as simple at that.

To me, the disposition of the deer seemed eminently fair. But what a howl went up from the litigants! The men smote their foreheads. The women pulled at their gorgeous long hair as if to tear it out by the roots. The children hissed at each other like vipers, while the grownups trembled in rage and stared at one another and at Father George with incredulity. Yet as he firmly reminded them, they had given their word to accept his ruling.

Next time, both parties vowed on their way out the door into the night with their spoils. Next time there would be no recourse to the priest, and matters would turn out very differently indeed, with all due respect, Father. Afterward Father George laughed and told me not to worry, he'd been through similar charades with the feuding families a dozen times before.

Maybe so, I thought. But, young as I was, I could not help thinking that the trouble between the Lacourses and the Gambinis was far from over and, as both families had earnestly promised, that the end, when it came, would be a tragic one.

❦

The feud continued straight through my boyhood. At length it reached such a pitch that Father George warned me to steer clear of both places on my hunting and fishing expeditions so I wouldn't get caught, perhaps quite literally, in the crossfire. In fact, the spring that I turned ten, when Emile Lacourse stumbled upon Pietro Gambini manufacturing *acquavite,* the hundred-proof Italian brandy used by the Gambinis at holidays and birthday celebrations, at his homemade still high on the brook between their properties, they argued, and Emile drew a pistol and put a bullet through Pietro's hat. When word of this near-tragedy got back to Father George, he lost patience with both adversaries. "For God's sake, Pietro, go tend to your distilling on some other stream," he admonished the moonshiner, supposing that the matter would then be closed.

Far from it. To avenge himself on his neighbor, on the night before hunting season opened, Pietro cunningly affixed the mounted head of his fabled seventeen-point buck to the trunk of one of his brookside beeches, as if the animal were peering out around the tree at the Lacourse maple orchard. When Emile shot it the following dawn and crept across the brook to drag it back to his property, Pietro, who'd been lying in wait in a barberry thicket, sprang out to accost him for unlawful trespass. Father George gave both men a furious dressing-down, pounding the bird's-eye table and condemning the souls of both men to eternal perdition before forgiving them and thanking them, not without irony, for providing him with something interesting to write about in his "Short History." But what was clemency to one party was invariably gall to the other, and both men went home more infuriated than ever.

You might think that as the two men grew older, they would gradually run out of the enormous energy required to sustain such a vendetta. Much the opposite. Over time the feud seemed to intensify in virulence, like Pietro's acquavite. Each fall the families fought over who would pay the negligible taxes on the water-filled old granite pit, until finally Father George persuaded the town assessors to stop listing it. Then they fought over who owned the speckled trout in the brook. How, Father George inquired, can a man possibly own a wild trout? He was assured by both parties that they would show him exactly how, if either caught the other angling there. At town meeting in March they debated every last item on the warning, preparing interminable eloquent speeches ahead of time, masterpieces of withering rhetoric that Father George said would have done credit to Pietro's ancestors in the Roman senate. Their lovely daughters found a hundred different ways to snub one another in school. Their sons fought with fists, wild apples, BB guns, rocks. A few months after the fiasco of the championship basketball game, Rodolfo Gambini and Etienne Lacourse asked the same girl to their graduation prom. When she prudently declined to go with either, they drove their father's expensive cars at each other full tilt, discharging guns out the windows like gangsters. That no one was killed or maimed was a miracle.

Father George worried constantly about the children of the feuding families. Over the years he resorted to every expediency to bring the trouble to an end. But how can you solve a problem whose source no one can identify? True, the feud seemed rooted in property. But since even the principals conceded that no one could really own the brook separating their land, it seemed more rooted in some dark recess of human nature. Furthermore, as Louvia the Fortuneteller liked to observe, no one likes change, especially in a small village. And what greater change could either family imagine than a cessation of hostilities? Wouldn't that amount to acknowledging that the trouble that had informed their lives with a unique significance had been not only unnecessary but meaningless? In short, the feud had become a way of life. In his lively chapter on the Lacourses and Gambinis in his "Short History," Father George likened the feud to a force of nature, like the water that ran into the granite quarry each time the Gambinis pumped it out to obtain a few more slabs of granite for their youngest boy, Peter, a gifted sculptor. Within three or four days the pit would again be inundated and, just as surely, the feud was bound to break out again, usually sooner rather than later.

The spring I turned twelve, Pietro Gambini hired the local

volunteer fire department to pump out the quarry. On its way back to the village, the pumper, with an inebriated Harlan Kittredge at the wheel, made a wrong turn, jumped the brook, and crashed into Emile Lacourse's sugarhouse. Down to the Big House rampaged both families. This time Father George banished Emile and Pietro to the porch while he spoke at length with their wives. Laying matters directly on the line, he said that like himself, neither of the two quarreling couples was getting any younger. He told them that too often in cases of this nature it was the children of the feuding parties who paid for their parents' stubbornness. He inquired quietly, did Rosa Gambini and Mimi Lacourse know how fortunate they were to have children in the first place? Surely, he said, these two good mothers did not wish to follow their sons and daughters to the grave.

Madame and Signora burst into tears and embraced. The husbands were peremptorily summoned. Mary, Joseph, Jesus, and all twelve of the sainted apostles help Pietro Gambini and Emile Lacourse if either henceforward uttered a single litigious word to the other. Never again would they be admitted to the marriage bed, a deprivation that would signify only the beginning of their tribulations.

The men shook hands stiffly and muttered apologies to each other. The women embraced again, exchanging tearful vows of eternal sisterhood. But the very next week Pietro's heifers broke down a fence, crossed the brook into Emile's prized old-fashioned apple orchard, and girdled the trunks of six young Duchesses and four Northern Spies. Emile impounded the animals in his barnyard and threatened to slaughter one a day until Pietro printed a public apology for the invasion in the *Kingdom*

County Monitor. In a searing white fury Pietro went to get his heifers back at gunpoint. A shootout ensued, in which Pietro took a few pellets of birdshot in his right calf. That evening, from my cupola bedroom in the Big House, I could hear the Lacourses discharging shotguns and rifles into the air long past midnight, in celebration of the wounding of Pietro Gambini. Father George lost his temper completely, and the following Sunday he threatened from the pulpit, in a thundering voice, to excommunicate them from Saint Mary's, if not from the church altogether, and administer a public horsewhipping to Emile and Pietro besides.

❦

In school, Thérèse Lacourse, Emile's youngest daughter and the apple of his eye, was one year ahead of Pietro's youngest son, Peter, the stone sculptor. She was a quiet and intense girl, a straight-A student at the top of her class. Peter, for his part, was a slightly built boy with serious brown eyes and brown hair that curled up at his shirt collar. In early boyhood he had contracted infantile paralysis, and though he had recovered completely from the disease, he never did become an athlete like his older brothers. During his convalescence he discovered his great-grandfather's carving tools, wrapped in oilskins in the old stone shed near the quarry. From the moment he first held the hammers and chisels in his hands, Peter knew that he had found his life's work.

Peter Gambini studied the carvings on the pink granite tombstones in the village cemetery. He hitchhiked to Barre to familiarize himself with the great stone figures in the Rock of Ages cemetery. Then he began to carve memorials of his own. Soon customers were flocking to the Gambini place from all over Vermont and across the border in Quebec as well, to commission the young genius to carve their tombstones. Horse-loggers wanted to be laid to rest beneath stones engraved with etchings of their teams. Farmers wanted representations of their barns and houses. Woodsmen coveted leaping granite bucks and trout.

By the time Peter was fifteen he'd left school altogether to work full-time in his great-grandfather's granite shed. Emile's sons left him alone, in deference to his childhood illness, and Peter's own brothers treated him differently. After all, he was special, an artist. But the entire village knew that when Peter was sixteen, Emile Lacourse had happened upon him and Thérèse skinny-dipping together in the deep green water of the quarry and, as Father George himself put it in his "Short History," it was well for the stone carver that afternoon that he was fleet of foot. But despite all that their parents could do, the young couple took every opportunity to be together. So it was really no great surprise when, one December evening in my thirteenth year, while Father George and I were decorating the Big House for Christmas, she and Peter showed up on the porch together.

It was snowing lightly, and a few flakes clung to Thérèse's long dark hair, reminding me of the dark-haired angel that traditionally went on top of the huge tree in the rectory parlor.

"Are your folks squabbling again?" Father George said, knowing better.

"Not tonight, Father, for a wonder," Thérèse said. She jerked her head at Peter. "This one wants to get married."

The couple sat down side by side at the bird's-eye table on which, years earlier, Father George had divided the buck between their fathers. Now he heated coffee. Once again I sat quietly on the woodbox by the blue porcelain stove.

Father George sat down across from the couple. "How old are you, Thérèse?"

"Eighteen."

"And you, Peter?"

"He's eighteen, too."

Father George frowned. But with children and young people, he almost never lost his temper. "Let him answer for himself, Thérèse. Are you seventeen, Peter?"

"And a half."

"He does the work of a man and is a man," Thérèse said.

Father George looked at Peter. "Do you have a job, son?"

"Certainly. I'm a granite carver."

"You should see 'The Magdalene Standing Vigil at the Tomb of Christ Our Lord,' commissioned for the cemetery entrance in Memphremagog," Thérèse said.

"I have," Father George said. "It's a masterwork."

"I was the model for the Magdalene," Thérèse said. She pulled her chair closer to Peter's. "Think what he'll be accomplishing at thirty." She took Peter's hands in hers and held them up. "Look. Strong and slender. The fingers of a master."

Father George took off his glasses and then put them back on again. "How do you feel about marrying Thérèse, Peter?"

Peter smiled. "We've made our decision," he said simply. But the way he held Thérèse's hand answered the question far better.

Father George poured coffee into the bone china cups he had bought in London on his way home from the Great War. From time to time Thérèse and Peter glanced at each other over the steam rising from their cups. Peter's features were very fine, like those of his statues, yet in his face there was already considerable strength as well, an artist's single-minded determination.

Father George poured more coffee. Then he came right to the heart of the matter. "You two love each other very much."

It was a statement.

"Yes," Thérèse said simply.

The clock on the mantel ticked; the snow gusted against the window. The wood fire flickered orange and red through the isinglass window of the blue stove.

"One more question, Thérèse," Father George said. "Do you love Peter enough to leave your mother and live with him forever?"

"Yes. And enough to forfeit a big church wedding with a white dress, besides."

Peter stood up. "Come, Thérèse. We'll wait on the porch. Let Father decide."

Father George sat thinking. "It's all so improbable, Frank," he said. "That this could ever work out. On the other hand, life is full of improbabilities that work out. I'm sitting at one."

He touched the bird's-eye table. Then his eyes flashed. "You see how God puts us in impossible situations. I'm beginning to think I'll be damned if I do marry these kids and damned if I don't. Quite literally." He clenched his big fist and shook it at the ceiling. "Oh, you're a rough old cob," he told God. "You don't ask for much, do you? Just our souls. See how He operates, Frank? He catches us in a pickle, like a man in a rundown between second and third. We can't go forward and we can't go back. Well, well. 'Whom He loveth, He chastiseth.'"

From the porch came laughter. I ran to the window and looked out around the curtain. "They're kissing on the glider!"

Father George sighed. Then he laughed. "Well, it's in their hands. Thérèse's and Peter's. Not mine. I'm not God, I'm a country priest. My job is to marry people who want to get married." He glanced up at the ceiling. "I'm sorry," he said, grinning. "I had no business saying what I did."

Now I laughed. Father George was always getting mad at God and then apologizing to Him.

"Call them in, Frank," he said. "An idea just occurred to me. You wait here in the kitchen with Peter while I talk to Thérèse in the parlor for a minute."

"I already know everything there is to know about such matters," Thérèse told Father George as they left the room together. "I grew up on a farm, you know, not in a convent."

Five minutes later Father George rejoined us in the kitchen. "Thérèse will be back shortly," he said. He got a bottle of Pietro Gambini's acquavite and two shot glasses from the cupboard and poured a drink for Peter and himself. "*Salute!*" he said, lifting his glass.

Peter grinned. "*Salute!*" He emptied his glass in two swallows. "So, Father. What advice do you have for me about being a husband?"

Father George finished his drink while he considered. Then he said, "Listen to your wife and try to do as she says. Apart from that, no man knows very much about being a husband. It's like being a priest. All you really need to know you'll learn as you go along."

Peter nodded. "This is an important night in my life," he said.

"Yes," Father George said. He poured them both a little more brandy. Peter swirled his around the bottom of his shot glass. The snow beat harder against the window. I got a stick of yellow birch out of the woodbox and put it into the stove. As its curling bark caught fire, a sharp wintergreen scent filled the kitchen. Father George had stepped into his study. He returned with a Bible and a long sealed envelope, which he laid face down on the table.

Suddenly whiteness filled the doorway from the parlor. Thérèse Lacourse appeared, wearing the wedding dress that had belonged to Father George's mother, her dark eyes full of shyness and triumph and expectation. "Well," she said. "What are we waiting for?"

"I'll marry you," Father George said. "But you'll both have to promise to listen to my advice after the ceremony and make every effort to follow it."

❦

Afterward there was a little more brandy. Then Thérèse said she'd change and give Father George back the wedding dress.

He shook his head. "The dress belongs to you, Thérèse. I want you to have it."

"Some day this watching boy on the woodbox will marry a young woman."

"She'll want her own dress then. This one is yours."

Thérèse made a curtsy. "Naturally I will treasure it."

Father George put his arm around Peter. "Where are you and your wife going to live?" he asked in the voice of one man addressing another.

"My great-uncle, a master stonecarver, wants me to come to Barre to work for him."

Thérèse said quickly, "You already know far more about carving than your uncle. We'll live in my folks' empty tenants' house near the brook between our families. You can walk up to the stone shed each day. I'll go to work for my cousin, Manette Riendeau, at her hairdresser's shop here in the village."

Father George shook his head. "You haven't asked my advice on this matter. The agreement was that I'd marry you if you'd follow my advice. Don't try to live on the disputed land or near either set of parents. They'll continue to quarrel, and sooner or later you'll get caught up in it despite your best intentions not to."

"I think Peter and I can stop this foolishness between our families," Thérèse said. "Now that we're married."

"No," Father George said firmly. "Emile and Mimi Lacourse and Pietro and Rosa Gambini will go on fighting until they're too old to fight any longer. Don't put yourselves and your new marriage in the middle. You'll have disagreements enough of your own. You don't need to assume your parents'."

Now Father George put his arm around Thérèse. "Go to Peter's great-uncle in Barre. Peter needs to learn all he can about his chosen work. His art. Then, when you have a family of your own and your folks are elderly, come back to our little village if you still want to."

"All this is good advice from a great man," Peter said to Thérèse.

"I'd miss ma mère," Thérèse blurted, and wiped at her eyes with the lace sleeve of her wedding gown.

"You have me now," Peter said, taking her in his arms. "I'll see that you miss no one."

"You'll both miss your parents," Father George said. "But you'll visit them frequently. In time you can come back here to live if you want to."

"What should we do?" Thérèse said to Peter.

"I love you," Peter said. Then, with a quick, desperate look at Father George, "I'll leave the decision to you, Thérèse."

Thérèse took a deep breath and looked at the priest, who smiled back at her. "Well, then," she said. "What must be must be. No doubt they have hairdressing shops in Barre, too."

Father George took Thérèse's hand. "Everything changes in the fullness of time, Thérèse. This feud will end with your parents' generation. Your children will laugh about how the old folks carried on."

"We'll have to find a rent," Thérèse said to Peter. "I won't live with your relatives. How can we afford a rent?"

Father George handed her the envelope. On it he had written "To Peter and Thérèse Gambini." She smiled at her new name on the outside, then gave it to Peter to open.

"Thank you, Father," he said, looking inside the envelope. "Come, Thérèse. Now we can afford a rent. But tonight we'll stay in the little motor court on Lake Memphremagog. An hour from now Barre will be the last thing on your mind."

❧

Peter and Thérèse set up housekeeping in Barre, near the Rock of Ages quarry. Peter apprenticed himself to his great-uncle, the master carver. Thérèse found work at a hairdresser's shop.

And what of the great feud? Well! To no one's astonishment the two enemy families descended on the Big House the day after Father George performed the marriage, threatening him and each other and even the young couple themselves. But what's done is done. At first Father George shouted back, giving them as good as he got. He threatened them with excommunication, asked me if his face was getting red, and ran to the cupboard for a drink of acquavite. Then he talked to the families for a long time, and in the end they went home, the husbands with grim expressions on their faces, as though they sensed the impending end of the trouble that had sustained them for so long, the wives looking not terribly displeased.

For a few years the older generation continued to quarrel. No one repaired the right of way leading up to the quarry. Occasionally there was a run-in, shouting, threats. But their hearts no longer seemed to be in it. When Pietro had a near-fatal heart attack, Mimi Lacourse personally delivered two baguettes and a maple sugar pie to the Gambinis. Eight months later, after Mimi Lacourse slipped while gathering eggs and fractured her hip, Rosa Gambini appeared at the door with a jug of wild grape wine and a piping hot lasagna.

"They're killing each other with kindness," Father George told me. "Now they're fighting with food."

For two or three years Thérèse and Peter and their daughter returned to live in Kingdom Common so that Peter could work the pink granite from the quarry above their folks' places. It was Peter, in fact, whom Father George had commissioned to carve the stone memorial loaves to Sylvie and Marie Bonhomme. But it proved impossible to keep the water out of the quarry for

more than a few days at a time, and the sunset-colored stone itself seemed to be about played out, like the hill farms and big
woods and the mills of Kingdom County. Peter and Thérèse returned to Barre, where, as Thérèse had predicted, he soon became recognized as one of the finest stone sculptors in the country. The elder Lacourses and Gambinis all died within two years
of each other; one way or another, even feuds come to an end.

During the summer after I graduated from college, Peter and
Thérèse traveled north to the Common again, this time to un-
veil, in the cemetery behind the church, a life-size memorial
sculpture that Peter had carved the previous winter and had
trucked to Kingdom Common under canvas the night before.
Half of the village was on hand for the ceremony, including Father George and me.

"Here it is," Peter said as the ropes and canvas fell away. "It's
called 'Sleep after Love.'"

From the crowd of Commoners came a rising murmur of astonishment, of delight, of awe. Even Louvia the Fortuneteller
lifted her hand to her wax bridgework in amazement.

On a plain bed of white Vermont marble, in an open spot
overlooking the village and about midway between the burial
plots of the Gambinis and Lacourses, reposed two sleeping figures of pink granite, a young man and a woman, folded together in eternal embrace, their heads close together on the marble pillow.

"Love conquers all," someone whispered — Louvia!

Even Father George was speechless. All he could do was nod
in recognition of this wonderment.

"I was the model for the woman," Thérèse told him. "When
we sleep we don't quarrel."

"We don't quarrel anyway," Peter said. "We're lovers, not fighters."

Thérèse laughed. "We quarrel all the time. It's in our blood. Isn't that so, Rosa?"

The small dark-haired girl between them laughed, either in delight at the sculpture or at Thérèse's remark.

Father George smiled, too, though his face was abstracted. I wondered what he was thinking of.

❦

All that was a long time ago. Thérèse Lacourse and Peter Gambini have grandchildren of their own now. The special world of the village has become much like the rest of the world. Yet the stone lovers still lie entwined in the graveyard above the town, and the inscription chiseled into the foot of the marble bed is still sharp and clear.

SLEEP AFTER LOVE

To the Memory of
Pietro and Rosa Gambini
Emile and Mimi Lacourse
Peter and Thérèse Gambini
Father George Lecoeur

May They Rest in Love Eternal

♦4♦
The Daredevil

Just as it is impossible to define the village of Kingdom Common separately from the railroad that informed it with so much of its character, it is impossible to define the Murphy family of Irishtown, that tiny enclave of a dozen battened houses just north of the village, apart from the context of the railroad that had brought the Murphys to Vermont and the Common the first place.

—Father George, "A Short History"

I T WAS CIRCUS DAY in Kingdom Common. The dawn sky was reddening quickly, though the lurid strip of crimson along the horizon was caused in part by the Canadian forest fires that had been burning out of control two hundred miles to the northeast for the past two weeks, creating in that quarter of the night sky a glow like embers. The wildfires had suffused a haze over the entire Kingdom, through which everything took on a slightly illusory quality.

At the same time, though it was now mid-July, there had been a sharp frost overnight, and those of us drinking our early morning coffee at the hotel could look out and see, on the glaze of frost on the green, the faint reflection of the red dawn sky.

"That could almost get to be discouraging," Bumper Stevens said, meaning the summer frost.

"It's the sky I'm more concerned about," Doc Harrison said. "Red sky in the morning, circusgoers take warning."

"Today will be just fine, Doc," Father George said. "Look at Blackhawk."

Everyone's eyes moved across the common and up the one-hundred-foot-high granite clock tower of the courthouse. Above the clock was a lookout with four tall paneless windows, one in each side of the tower. Some twenty feet above the lookout, looming high over the tallest elms on the common, was the copper weathervane, set in place half a century ago, of the fabled thoroughbred Morgan pacer Blackhawk, mane and tail flying. Today Blackhawk's head was into the north, from which quarter both the recent run of good weather and the filmy haze of smoke from the Canadian fires were coming.

"His nose never lies," Father George said, and everyone nodded.

That, at least, was a relief. For in those years in Kingdom Common, when the circus came to town, we all prayed for good weather. Now it only remained for the Slade Bros. Last Railway Extravaganza and Greatest Little Show on Earth to arrive in the village. It was due at any moment.

*

The circus handbills promised wonderful things. See the grand, free, mile-long parade and the Four Horses of the Apocalypse! See the Bestiary of Antipodean Rarities! See two three-ring performances! In fact, the Slade Bros. Railway Extravaganza was a shabby little affair. A couple dozen dingy blue-and-yellow circus wagons chained on rusty flatbeds, a few boxcars, and two faded Pullman sleepers that had formerly belonged to the Santa Fe

Line, pulled by a single, grimy, snub-nosed diesel locomotive that limped into town every two or three years for a one-day stand on the common, then departed, leaving a trampled ring in the outfield grass of the baseball diamond where the Big Top had been pitched and a sad litter of crushed lemonade cups, popcorn boxes, and hot dog wrappers.

My job for today, as Father George had explained it the night before, was to chaperone Kingdom Common's seventeen-year-old tomboy and self-declared daredevil, Molly Murphy. Until three years ago, when her parents were killed in a railroad wreck on the trestle a mile north of town, Molly had lived in one of the half dozen shanties near the trestle, an area known as Irishtown. After she was orphaned, Father George had arranged for her to go to the convent boarding school in Memphremagog. For almost as long as I could remember, she had wanted to run away with the circus—which was just now pulling into town, with Molly herself waving from the cab of the locomotive.

"Are you responsible for this redheaded she-hooligan?" the engineer said to me a few minutes later in the rail yard. "She stood smack on the trestle outside of town and flagged me down. Refused to budge an inch. Animals all shaken up, performers thrown out of their berths, not to mention my old ticker here. A person could go to jail for that."

Molly laughed and vaulted out of the cab. In her baseball cap, jeans, T-shirt, and sneakers, she looked like a boy with a ponytail. "How's my best friend and future intended this morning?" Molly called out to me. And she ran up and gave me a big hug. "I can still pin you in ten seconds flat, Frank."

I laughed. "You're too big to wrestle now."

"Am I big enough to marry yet?"

Ever since she was a tiny girl, Molly had declared it her intention to marry me, though the idea of Molly Murphy marrying anyone was inconceivable.

To the engineer she said, "I'm not going to jail. I'm going to join your circus."

"Yes, sir," the engineer said. A gaunt man of about fifty, he wore a denim jacket, a red bandanna, wrist-length gloves, and a blue-and-yellow cap that said Slade Bros. over the bill. He appeared more weary than angry. "Flagged me down and swarmed up into the cab and insisted on riding into town in the circus train," he said. "You don't get killed by a locomotive, little missy, I imagine you'll wind up in the penitentiary."

The engineer made it sound as though winding up in the penitentiary might be rather desirable, causing Molly to double over with laughter.

"I'm Frank Bennett," I said. "This is Molly Murphy. She's wanted to join the circus since she was five."

"Four," Molly said.

"Well, Frank Bennett, here's a word of advice from an old railway circus hand. Tell your redheaded best friend and future intended here not to be jumping in front of no more locomotives. It will cut short a circus career quicker'n anything."

❦

When Molly and I next caught up with the engineer, he was pounding with a gloved fist on the door of a boxcar just in front of the circus train caboose. Out of it stumbled a couple of dozen roustabouts and tent riggers, men with unkempt oily hair and dark, pocked faces. A few minutes later there emerged a tall man in a blue shirt, a yellow vest, and a blue-and-yellow-striped straw hat. Under his terse directions the roustabouts bridged the gaps between the flatbeds with wooden planks and began un-chaining the circus wagons and rolling them forward and down a ramp off the lead car.

While the performers slept on in their Pullman cars, a dusty half-grown elephant and four Appaloosa horses, white with gray speckles, pulled the tent and pole and the cook wagons from the railway siding over to the common. All this was done with a minimum of conversation, but a great deal of cursing and spitting and scowling, under the direction of the tall circus master in the jaunty straw hat, who, when Molly approached him on the green, turned out to be none other than the train engineer who'd wanted to send her to prison.

"Mr. Slade?"

He gave an abstracted nod.

"I intend to go to work for you," she said. "I can do any job you've got. Bareback rider, aerialist, head clown, whatever."

"Big Top in center field," Slade called out to the roustabouts. "Cook tent this side of second base. Midway in left field, carousel by home plate." He thrust a collapsible canvas bucket at Molly. "Here, Missy. Run this full of cold water for Rudyard Hefalump."

Molly dashed to the water spigot behind the backstop and filled the bucket for the undersized elephant, which watched the circus master narrowly out of malicious little eyes, waited until he wasn't looking, then filled its trunk with water and played a great arcing jet full in his face.

"Hosed down!" Slade exclaimed in a strangely satisfied tone of voice as he wiped at his face with his blue-and-yellow handkerchief. "Even my elephant's hand is set against me this morning. I suspected when I billed this town that it was a mistake. What's all this haze and smoke in the air?"

"Forest fires up in Canada," I said. "We get it nearly every summer."

He nodded. "Hop to, gentlemen," he told the tent riggers. "There's a major conflagration headed this way."

The riggers set up the dining tent, open at the sides like a pavilion, then, with the help of the horses, dragged the three center poles of the Big Top onto the outfield grass and spread the vast blue canvas tent with yellow stripes out over them. It lay there on the common like the biggest parachute in the world. How many side stakes did the Big Top have, Molly wondered. One hundred and eighty, if she must know. How long were the center poles? Sixty by God feet, Douglas firs shipped east from Washington State to the tune of $535 apiece. Was Rudyard an African elephant or an Indian elephant?

"See what I mean?" Slade said to me.

"About what?"

"Redheads. When they aren't throwing your locomotive off the tracks they're beleaguering you with questions. Don't never marry one. I did once and it was the worst mistake of my life." He turned to Molly. "Indian," he said.

"Where are the other Slade brothers?" she said.

"Who, Brother Beeb? Up yonder."

"Up yonder?"

"Canvas coliseum in the sky." Slade jabbed his thumb upward at the hazy zenith, in commemoration of the passing of Brother Beeb.

"What did he die of?"

"Too much circusing," the remaining Slade brother said. "That will do it every time."

❧

Underfoot the frost was evaporating. In spots the grass was already dry. As more Commoners ambled over to the green to watch the setup, the riggers hitched Rudyard to the free end of a three-inch-thick hawser attached through a massive pulley to the top of the center pole. The Four Horses of the Apocalypse were separated into two pairs and hitched to hawsers connected to the two other poles. At a command from Slade, Rudyard and the horses plodded off in three separate directions. Majestically and magically, the Big Top billowed up and outward, taking shape before everyone's eyes. This was always a great moment on circus day, and, viewed through the haze from the forest fires, the scene had a certain anachronistic and dreamy grandeur, like a fair on a medieval green. Molly squeezed my hand hard and sighed.

We were immediately jolted back to the present by the staccato clanging of riggers driving side-flap stakes with sledge hammers until it sounded as though the last railway circus was laying its own tracks across the common. From the rail yard, Rudyard and the Four Horses were pulling wagons containing the animals, the midway concessions, the sideshow tents, and the Bestiary of Antipodean Rarities, as well as two flatbed wagons, like hay wagons, upon which reposed an old-fashioned steam-driven calliope and a merry-go-round with painted wooden mythological monsters instead of circus animals.

By now the performers were beginning to drift over to the

dining tent from the gold-striped Pullman cars. Molly jumped back from the path of a yellow forklift driven by a tattooed man with a black eye patch. Riding on the forks was the largest woman I'd ever seen.

"You lot lice keep outen the way," the tattooed man snarled as he went careening past, but the colossal woman, who had long blond hair and blue eyes and pink cheeks like a doll, smiled at us and waved.

"Beautiful Giantess from the Hippodrome of Grotesqueries," Slade explained. "Tips the scales at ten hundred and fifty pounds, wonderfully good-natured, good draw for the barker's ballyhoo. Plays the calliope like a concert pianist."

Molly's eyes shone with delight at Slade's circus lingo. It was plain that she loved everything about the strange and embattled world of the Last Railway Extravaganza.

"Back some years ago," Slade was telling us, "when the Flying Zempenskis come on board, I and Brother Beeb had to go out and purchase a higher tent." He nodded toward the Big Top. "Holey old spread of canvas, bought it off the Adam Forepaugh outfit that went bust in Skokie in '57. Why come, the Flying Z's needed more clearance for their trapeze act."

"I intend to join that trapeze act," Molly said.

"The Zempenskis will be gratified," Slade told her.

I laughed. But Slade looked up at the Big Top as if fearful that it might collapse at any moment. "This is a failing operation," he said. "In the meantime, we may as well slide over to the eating tent and have some breakfast."

Breakfast was steak, eggs, bacon, oatmeal, ham, mountains of toast and pancakes, and oceans of hot strong coffee, all served on scarred wooden tables with fold-out benches. The lean Slade brother heaped up his tin plate with some of everything and ate like a trencherman rather than a man on his last legs from too much circusing.

"Yum," Molly said. "I wouldn't mind a breakfast like this every day. You ought to see what they feed us up at the convent school."

"You could say yum and not be too far off the mark," Slade said. "Other side of the coin, beefsteak beefsteak beefsteak, three times a day, seven times a week, adds up." He pushed back his straw hat, which made him look momentarily younger. "Di-fugalties," he said. "They did for Brother Beeb. Soon enough they will do for me."

For all of his animadversions on redheaded hooligans, Slade seemed to have taken a paternal shine to Molly. "Look around, girlie, without staring at nobody. Note that the performers eat by theirselves. Grotesqueries chow down together. Animal trainers have their own table, same for the clowns. Riggers and roustabouts feed last."

"That's not fair, Mr. Slade. The riggers do all the work."

"Life ain't fair," Slade said happily. "No, it is not. Where's my fire eater? Stole away by King Cole Amusements. Cat man's serving out a stretch in Macon for statutory with a cracker gal, redheaded, naturally, looked a hard-bitten thirty if she was a day and turnt out to be fifteen. Saddest joey clown I ever employed, another Emmett Kelly when it come to sweeping up a spotlight, jumped ship for R, B and B in Sarasota last winter. Here's my bread and butter coming in now. Flying Z's. Don't stare."

A slim, dark-haired young man, an older man with silvering

temples, and a women with platinum hair came into the dining tent and sat down at a nearby empty table. All three wore dark warm-up tights. The two men looked like weight lifters. The woman, though middle-aged and almost as ruggedly built as the men, was astoundingly good-looking. As they ate they talked quietly in a Slavic-sounding language. Instead of ham and steak and eggs they had cold cereal and brown bread.

Molly watched the newcomers intently. "They can't talk English? That's why they sit off by themselves?"

"Oh, they can speak English," the Slade brother said. "Reason they set alone is what I was telling you, circus is the worst old caste system in the world." He lowered his voice. "Flying Z's, they're the aristocracy. They won't break bread with nobody, including yours truly. It drives this old circus master to distraction, but it's tradition, and if you're circus, tradition's religion. Say you were to come on board? Running a midway concession, say? You'd be at the bottom of the heap. Lower'n the riggers even. How old would you be, sis?"

"Seventeen."

"Well, I don't want to hold out too much hope, hope being by 'n' large a poor proposition. But if you ever live to be eighteen, there might be something for you on the midway, you promise not to pester the Flying Z's today." He lowered his voice. "For one, Count Z and the Countess lost a gal, Young Count's sister, offen the high wire in Manhattan, Kansas, this past spring. You probably read about it in the rags and mags. Second most terrible catastrophe I ever witnessed under canvas. She was riding a unicycle over a wire with too much sag in it. Gal and unicycle and all plunged forty feet and shot clean through the safety net. Since then the Z's have been about one more small di-fugalty away from throwing in the towel and striking back to Warsaw."

"She was killed?" Molly said.

"Yes, and don't you be getting no wild ideas. She was twenty-one, and she'd been in training since she was two."

"I can do three flips off the high trestle over the river outside of town, and if I had another fifteen feet to work with I could do four. Isn't that right, Frank?"

I nodded.

"Flying trapeze ain't no train trestle." Slade stood up and fished in his vest pocket. "Here's your passes, good for the matinee only. Keep little sis here away from the Zempenskis, Frank."

"What was the worst catastrophe?" I said.

"Under canvas? Conflagration when Uncle Phineas Slade's Big Top took fire in Toledo in '29. Eighty-one circusgoers, twelve performers, five handsome show gals, and thirteen large circus animals incinerated alive. Funeral cortege estimated in excess of forty-five thousand."

The brother thought for a minute. Then he shook his head. "Circusing," he said. "If it don't get you coming, it will get you going. Brother Beeb was here, he'd tell you the exact same."

❧

It was hazier now, and the acrid smell of smoke was stronger. In the west an optical illusion of the northern Green Mountains quivered high above the horizon, like mountains in a dream. The sun looked like a red-hot stove lid. I glanced up at Blackhawk, still facing into the north.

In the meantime, Rudyard and the Four Horses were hauling

into the Big Top wagons that unfolded into blue-and-yellow bleachers. The forklift raced past us, carrying the Zempenskis' rolled-up safety net and trapeze apparatus. The driver glowered at Molly out of his single eye.

Inside the tent, roustabouts were setting up flood lamps on metal poles. Underfoot, electrical wires as gaudy as tropical snakes ran everywhere. The sunlight filtering through the faded blue canvas tinted everything a strange pale violet, including the Count and the Young Count as they climbed up rope ladders to rig their high wire and trapezes.

Molly held out her blue hands. "Look, Frank. Magic!"

I laughed and put my arm around her shoulder. "You love everything about the circus, don't you, sweetheart?"

"I do," Molly said. Then she said, "Frank? Are you really going into the seminary to be a priest like Father George?"

"Probably. I guess so."

She looked at me hard with her intense green eyes. "And we'd still be best friends?"

"Sure."

Molly nodded. "That's good," she said. "Because even if you never marry me, I can stand it if you don't marry anyone else and we stay best friends. Oh! Look."

Nearby, the Countess had begun warming up on a small trampoline. In her black leotard, with her heavy blond hair in a ponytail, her fine features, and her sparkling teeth, she looked like a veteran movie actress. But her eyes were remote and expressionless and trained on the faraway distance, as though looking for something she'd given up hope of seeing, something she looked for out of habit alone, in much the same way she did flip after flip on the trampoline, without thinking about what she was doing.

Molly edged closer. "I'm sorry about your daughter," she said. The Countess didn't reply.

"I can do three flips off the flying trapeze," Molly offered. "Probably four."

"Please not to stand so close," the Countess said without interrupting her workout. "No insure."

"No insure is right," said Slade, who'd appeared from nowhere accompanied by a large monkey, black with a white face. "What did I tell you about no redheaded scalawags pestering the Zempenskis? Do you want me to revoke them passes?"

Molly bent over and extended her fingers to the monkey, which stood up on its hind legs and solemnly shook hands with her.

"This gentleman is a white-faced Kilimanjaro monkey, performs on the high wire with the Zempenskis," Slade said, as the monkey ran up the center pole and scampered across the high wire. "It's a climbing fool, if you want the truth. They have it with Lloyd's for ten thousand dollars—you'll see why at the matinee. Meantime, I imagine you're going to the parade?"

❦

The circus parade started at the southeast end of the common. It came lurching up the east side of the green past the railroad station, the courthouse, and the Academy, turned jerkily onto the short street between the north end of the common and the hotel, swung down the west side past the brick shopping block, then hooked back along the south end of the green to complete the circuit. Three times the parade circumambulated the common: a

sorry little progression nothing at all like the mile-long caval-
cade promised on the advance posters. But what the grand free
parade of the Last Railway Extravaganza and Greatest Little
Show on Earth lacked in size and splendor, it more than made
up for in its sweet small idiosyncrasies and a certain brave
razzmatazz, staggering along under the direction of the benignly
cynical Slade, in spite of every conceivable di-fugalty.

The procession was led by a blue bandwagon pulled by Rudyard, on whose back, in a rickety howdah, sat the big Kilimanjaro monkey. The four-piece band consisted of a saxophone, a
trumpet, a slide trombone, and a gleaming sousaphone played
by none other than the versatile Mr. Slade, in a major-domo's
uniform with a tall beaver hat like a palace guard's. Behind the
bandwagon walked the one-eyed roustabout, now wearing a
turban and whapping, at arrhythmic intervals, a bass drum.
Around his neck was a placard that said "150-Year-Old Drummer Boy and Parsee."

Straggling behind the elderly drummer boy were the Four
Horses of the Apocalypse, each pulling a float. First came the
Bestiary of Antipodean Rarities. Reposing at the feet of a
roustabout in a big-game hunter's leather hat were a dark-
maned Nubian lion, looking suspiciously like an emaciated
tame puma with a few dollops of black paint splashed on its
scrawny neck; a rare Tibetan ram that bore more than a passing
resemblance to Bumper Stevens's evil-tempered old billy goat,
Satan; the twenty-six-foot-long Pythoness Sapienta, stretched
out in the sunshine inert as a fire hose; and a Nile river horse, a
Cape buffalo, and a white rhino, all three of which appeared to
be stuffed.

On the next wagon were the sideshow performers from the

Hippodrome of Grotesqueries. Arrayed upon packing crates or squatting in the straw strewn over the wagon bed were the fire eater's replacement, the sword swallower, the armless-legless child, and the beautiful half-ton giantess with golden curls. They were followed on a third float by the Flying Zempenskis, doing a mechanical routine of handstands, pyramids, and flips. Three clowns, dressed as a jester, a tramp, and a rube farmer, capered on a fourth wagon to the band's bright and discordant rendition of "Stars and Stripes Forever."

The bass drum boomed and vibrated from one end of the village to the other. The pungency of the circus animals was sharp on the air; and the entire parade had about it a picture-book quality. For a few minutes that morning, as I stood with Father George on the cracked slate sidewalk in front of the hotel, watching this strange conjunction of the wondrous and the absurd thrice circle the village green as if weaving an ancient spell over the town, I was caught up in its old, shabby glory, and my heart beat a little faster.

"Where's Molly?" Father George said suddenly, looking around.

"I'm not her keeper, you know."

"Well, if you aren't, I don't know who the hell is," Father George said, his face getting red. "By the bald-headed baby Jesus, Frank, I thought I told you—oh, no!"

And he began to laugh.

I looked in the direction he was pointing. As Rudyard headed up the west side of the green for his third and final circuit, a girlish figure with a bright red ponytail appeared on his back in front of the monkey's howdah. Having evidently dropped onto the elephant from the drooping branches of an overhanging elm, she stood now on one foot, now on the other, now on her hands. Finally she danced on the elephant's back with the monkey while the band played and the crowd laughed and clapped and cheered, as though nothing that they had seen thus far could exceed, for sheer bravado and hoopla, the escapades of our hometown tomboy and daredevil, Molly Murphy.

❧

"Acting up," the Commoners called Molly's behavior when she was younger. Once she appeared at the Big House in a home-made green spaceman's costume. "Come quick, Frank. I just told Welcome Kinneson a man from Mars was going to land on the roof of Ben Currier's sugarhouse at high noon."

Or, while she was playing flies-and-grounders with a gang of us village boys on the Common, and Louvia DeBanville appeared with her enormous reticule: "Louvia! I dreamed that the world is going to end tonight at the stroke of midnight. What should I wear for the event?"

Molly teased me, too, from the time I was ten and she was six, the way a younger sister teases a big brother: constantly and devilishly, tagging after me everywhere, horning in on my ball games and fishing excursions, inventing any number of objectionable nicknames for me at the same time that she swore she would marry me "before I marry anyone else in Kingdom Common." And woe betide Molly Murphy's enemies in the village. Long before she was a teenager, she was more feared for her merciless tongue than Louvia herself.

Even the auction-barn gang respected her. Actually, she was a great favorite with them because she cooked up her own escapades, most of which were far more imaginative than any that the town rowdies could have devised for her. At twelve, Molly became the first person in the history of the village to go over the High Falls of the Kingdom River behind the hotel in a barrel, choosing for her maiden voyage opening day of trout season, when the banks below the thundering cataract were lined with an audience of fishermen. Miraculously, she emerged from this performance with only a broken little finger, a cracked collarbone, and more bruises and contusions than Doc Harrison could remember seeing on anyone other than a few scarcely recognizable automobile and farm-machinery fatalities. Her parents tried to rein her in, to no avail. Two months later she swam the entire twenty-five-mile length of Lake Memphremagog. She rode standing up on the back of Ben Currier's prize racehorse as it galloped around the track at the county fairgrounds; and at every possible opportunity she practiced her flips off the high trestle near Irishtown, never doubting that when the time came, she would run off with the circus and become an aerialist.

"Where do you calculate she'll strike next?" Slade asked after I'd filled him in on Molly's history.

"I don't have any idea."

"Well, be warned, Frank Bennett," he said. "Next time your best friend and intended breaks out, I aim to prefer charges. Like Brother Beeb said just before heading West, enough is enough."

He was standing with his head inside the workings of the

merry-go-round, twisting something with a wrench as long as a Louisville Slugger. Nearby stood a crowd of expectant kids, marveling at the old-fashioned carousel with its strange company of mythical beasts. Chipped and faded, they were still recognizable as a sphinx, a gorgon, a basilisk, a Cyclops, two Furies, a three-headed Cerberus, a siren, and an assortment of Greek and Roman gods and goddesses. Molly was perched astride Cerberus. But the merry-go-round refused to budge, and the steam calliope emitted only a puny whistle, like a sick teakettle.

"Thirty days on bread and water can work wonders for a young female felon," Slade muttered into the frozen gears of the carousel.

He gave a last exasperated two-handed heave on the wrench, then looked up at the soaring courthouse tower, as though seeking consolation there. His eyes seemed to be following the progress of the century-old bittersweet vine that ascended the sheer south wall of the building, snaked along the ridgeline of the roof, then traced its way, in a delicate lacy green pattern, nearly up to the defunct clock on the west side of the tower.

"You can't imagine what a draw I'd be as the main attraction of your aerial show," Molly wheedled.

From deep in the carousel's workings, Slade's voice said, "You can't imagine what a draw I'd be as ringmaster of Ringling Brothers and Barnum and Bailey."

The words were no sooner out of his mouth than the merry-go-round gave a screeching howl and lurched into motion. The calliope broke into the strains of "Go Tell Aunt Rhodie." Wrench in hand, Slade tiptoed backward so as not to break the charm. The merry-go-round picked up speed as the calliope elided into a squawking rendition of "The Sidewalks of New York," and the battered wooden monsters seemed to beam in the smoky sunshine.

"A thousand thank you's, gentle friend," Molly said as she vaulted off Cerberus a few minutes later. "On to the Hippodrome, Frankie-boy!"

Inside the Hippodrome tent, the Grotesqueries lounged on trunks and packing crates, visiting companionably with a handful of spectators. They were dimly lighted by a single flood lamp attached to a pole. The air smelled of mildewed canvas.

Near the entrance, on a rounded wicker laundry hamper, sat the 150-year-old drummer boy and Parsee, formerly the one-eyed roustabout. The Pythoness Sapienta was draped over his shoulders, her little wedge-shaped head swaying gently from side to side, surveying the small crowd with sleepy curiosity. "Gaze into the eyes of death," the Parsee said to Molly.

Before the snake handler had any idea what she was doing, Molly slipped in under the first several feet of the great somnolent Pythoness.

"Jesus, girlie, look out!" exclaimed the Parsee in an accent much closer to that of Indiana than of India.

"The eyes of death!" Molly said. She smiled at the snake's head, six inches from hers. "You go back to sleep, Sapienta." She ducked out from under the constrictor's loops and said, "Do you need an assistant, Parsee darling?"

"I'll tell you what I don't need," the one-eyed snake handler said. "I don't need no smart-alecker young gal bedeviling me at every turn. You clear out now or I'll holler for Brother Slade to run you off the lot."

"Your threats don't frighten me in the least," Molly said.

The Parsee gave her a sinister smile. "Do you want me to frighten you, Missy Know-All?"

He rummaged in his hamper and pulled out a gallon glass jar with a wide mouth. Inside, floating upside down in a clear liquid, was a deformed human fetus with webbed fingers and toes, a dorsal fin and a short tail.

"Old Grandpop's been putting up preserves," the Parsee said. He unscrewed the lid, releasing the penetrating odor of formaldehyde. He lifted the deformed creature out of the jar and sat down on the hamper with the fetus on his knee. "Meet Nostradamus, girlie. The four-hundred-year-old infant prophet. Ask him a question, he'll give you an answer."

"That's no prophet, it's a little child that didn't turn out right inside its mamma," Molly shouted, jabbing her finger into the Parsee's chest.

She grabbed Nostradamus off the Parsee's knee and held him up to her face and looked deep into the slits where his eyes should have been. He was about as large as a cat, and a shocking instance of what can go wrong in the universe. "It's a bad thing they've done to you, little one," Molly said. "I wish I could give you all the love your ma would have."

She gently kissed Nostradamus's wizened gray cheek, eased him back into his jar, clapped on the lid, and shoved it hard into the Parsee's stomach. "As for you," she shouted, "you should be electrocuted for making a spectacle of him."

Not far from the Parsee and the Pythoness was the fire eater's replacement, a man with a gaping hole in the side of his skull. In a husky voice he explained that a crowbar had been driven completely through his cranium in a blasting accident in a West Virginia coal mine. He put down his gasoline-soaked fire-eating tongs, picked up the offending bar, and inserted it several inches into a hole above his right ear. "I read about you in *Ripley's*," Molly said. "You're famous. Soon I will be, too."

The fire eater made a charred noise, like a burning log collapsing into its own coals.

Gawain, the armless-legless "child," signed his autograph for Molly with a tiny flipper attached to his shoulder. The beautiful giantess complimented her on her performance on Rudyard during the street parade. And for a brief time in the Hippodrome, the daredevil withdrew, leaving good-natured Molly Murphy visiting amicably with the sideshow family of the Last Railway Extravaganza and Greatest Little Show on Earth.

"Why come it's always the redheaded ones?" Slade was saying to me. "Every town has its Peck's bad boy or gal, and seven in ten of them sport a head of hair the color of barn paint. That gal is bidding fair to disrupt my entire show—complaints about her are pouring in from all quarters."

"She really does want to join your circus," I said. "Why don't you give her a shot?"

Slade shrugged. "She'd only come back home in six months, damaged goods."

"I don't think so. She knows what she wants."

"I want to run the Moscow Circus," Slade said. "At this moment, my odds are considerably better."

He picked up his blue megaphone and climbed up into a tall yellow ballyhoo stand at the entrance to the Big Top. "Hurry,

hurry, hurry. The matinee of the Greatest Little Show on Earth begins at two o'clock. See the Flying Zempenskis' death-defying aerialist act. See the Four Horses of the Apocalypse Equestrian Exhibition. See clowns, clowns, clowns..."

The common was filling up with spectators, mainly parents with kids in tow. Flashing our passes, Molly and I crowded into the Big Top and sat as close to the single ring as we could get. At five of the hour, Rudyard Hefalump drew the steam calliope wagon inside. The beautiful giantess sat at the keyboard playing a booming rendition of "Give My Regards to Broadway." Out ran Slade, tall and imposing in a crimson ringmaster's coat and a shiny stovepipe hat. He cracked a long whip in the fresh saw-dust and gave a blast on a silver whistle. To the coughing strains of "Broadway," punctuated by the rifle reports of the ringmas-ter's whip and his piercing whistle, two of the Apocalyptic Horses galloped into the ring side by side. Standing with one foot on the back of each animal was Count Zempenski.

The giantess played an anticipatory riff simulating a cavalry charge, whereupon the Countess and the Young Count rode into the ring single file on the other two horses, crouched low on their speckled backs like attacking Indians. Galloping a yard apart, the Count's teamed pair tore around the ring with the Countess and Young Count in pursuit. Suddenly the Countess and Young Count wheeled their steeds around and rode straight between the Count's horses, under his wide-spread legs.

The matinee sped by. Clowns dressed as demons plagued Slade with water pistols. Rudyard reared up on his wrinkled hind legs on a low stool. A trained seal balanced a ball on its nose and played "Row, Row, Row Your Boat" on six rubber horns while the Young Count rode a bicycle across the high wire with the Count standing on his shoulders and the Kilimanjaro monkey clinging to the Count's back. Roustabouts and riggers as sober as you would ever see them trotted in and out of the ring with props and worked their way through the cheering crowd, selling pink lemonade and Slade Bros. Circus caps. And for a few fleeting moments, the failing little one-ring circus under the patched old tent became a magical, blue-tinted fairyland.

Before the trapeze finale, the circus was interrupted by the obligatory drunk who wanted to perform. He was barefoot and dressed like a hayseed farmer in torn overalls and a straw hat. The ringmaster expostulated with him to no avail. The sheriff, Mason White, was called forward to evict the interloper; but when the law officer lunged for the drunk, he missed and, to the crowd's delight, sprawled face first in the sawdust. Then Slade rushed at the rube farmer, who sprang up the rope ladder to the trapeze rigging. Flinging off his overalls and hat as he climbed, he revealed himself as Count Zempenski. In the meantime, the Young Count mounted to the trapeze opposite his father. As the crowd cheered they launched themselves into the air, flipped, exchanged trapezes, seemed to fall only to catch themselves by their ankles, and performed a dozen other next-to-impossible feats.

To a gathering drumroll, played by the 150-year-old drummer boy, the Countess took her husband's place high overhead. In a bold voice Slade announced, "Ladies and gentlemen, boys and girls. Countess Sophie Zempenski, world-renowned aerialist of the Last Railway Extravaganza and Greatest Little Show on

Earth, will now perform three somersaults off the flying trapeze. From Warsaw, Poland, just returned from a triumphal European tour, I give you—Countess Sophie."

Assisted by her husband, who pulled a long rope leading up to the trapeze, Countess Sophie, in the briefest of spangled blue costumes, began to swing back and forth in widening arcs under the roof of the tent. Opposite and below her, some thirty feet away, the Young Count stood on a tiny platform holding his trapeze in one hand, the other hand and arm directing the crowd's attention to his mother. Molly was on the edge of her seat, no doubt thinking about the Young Count's sister and the terrible accident in Kansas. At a nod from the ringmaster the giantess struck up "The Man on the Flying Trapeze" on the calliope. The Countess dropped from her sitting position and hung from the trapeze bar with both hands. As she swung higher, the drumroll intensified. Alone in the spotlight, blue as a mermaid glimpsed far beneath the sea, the Countess released her hold, tucked into a glittering ball, and spun over.

"One!" the ringmaster shouted.

The countess spun again.

"Two!" shouted the ringmaster and half the crowd.

In unison the crowd rose. "Three!" they roared as Countess Sophie performed her final revolution and the Young Count, hanging from his trapeze by his legs, catapulted himself out over the ring, reached for her outstretched taped wrists, and plucked her from thin air as surely as a father catches a child tossed over his head for play, while the Common cheered its heart out.

The spectators continued to applaud as Countess Zempenski and her son dropped lightly onto the safety net and somersaulted out onto the sawdust. There they were joined by the Count and the other circus performers. Even a few smirking roustabouts bent a leg to the thundering applause.

Only Molly remained silent until, at last, the cheering died down and the performers ran out of the ring. Then, over the last smattering handclaps, over the calliope playing "Under the Hippodrome," she shouted, "That's nothing! I can do four full flips, and I will before this day is out."

*

"So she's given you the slip again," a very unhappy Father George was saying as he caught up with me on the circus midway late that afternoon. "How the hell did that happen?"

"I don't know and I don't care," I said. "Do you know what that damned kid did right after the matinee? She—"

"Good God almighty, the monkey's broke loose!"

It was Slade, rushing toward us, raising the hue and cry for his missing animal.

"Look!" someone shouted, pointing across the green and up at the courthouse tower.

Sure enough, the big white-and-black monkey was making its way swiftly up the bittersweet vine clinging to the side of the tower. By the time I joined the gathering crowd on the courthouse lawn, the runaway monkey was already higher than the limp blue-and-yellow pennants on the Big Top.

In the meantime, the hook-and-ladder truck, driven by Sheriff White, had skidded up onto the lawn beside us, siren screaming. But the ladder, when fully extended, still came up a few feet shy of the roof.

Slade paced back and forth on the lawn, while the Young Count called for the animal to come down. But the ten-thousand-dollar monkey continued its desperate ascent up the bittersweet vine, from time to time looking down over its shoulder in absolute terror, as if trying to escape not only from the village and the circus but from the earth itself.

"If it isn't redheaded scalawags, it's runaway apes," Slade said in a distraught voice.

"Or both," said Bumper Stevens. Bumper removed his cigar from his mouth and pointed its glowing end at the clock tower. Coming over the ridge of the roof below the tower, clinging to the bittersweet vine for dear life, was Molly Murphy.

She stood, ran along the roof peak to the base of the tower, paused, leaped high into the vine again, and continued to pull herself up nearly as fast as the monkey was climbing. Her left Ked came loose, and she kicked it far out over the steep slate roof below. It landed in front of the hook-and-ladder, bounced once, and came to rest right side up, like a single shoe in the road near an unspeakably bad automobile accident.

"Molly!" I shouted with my heart in my mouth. "Come down from there!" But I might as well have been shouting at the monkey, which, high above her in the hazy air, was resting just below the tower clock.

Here, some ten or twelve years ago, a professional human fly who called himself the Great Zeno had been stymied in his attempt to climb the courthouse tower. Zeno had come to Kingdom Common claiming grandiosely that human hands had not yet erected the structure he couldn't scale. In his résumé he had alleged conquests of the Eiffel Tower, the Empire State Building, and the Golden Gate Bridge, but after ascending to the uppermost reaches of the bittersweet vine, he'd been stopped in his tracks by the smooth face of the clock. He was obliged to descend in ignominy and return to the town his fee of five hundred dollars.

Yet a human fly was, after all, a human being, not a monkey, and the monkey, though visibly trembling, when it finally looked down and saw Molly climbing up the bittersweet vine like a monkey herself, made a desperate leap to the long iron minute hand of the clock. It scampered up that to the hour hand, and up the hour hand to a slight foothold atop the black iron XII. From there it sprang to the granite sill of the lookout window in the tower wall. Still trembling, it ducked inside. A few moments later it appeared on the railed walkway atop the tower, where it clung, shivering, to the base of the weathervane in the likeness of Blackhawk.

To my horror, Molly was at least three quarters of the way up the tower now. Here the bittersweet vine was so slender that the tendrils holding it to the granite blocks were almost too slight to see from below. Yet surely and steadily she crept upward, barefoot now, splayed against the perpendicularity of the battlement-like tower, which seemed to have been built just for this moment. From where I stood, far below, she looked no larger than a small child, pressed against the pink granite made even rosier by the haze in the air. Once she momentarily lost her foothold and slid a foot or so down the face of granite blocks, her legs dangling. A short length of the vine pulled away, and for a dreadful moment, Molly started to sway out from the tower. Somehow she lunged for and found another handhold; but as she did, a chunk of mortar, worked loose over the decades by the vine, broke free and fell to the slate roof below, where it shattered into several pieces with the heart-stopping sound of ice falling onto a hard pavement from a great height.

Now Molly was testing the vine with short tugs before putting her weight on it. The clock face that had ultimately thwarted the Great Zeno loomed just above her, its hands eternally frozen at twenty of twelve. Meanwhile the monkey had climbed up onto Blackhawk's back and was clinging there like a jockey riding down the home stretch.

At this point a new element was introduced into the drama unfolding high above our town. As the monkey, chittering with terror, clung to Blackhawk, and Molly clung to the uppermost tendrils of the bittersweet vine, a blue-clad figure appeared, running up the extended ladder of the fire truck. It was the Young Count, still in his circus tights, rushing to the rescue of Molly or the monkey or both. When he reached the top of the ladder he did not pause at all but simply leaped across the yard-wide space to the roof and sprinted up the slates, only sheer momentum preventing him from slipping backward and plunging forty feet to the steps below.

Just as the Young Count reached the base of the tower, Molly gave a powerful surge and scrabbled up the last few feet below the clock supported by her toes and fingers alone. She got one hand over the narrow projecting cornice at the base of the clock and pulled herself to her knees, then her feet. Using the VII as a foothold, she followed the monkey's route up the minute and hour hands. On top of the XII, she reached for the windowsill of the lookout. But, like the monkey, she would have to jump for it.

She glanced down at the Young Count, now more than

halfway up the tower, bent her legs to the degree that her perch, almost flush with the clock face, would allow her to, and leaped for the sill. Just then an unearthly scream rent the smoky air.

My first thought was that Molly had missed the sill and was already falling. In fact, it was the monkey that had screamed. Molly was hanging by her fingertips from the granite windowsill, now hauling herself by main force up to her elbows, now crouched in the lookout window, and now out of sight, presumably on her way up the inside of the tower to the trap door in the roof and the railed walkway, by whatever means she could find, the wooden stairway from below having rotted away years ago.

Abruptly the monkey screamed again, a scream more piercing than mill whistle, fire whistle, train whistle. It screamed yet a third time as Molly emerged onto the iron-railed parapet atop the tower, where no man or woman had stood for more than half a century. And thirty feet below, at the uppermost extremity of the bittersweet vine, the Young Count stopped short where Zeno the Human Fly had stopped.

Now a contingent from the fire brigade came running with the town's big white nylon safety hoop with a red circle in the center. They stood on the courthouse steps—Harlan Kittredge, Stub Poulin, Abel Feinstein, and Armand St. Onge—holding the net and looking about as foolish as four well-intentioned firemen can look. What good would the hoop do if Molly fell from the tower onto the slate roof?

Another murmur rose from the crowd, a concerted suspiration, as Molly started shinnying up the pole supporting Blackhawk. The entire weathervane wobbled as she set one foot on the extended back leg of the famous pacer, and shifted her weight onto the horse. She reached up and eased the monkey onto her back, where it remained, its teeth chattering, as she descended to the lookout, vanished inside, and reappeared at the window, this time with a length of stout rope, apparently left there decades earlier by the steeplejack who'd erected Blackhawk. The monkey still on her back, she lowered herself, with the assistance of the rope, to the clock and down its face to the bittersweet vine. Motioning for the Young Count to precede her, she continued down the vine with the monkey.

Their descent took perhaps ten minutes. Each time the Young Count reached up to give Molly a hand to step on, she waved him away; when they reached the ridge of the slate roof, she motioned for the firemen, still jockeying around the steps below, to take the safety hoop around to the side of the courthouse, down which she proceeded on the ancient vine. Some twenty feet above the ground, she let go and dropped triumphantly into the middle of the red circle, still carrying the monkey.

As Molly landed, a great roar went up from the crowd.

"Upstaged," said Slade. But he was unable to keep a trace of admiration from creeping into his features as he turned to Bumper Stevens and me and said, "Well, boys, if I could contrive to lug a courthouse with a hundred-foot tower around with me from town to town, I might actually have a place for her."

❦

"You were right," I said to Father George. "I should have kept better track of her."

"You bet you should have," he said bluntly. "However, all's well that ends well. Did you get her on the 6:04 all right?"

I nodded. "She's back at the convent by now — if she hasn't commandeered the locomotive and headed to Montreal or Vancouver, which I'm inclined to doubt. She seemed pretty well satisfied with her day's work and willing to go back to the convent by the time she left."

Father George and I were on good terms again now, laughing about the events of the day over steak sandwiches and beers in the hotel dining room before the circus's evening performance.

"She certainly knows exactly what she wants to do with her life," I said. "I'll give her that."

"She does," Father George said. "I've no doubt that in another year, after she graduates, she will, too. If she survives that long, of course."

He looked out the window at the Big Top and rides and concessions on the green, their brightly colored lights glowing in the settling dusk like Christmas lights. "How about you, son? Do you still know exactly what you want to do with your life?"

"Sure. The same thing you have."

Father George smiled. "You mean spending every minute of your spare time hunting and fishing? Writing stories?" He gestured out the window toward the common. "Playing baseball?"

"You know what I mean — being a priest. But sure, I want to do those other things, too. You always have."

"I have," Father George said. "And I've been damn lucky to be able to. But I'll tell you something, Frank. The days when a priest could play ball, fish, and hunt are drawing to a close. Even up here in the Kingdom. If I were just starting out in orders now instead of forty years ago, I'd have to live my life differently!"

"So what should I do? I've had my ups and downs this summer, with Foster Boy and even today with Molly. I could have gladly wrung her neck when she started up that damn tower. But I like working with the people of the parish better than anything I've ever done."

"Your experience with Foster Boy didn't shake your faith?"

"Not really. You always told me that the best way to express faith in God is to help other people. I believe that as much or more than ever. But when Louvia and I went to Little Quebec that afternoon—"

"What about when you went to Little Quebec?" Father George said, smiling again.

"I met a girl," I said. "A girl I've thought about a lot lately."

"Good," my adoptive father said, to my surprise. "Good for you, son. Keep thinking about her. And as far as this fall is concerned, nothing's cut in stone yet. Remember that."

Relieved that I'd been able to talk about this matter, I ordered another beer, and then we drank coffee and talked about baseball. I had little interest in seeing the circus performance again, but around nine o'clock Father George went home to work on his "Short History" and I ambled over to the green for a final look at the Last Railway Extravaganza and Greatest Little Show on Earth.

I arrived at the Big Top entrance just as it started to rain. The tent gave off a translucent blue glow, and its pennants snapped in the breeze that had brought the rain. Like a huge beating heart, the whole Big Top seemed to contract and expand to the calliope's strains of "The Man on the Flying Trapeze." Nearby, in the slanting raindrops, the roustabouts had already begun to dismantle the midway rides and booths. The mythological carousel rolled by on its wagon, the sphinx and basilisk and Cyclops appearing to grin at me in the rain.

"Where's little carrot-top sis?"

It was my friend the Slade brother, who'd stepped outside the Big Top for a breath of fresh air during the aerial finale.

"She's gone back to school," I said. "I think she figured the evening show would be an anticlimax after her performance at the courthouse this afternoon."

"No doubt," Slade said. "Well, next time you see her, you tell her for me, when she turns eighteen, supposing we don't go totally under in the meantime, I might be willing to start her out on a popcorn concession."

The rain drove harder. I looked around at the wagons heading back through the rain toward the flatbeds in the railyard. The dismantling of the circus had none of the glamour and romance of setting up; the roustabouts were racing the downpour, the train schedule, the next afternoon's performance deadline. I wandered into the tent out of the rain, past the empty ballyhoo stand, and emerged into the blaring music and lights just as Slade was bowing the performers into the ring for their encore. Two of the riggers were dismantling the Zempenskis' safety net and rolling it up. Others were yanking up the stakes pinning down the side panels of the tent. Rain gusted in on the spectators crowded onto the bleachers. The whole town seemed packed into the Big Top tonight, standing to applaud the performers.

As the calliope swung into "Daisy, Daisy," the Zempenskis ran hand in hand into the ring. At the same moment, one of the Four Horses of the Apocalypse came prancing out into the spotlight. Clinging to its back, flopping from side to side like a cloth doll, was the circus drunk, dressed tonight like a railroad tramp, an old-fashioned bindlestiff in a long seersucker suit jacket, baggy trousers held up by a rope, a red bandanna around his neck, and a slouch hat pulled down over his eyes. It was an odd moment, coming as it did after the Zempenskis' finale. Some in the audience were already leaving.

The flopping tramp rose unsteadily to his feet on the back of the Appaloosa and circled the ring once, scattering performers in all directions. He leaped onto the rope ladder leading to the trapeze rigging, still swaying in the top of the tent. As he ascended, casting off jacket and trousers and bandanna, I realized that Count Zempenski was still standing with his wife and son near Slade. The climbing figure pulled off his slouch hat and sailed it out over the crowd—revealing a cascade of bright red hair! A moment later Molly Murphy was standing high above the ring on the tiny platform attached to the center tent pole.

As the Count started fast up the rope ladder after her, Molly reached out and caught the swinging trapeze. The calliope faded out. And far below, standing near the circus performers who, like the townspeople, were all gazing upward, the 150-year-old drummer boy and Parsee smiled a wholly evil smile and started his rolling accompaniment to the aerial show.

"And now, ladies and gentlemen," Molly shouted, "in a death-defying encore, using no safety net, the Magnificent Molly Murphy will attempt the never-before-accomplished feat of executing four complete midair revolutions off the flying trapeze, into the hands of Count Zempenski the Younger. Count, ascend to your trapeze."

Her announcement actually halted the old Count midway up his ladder. After the briefest pause, his son raced up the rope ladder across the ring to the trapeze opposite and below Molly, who now shouted in a triumphant voice, "Ladies and gentlemen, boys and girls. I give you—Flying Molly Murphy!"

With the rolled-up safety net lying limp in the sawdust and the eyes of all Kingdom Common upon her, Molly grasped the trapeze ropes, swung up into a sitting position on the wooden bar and launched herself out into the spotlight. The drumroll intensified. Molly dropped down to hang from the bar by her hands. The trapeze swung in a wider arc. The vibrating drumroll reached a deafening crescendo, then stopped altogether as Molly released her grip and spun over like a hooked trout, her bare feet brushing the blue roof of the tent.

"One," she cried out.

"Two!" This time, as Molly twirled in the air, a few members of the crowd counted with her.

"Three!" Molly was plummeting like flaming Icarus, her red hair streaming behind her.

"FOUR!" roared the circusgoers of Kingdom Common, as Molly completed the unprecedented quadruple somersault.

The Young Count, flying toward her upside down on his trapeze, reached for her hands. He missed, just grazing her outstretched fingertips. But as she shot past him toward the netless void, he caught, in his iron grasp, one slender ankle, as if they had done the act together a thousand times.

The Young Count and Molly descended the rope ladder, clasped hands, and raised their arms over their heads in the sawdust under the Big Top, turning and bowing to the thundering ovation like clockwork figures. The waves of applause continued as, hand in hand, they ran out of the ring, out of the lights, out of the tent, and shortly afterward, out of Kingdom Common. For weeks I felt almost as desolated as if the Young Count, soon to be Molly's husband, had missed my best friend after all, though in fact he never would.

❧ 5 ❧

The Land
of the Free

Outsiders—French Canadian farmers and mill workers, Irish railroadmen, even teachers and clergymen from Away—have often found Kingdom Common, at least at first, to be a hostile place.

—Father George, "A Short History"

RIDING THE RATTLER south through the midsummer night, I read the postcard once more. "Hello Frank Bennett. Send box from Chinese Bank behind bin right of door in Land of Free to 8247 Liberty St. Staten Island New York. I fine. How you? Yr. friend Dr. Sam E. Rong."

The message was printed in small red letters precise as typescript. On the reverse was a glossy photograph of the Statue of Liberty at night, torch aglow, the multicolored skyline of Manhattan in the background.

As the eight-car Rattler crossed the height of land south of Kingdom Common and began to pick up a head of steam on the long downgrade toward St. Johnsbury, I wondered again why Sam wanted the rectangular lacquered teakwood box, somewhat larger than a shoebox, full of envelopes with postmarks from Chicago, New York, Los Angeles, Vancouver, Hong Kong,

Singapore, and a score of other North American and Asian cities. Why, if it was important to him, would he have left the box behind in the first place? Two days before, right after the card arrived, I'd gotten the key to the padlocked front door of the Land of the Free Emporium from Bumper Stevens and dug the box out from behind the bin by the door. When I'd opened it, it had given off a sharp herbal aroma that I recognized immediately. And at exactly that moment I decided to make the trip from northern Vermont to Staten Island to see my old friend Sam Rong in person.

❧

It had been eight years, but I still remembered the evening vividly. I was just thirteen at the time, and a gang of us town kids were playing a pickup ball game on the common. I happened to glance over at Bumper Stevens, sitting on his three-legged milking stool behind the backstop and calling balls and strikes, and noticed a slender, dark-haired stranger standing nearby in white pants and a white jacket, his arms folded, frowning out at the diamond. He was the first Chinese person I'd ever seen in the Common, but what surprised me even more was my absolute certainty that a moment earlier the man hadn't been there. It was as though the frowning newcomer dressed in white had simply fallen out of the sky onto the village green. Or perhaps materialized, like a genie from a fairy tale, out of the faint blue haze of Bumper's cigar smoke.

"Yes, sir," Bumper said by way of greeting.

"What game?" the Chinese man said abruptly in a disapproving voice.

"That would be baseball," the auctioneer said. "Basey-bally. The great American pastime."

"It figures," the man in white said.

Bumper looked at him sharply. But the stranger's face was as expressionless as the pale moon just coming up behind the courthouse tower across the street.

"You no pray basey-bally in Chiny?" Bumper said, not unamicably.

The man in the white pants and jacket gave him a pitying look. "That's the silliest game Dr. Sam E. Rong's ever seen," he said. "Smack ball with stick, run like hell to get back where starting. What jobs you got this burg?"

That made Bumper laugh out loud, so on the spot he asked Dr. Sam E. Rong to dinner at the hotel. The next time I saw the Chinese man was the following Tuesday evening at Bumper's weekly cattle auction, where he seemed to be very capably doing several jobs at once: parking farm trucks, selling coffee and hot dogs, brandishing a blue cow cane, and herding doomed Jerseys, Holsteins, and Guernseys from failed local dairy farms into the makeshift wooden ring inside the commission-sales barn, all the while bantering with the auctioneer a mile a minute, giving back everything he got, with interest.

"Chinka chinka Chinaman, settin' on a fence, tryin' to make a dollar out of fifteen cents," Bumper chanted into his microphone between herds. "Fifteen cents, fifteen cents, who'll start off the bidding on this sorry-looking Chinaman in the white coat for fifteen cents?"

"Ha," Sam replied from atop the high board enclosure of the auction ring, coolly surveying Bumper and the crowd. "Red nose auctioneer too old too fat too full cheap beer to sit on fence at all."

"Chop chop chop! Wrastle that next bunch of critters in here pronto," Bumper roared into the mike over the general laughter.

"Chop chop yourself," Sam said in a plainly audible voice as he jumped lightly off the fence into the sawdust and opened the gate. "Sam E. Rong's the only fella does anything chop chop round this joint. Bump Steve ever try to move chop chop, have thundering big brain stroke, wind up six feet under Celestial Kingdom. Then Dr. Rong run auction, things round here get done right for change."

Soon Sam was holding his own in Bumper's after-hours poker games, too. For the first several weeks he'd watched the players, gone to the cooler at his own unhurried pace to fetch them beer, and conducted a constant running repartee with Bumper. Then Sam began to sit in, keeping track of his winnings on a tall red abacus with green wooden rings. Of course the abacus amused the auctioneer and his cronies, who continued to laugh and shake their heads the following spring when Sam used part of his poker winnings to buy the disused feed store on the edge of Little Quebec and opened the Land of the Free Emporium.

"Chinka chinka Chinaman," I yelled out as I raced past Sam's place that summer. "Settin' on a fence!"

"Boy!" he called back sharply. "Snooping young neighborhood boy, always round where not supposed to be. Why you scared of Sam?"

"I'm not scared of you," I yelled back from a safe distance.

"Are too. You scared because you very, very ignorant. Tell what. Make self useful, you going to spy on Dr. Rong every waking minute anyway. Run home for twenty-two rifle, hurry back. Got job for you to do."

I ran home with no intention of doing what he had asked, for I was frightened half to death by Sam, as well as fascinated by him. But when I got home, Father George, who'd overheard my taunts, ordered me in no uncertain terms to get the hell down to Sam's with my .22 before he horsewhipped me all the way back there himself.

"I—I don't want to."

"You don't want to! Of course you don't want to. You're ashamed. I would be, too, if I were you. You goddamn well ought to be ashamed."

"I don't like the way he looks at me."

"What you mean is, you're scared of him because he's different. Well, Frank, I guarantee that Sam Rong won't hurt you. But you are by God going to help him out, starting this afternoon, or I will know the reason why."

Which was how, the summer I turned fourteen, I went to work for Sam Rong, waging war on the colony of rats that had taken up residence in the abandoned feed store. When the rats were gone, I swept out the old wooden bins and helped Sam paint the exterior of the store red, yellow, and green. Over the summer he added swooping eaves and a pointed cupola. After the renovations were complete, the store resembled a jerry-built pagoda. A pagoda on the edge of a French Canadian enclave in a northern Vermont village!

"Ha," Sam exclaimed, delighted by the irony, as he painted "The Land of the Free Emporium, Dr. Sam E. Rong Prop" in shiny black letters over the entrance. On the inside walls of the store, on a sixty-foot-long scroll of blank newsprint that Editor Kinneson gave him, Sam began drawing a pen-and-ink representation of market day in a Ming dynasty village. The town, which had a rectangular central green and bore just enough resemblance to Kingdom Common to make me hope Sam might be parodying our village, was crowded with merchants, fishermen, barterers, wrestlers, musicians, bricklayers, carpenters, revelers, storytellers, aristocrats in sedan chairs, hunters, warriors, potters, silversmiths, and children. A fat cattle drover with a long goad looked suspiciously like an Oriental Bumper Stevens. A sharp-featured woman haggling over a turnip resembled Louvia the Fortuneteller.

Here and there on his tableau, as the spirit moved him, Sam inscribed proverbs of his own composition in red ink.

"You, Frank Bennett. Listen. This says, all the time a fella spends fishing can add on to life at the far end. That's how much older he'll live to be. You like to fish? Come here early tomorrow morning."

The following day Sam showed me how to set wire traps for northern river eels in the Kingdom River under the Irishtown railway trestle. That evening he fried up a tasty meal of moo gew eel kew in a wok made out of a discarded hubcap from a 1936 GM farm truck. Sam nodded at the fishing proverb on the scroll. "See?" he said. "Add two, three hour spent catching eel today on to other end of our lives. Other words, Frank Bennett, more you fish, longer you live. Very wise proverb, eh? I pay you in wisdom. Better than cash."

At fourteen, I was skeptical about this proposition. But I liked Sam Rong from the start, and soon we became good friends.

Before it was a feed store, the building had been a tenement for French Canadian mill workers. Sam took up living quarters in the rear, in an enclosed porch overhanging the river. He heated the store with a coal-burning Glenwood parlor stove that he bought from Bumper Stevens at a farm auction in Lord Hollow. Besides cattle feed, which Sam purchased in bulk from grain cars coming in from the Canadian West, he sold garden seeds, horse liniment, and his own brand of bag balm, good not only for sore cow udders but, as Dr. Rong liked to say, for whatever ailed you, including cuts and bruises, arthritis, hemorrhoids, even infant teething. He stocked a few staple grocery items like rice and noodles. From Hong Kong he imported a line of durable, inexpensive work shoes. He sold fifty different kinds of homemade medicines compounded from pennyroyal, mint, wild ginger, gill over the ground, goldenthread roots, sarsaparilla, and dozens of other plants that he foraged for in the woods and meadows outside the village. On raised beds on a sunny patch of riverbank below his jutting living quarters he grew several varieties of exotic vegetables to sell to adventurous Commoners, including bok choy, Chinese celery, and a savory pale green pole bean stippled as red as a brook trout's sides. He added a line of used books, representing every branch of learning from homeopathy to classical literature.

Two or three evenings a week, while Sam balanced his accounts in a tall black register book with bright green Chinese characters on the cover, he had me read aloud to him from an 1860 pirated American edition of Dickens, with illustrations by Boz. Sam's all-time favorite was *David Copperfield*. Uriah Heep and Mr. Micawber delighted him so much that he copied

Boz's depictions of them onto the wall scroll. And he personally appropriated Joe Gargery's line from *Great Expectations,* barking out at me, with ironical satisfaction, at the end of each of our reading sessions, "Ever the best of friends, eh, Frank Bennett?"

"How about I brew up some friendship tea," Sam said one evening. "We drink in evening, read Mr. Charles Dickens. First you tell me. Where butternut trees grow round Celestial Kingdom?"

"Butternut trees? There're a few north of town. Out along the river past the trestle."

"No, no. I know all about those. Too wet there. Where butternut trees grow in forest? Also maybe basswood. Where butternut and basswood grow in *forest* of Celestial Kingdom? There we find friendship root."

I told Dr. Rong that I'd noticed a few old butternut trees on the edge of a clear-cut on Little Quebec Mountain above Louvia's place. I thought I remembered seeing a stand of basswood nearby, too.

"Good. What doing this Sunday morning?"

I shrugged. "Mass with Father George in the morning, I guess."

"Ha. Church. Dress all up like funeral, sing sad song, listen fella in black nightgown talk talk talk, not say nothing. Church big fat bore, Frank Bennett. Second great American pastime. No further ahead at the end of church than at beginning. Behind in fact."

"How do you figure that, Sam?"

"Call Dr. Rong, not Sam. Use respect. Okay. Jungle ring jingle. Along comes church money basket on long handle. I know, I go to church one time. Afterward, I tell fella in nightgown, next time he pay me go church, not other way round. What you ever learn in church, Frank Bennett? Quick, name one thing."

I could not. Everything important that Father George had taught me, it seemed, he had taught me outside of church.

Sam made a noise in his throat, unknown in English and only distantly related to a laugh. "This Sunday morning, Frank. You forget all about church. Come to forest with Dr. Rong for friendship root. Maybe you'll learn something there. Doubt it."

❧

"Why you never bring me this good place before, Frank Bennett? Look at all treasure we find already. Yellow coltfoot, fine for Sovereign Cough Elixer. Watercress leaf, infuse in Celestial Fever Reducing Beverage. Here, by brook. Look! Cattail slime, good cure for running sore on elbow ankle. Not even come to butternut trees yet, already strike big bonanza."

As we continued along the old logging trace beside Little Quebec Brook, the pealing of church bells came floating up through the spring woods from the village far below. An idea occurred to me, one I hoped to impress Sam with. "Dr. Rong? Somewhere I read that nature is God's true cathedral. You know, out here in the woods?"

Sam gave me his pitying look. "How very foolish. Sounds like Sunday School talk, Frank. Stop and think. Here in forest, every beast eats every other beast. Fox eats bird eats bug eats Dr. Rong's medicinal plant. Law of wild."

I laughed.

"Not funny. Whether you know or not, you part of too. Say

you're out in woods, too busy being big philosopher watch where going. Whoop daisy! Catch shoe, trip over hobblebush, fall down, knock daydreaming head on granite ledge. Hungry beasts of forest come flocking to eat you up. Soon only white bones left. Fall comes, cover with yellow leaf, goodbye Frank Bennett. Very pleasant cathedral. Now. Where butternut trees? Where basswoods? Get show on road here."

❦

High on the mountainside, half a dozen sparsely limbed butternut trees had been left untouched by the loggers.

"Now look close on ground, Frank. Find tall proud plant, shy green flower in middle, three big pointy leaf. Here, see? And here. Five teeth on leaf. Friendship root. Jin-chen!"

"Jin-chen?"

"What else? Jin-chen. Ginseng. In fall, when Celestial Kingdom turns bright colors like Emporium, you and Sam Rong slip out here some Sunday morning when everybody else cooped up in church feeling sorry for self, telling Mr. Jesus how hard they got it. Dig jin-chen root. Keep a few for friendship tea. Sell the rest to Hong Kong for big money. You got something against money?"

"How much money, Dr. Rong?"

Sam frowned. He looked around the clearing. "Maybe hundred dollars' worth of ginseng here. We take one of three roots. Leave two of three to grow. You help dig, I give ten percent. Quick, how much that?"

"About—three dollars?"

"Yes. You right for once."

"What's ginseng good for? Besides tea?"

From his jacket pocket Sam removed a shard of china pottery with a purple peacock painted on it. He knelt and dug with the shard around the base of a ginseng plant, lifted it partway out of the ground, and shook off the damp black woodsy humus. "See where root fork like trouser leg? Some Chinese think jin-chen root shaped like a man, Frank. Think man-shape root makes very potent, have many son. You ask Dr. Rong, that nonsense. Like great American pastimes, church and baseball."

He broke off a small piece of the root and replanted the rest. "Makes good tea for friends to drink in evening. Otherwise, okay for upset stomach, I guess. Don't make any worse, at least."

"Maybe it's mind over matter."

"Maybe. I not put much stock in mind over matter."

"Dr. Rong, if you don't believe in mind over matter or in going to church or in nature being God's cathedral, what do you believe in? You must believe in something."

"Sure believe in something. Believe in two somethings. Believe in golden rule, do unto others. And believe young Frank Bennett ask too many questions. Don't need church for do unto others. Far as questions go, read this."

Out of his white doctor's coat Sam whipped a pencil stub, with which he scrawled three Chinese characters on the trunk of one of the butternut trees. "What, can't read? Okay, I read to you. Says, 'Ask less, listen more.' Don't forget. Now I ask you a question. Where this old road go?"

Sam pointed across the clearing, where the ancient lumbering road we'd walked up from the village continued north, almost indistinguishable in the raspberry brakes and saplings.

"It goes to Canada if you keep following it."

"Pretty big woods whole way?"

I nodded.

"How fella know when in Canada?"

"You don't really. Father George told me there used to be a cleared strip through the trees to mark the border. That was years ago. When he and I were up there deer hunting last fall, it was all grown up to brush."

Dr. Rong nodded. Then abruptly he headed back down the trail toward the village.

❧

"Eat less!" Dr. Rong shouted at Bumper Stevens. The auctioneer was sitting in a straight-backed kitchen chair with a red-striped sheet around him while Sam cut his hair and lectured him.

"Read proverb on scroll," Sam said, jabbing with his shears in the direction of a new set of characters on his ever-enlarging tableau. "Proverb say, 'Less you eat, better you feel.' Too much rare roast beef in hotel, too much beer, too much sitting round on foolish green milking stool holding court for hooligan sidekicks. Don't take better care of self, you die, Sam have to drop everything, make extra large coffin."

The Land of the Free Emporium had been open for several months now, and Sam was doing a brisk business, with a finger in every pie in town, as Bumper himself had put it. Besides cutting hair for a quarter a head, Sam was in fact retailing coffins, which he fashioned from knotty planks rejected by the American Heritage furniture mill and sold at half the price of a factory-made casket. For a nominal fee Sam would yank out an abscessed tooth, set a broken wrist, doctor a sick horse or cow. Wednesday evenings he turned the Emporium into a gymnasium and taught judo to us high school boys. For the women of the village he conducted a course in homeopathic medicine and another in Chinese cooking. "Don't stuff men with beefsteak, Aroostook County potatoes," he harangued them as he stirred his famous moo gew eel kew in the hubcap wok. "They get used to nice lean river eel on rice, like fine. They not like, tell do own cooking, see how they like that."

What amazed the Common was that Sam's nostrums actually seemed to work. Doc Harrison told Father George and Judge Allen over their regular six A.M. coffee at the hotel that Sam Rong was bidding fair to clear his slate of hypochondriacs. Not only was the Chinese doctor's advice medically sound, villagers seemed to go to him, as they did to Louvia the Fortuneteller, to hear the truth about themselves. Despite Sam's reservations about church, he and Father George soon became fast friends. As for Louvia, when her herbal clients from Little Quebec first started to consult Sam for a second opinion, she was consumed by professional jealousy. She flew down off her hill to the Emporium to threaten him with a quadruple hex if he didn't leave town immediately, then wound up staying for the better part of the afternoon to exchange remedies. She went back to visit Sam so often that it was rumored the two were having a fling. Some Commoners doubted this, others swore to it, but no one really knew. In the village in those days, nearly anything was possible.

"How you like stamp collection, Frank Bennett? From all over land of free and far beyond. Every week you get mail with stamps from New York, San Fran, L of A, Hong Kong too, maybe."

It was a Sunday morning in October. Sam and I had been digging ginseng in the clear-cut high on the ridge for about an hour, selecting only the largest plants and only about half of those, when out of the blue Sam asked me about the stamp collection.

"That sounds like a lot of pen pals, Dr. Rong."

"No pals. You get mail in box at post office. Bring all letters to Sam Rong at Emporium. Sam correspond with pals. You just keep stamps. Don't pick jin-chen so close together, Frank. What I tell you? You be good to jin-chen, jin-chen be good to you."

For emphasis, Sam waved the shard of china with the painted peacock that he used as a digging tool. "You all set now, start collecting stamps. Later today I give you cash rent post box. This enough jin-chen for now. Hope nobody else horns in on patch, eh?"

"Who'd even know what to look for? Much less where to look?"

"You be surprised who. What Sam tell you many times already? 'Hope for best, expect worst.' That way you ready for anything. Now you ready start collect stamps."

Which is how I became an amateur philatelist. Several times a week after school I stopped by the post office and picked up a letter or two or three and delivered them to the Land of the Free Emporium. Sam steamed off the stamps with the same chipped blue enamel kettle he used to boil water for his ginseng-root friendship tea, which we drank in the evening while I read aloud to him from *Bleak House, Oliver Twist,* or *A Christmas Carol.* Some of the stamps were from U.S. and Canadian cities. Others, as bright as butterflies, bore postmarks from Singapore, Borneo, even Australia. The envelopes and letters Sam stowed in the aromatic teakwood box that he referred to as his Chinese bank and kept hidden behind the buckwheat bin to the right of the Emporium's door.

At one of Bumper's farm auctions, Sam bought a Model A Ford in good running order. He equipped it with tire chains and a front-end winch and began driving out from the Common on all-night expeditions once or twice a month. That same fall a succession of Chinese helpers appeared at the Land of the Free. Most of these assistants were young men who stayed only a few days. Occasionally an entire family showed up at the Emporium. Soon it was apparent that Sam was using his store as a way station for aliens being smuggled into the country. One morning when Sam was stocking his shelves, Bumper lettered "The Orient Express" on the driver's-side door of the Model A. Everyone in town, including Sam, had a good laugh.

As for the letters tucked away in the Chinese bank, I suspected that they contained money, sent on some kind of pre-arranged payment plan by Sam's clients. Sam never said, though, any more than he said where he'd come from himself. He remained as much a mystery as the day he appeared in our village.

❧

Over the course of the next year Sam's wares and services continued to expand. From Minnesota seed stock he grew wild rice in the hidden backwaters of the Kingdom River beyond the railroad trestle north of town. Early in the fall, a week before Sam and I picked ginseng, we paddled a canoe out to the rice beds and bent the long wavy stalks over the gunwales and whacked off the ripe kernels with short sticks. Sam sold the wild rice by the pound, unhusked. From it he also made a delicious penny candy, which he scooped out of an old molasses barrel for the kids of the village, who flocked to the Emporium after school to see, on his famous scroll, drawings of undutiful children being swooped off by winged dragons and warlocks with tongs for fingernails. Out of another barrel he sold miscellaneous souvenirs, including a hideous squat green replica of the Statue of Liberty, made in Hong Kong. Inscribed on its plastic base was the legend "Send me your tired, your poor, your huddled masses yearning to breathe free."

To a select group of regular customers Sam extended personal and business loans at half the interest rates of the First Farmers' and Lumberers' Bank. At no interest at all he loaned young people money to go to college or get married or make a down payment on a first home. He insisted only that they pay something on their accounts each month, even just a few dollars if that's all they could afford; he kept track of these transactions in the tall black register book. Day and night he dished out blunt observations, shrewd advice, and witty proverbs to everyone who set foot in the Emporium, chuckling to himself over the incongruity of a Chinese wayfarer from no one knew where dispensing wisdom and irony in the wilds of northern Vermont, the Celestial Kingdom, the far end of the civilized world.

One chilly fall evening when Sam and I were drinking friendship tea and laughing over Mr. Micawber's latest sojourn to debtor's prison, an elderly farm woman in a man's slouch hat, a long denim barn coat, and rubber barn boots appeared at the Land of the Free. It was Mattie Kittredge from Lost Nation Hollow. Mattie's husband, John, had died recently. With her was Bumper Stevens, whose cigar smoke tonight was redolent not of thick stacks of well-thumbed hundred-dollar bills, or the selling off of family farms, or crude, sardonic humor and shady dealings, but of something like concern.

"I know my husband ran up a great long feed slip with you," Mattie told Sam. "I came to inform you that I can't make good on it until Mr. Stevens sells off my cows. Until the auction next month I don't have no cash money at all, only just what I need to get by on."

"You wait," Sam said. He opened his black account book to the page with John Kittredge's name at the top. Clicking his tongue mathematically, he did some rapid calculations on his abacus. He nodded to himself, reached into the souvenir barrel by the counter, and pulled out a rose-colored penknife shaped like a fish with the violet letters "U. S. of A." stamped on it. Sam opened the knife, cut John's page neatly out of the account book, crumpled it into a small ball, put it into his mouth, and swallowed it.

"You owe nothing," he said. "Very sorry to hear about John."

Mattie stared at him.

Sam shrugged. "Not that much anyway. John made whopping big payment couple weeks ago. Cleaned up all except few dollars."

Mattie started to object, but Bumper stepped forward out of a cloud of relieved cigar smoke. "Well, then, Dr. Samuel. We thank you kindly and I'll get Mattie here back on out to the Hollow."

"I am obliged to you," Mattie told Sam quietly as Bumper steered her toward the door. Then she stopped. "They say you —they say sometimes you tell folks comforting things. Like a preacher, only better. Would you tell me something?"

"Oh, sure," Sam said from atop his tall stool behind the counter. "You and John have son?"

"Sons? Yes. We have four sons. And three daughters."

"All son and daughter alive and well?"

"They be. Thank the Lord."

"Good. Got grandson?"

Mattie smiled. "Nine. And six granddaughters. One great-granddaughter."

"Good. Great-granddaughter very good. Now you watch."

Sam hopped down from his stool. He got out his fine-tip drawing pen and an inkwell. Under a funeral procession on the wall tableau he carefully inscribed several intricate red characters. "What say?" he demanded.

Mattie shrugged. "What does it say?"

"Say very good news, very comforting." Sam returned to his stool and reached again for his abacus. He dropped one green ring down the slender red pole. "Grandfather die," he said. He dropped another ring onto the abacus. "Father die." Adding a third ring, he said cheerfully, "Son die. Proverb say, 'Grandfather die, father die, son die.'"

"By the Jesus, now," Bumper muttered. "What the —?"

Mattie frowned. "The grandfather dies, the father dies, the

son dies. That would be comforting to an old woman who has just lost her husband of fifty-two years?"

"Oh sure, most comforting," Sam said. "What other order you want them to die in? Other proverb say, 'Old must die, young may.' You and John most fortunate, eh? No young die in family yet."

For perhaps five full seconds, Mattie Kittredge looked at Sam, who looked back at her, his eyes as humorous and wise as those of the snapping turtles he kept for soup in the watering trough in front of the Emporium. Then she nodded once, and headed out the door with Bumper.

For his part, Dr. Rong never seemed to look any older. No one had the slightest idea how old Sam was. He could have been forty, he might have been sixty. It was rumored that he had a large family in Mandalay, a beautiful occidental mistress in Toronto, a string of high-toned whorehouses in Vancouver and Mexico City. But no one knew. When it came to Sam E. Rong, everything was speculation.

❦

"Now then, Mr. Frank. This that I'm about to tell you, assuming I do tell you, ain't for public consumption. Do I make myself plain?"

I nodded. It was late summer again, with my first year of college fast approaching. I'd been walking back to the Big House late in the evening after visiting Sam when, out of the dark entryway of the commission-sales barn, Bumper's raspy, peremptory voice had summoned me inside. We now sat facing each other across the auctioneer's cluttered desk under a single fly-specked overhead light bulb.

While Bumper fired up a fresh cigar, I looked around. His office was crowded with piled-up wooden sap buckets, horse hames and harnesses, ox yokes tipped with brass ornaments, crates overflowing with lightning rod balls, fence insulators, cutter-bar teeth—the miscellaneous detritus of a hundred farm auctions and a hundred played-out farms. On the wall behind his desk, at a rakish slant, the auctioneer had tacked a lucky playing card, a smudged ace of diamonds. Above it was last year's calendar adorned with a photograph of a leggy young woman with long blond hair perched naked on the hood of a powder-blue Ford convertible with the top down. A few short years before, here in Bumper's tiny principality within the mostly self-contained universe of the village, Sam Rong had parlayed his good poker hands into the Land of the Free Emporium. And somehow, reflecting on those card games, from which Sam had long ago been politely banned, I knew that the confidential disclosure Bumper was all but threatening me with involved not only our mutual friend but trouble as well. For trouble, and serious trouble at that, was the unmistakable odor of the cigar smoke enveloping us in a thick blue haze that night.

"Yes, sir," Bumper said, meaning that he was ready to get down to business. "Now this is good sound information, Frank. Who or where I heard it from is immaterial. And who or where you heard it from is to stay here in this office between I and you and"—he jabbed the orange tip of his cigar at the calendar girl—"Miss Fairlane there. Do you understand that?"

I nodded again.

"According to reliable reports, Frank, some of our selectmen come together in secret last week to hash over a close associate of yours and mine. An associate with these initials." Bumper took the nub of a pencil from behind his ear and scrawled something on a grimy yellow slip of paper, which he shoved across the desk. The yellow slip was a receipt for a piglet with a ruptured belly. On the bottom Bumper had written the letters S. E. R.

"Sam E. Rong," I said.

"Did I say so?"

I grinned. "No."

"Did I tell you this close associate's initials?"

"No."

"And you would swear in a court of law I did not?"

"Yes," I said.

Bumper nodded. "Now, then, it seems these town fathers, these fine upstanding citizens and leading tradesmen and pious churchmen, was a tad riled that this gentleman in question, who might or might not be a foreign gentlemen with these initials" — Bumper reached across the desk and tapped the yellow sales slip — "that this gentleman is cutting into their custom and slicing into their profits. By underselling them. By extending out too much credit. By charging low interest. And in certain cases by forgiving some debts altogether."

"By doing unto others, in other words."

Bumper stared at me through the thickening cigar smoke. "Others are about to do unto him, Frank. Others are about to do him out of business and out of town and very possibly right out of this country."

"So what should Sa—what should our mutual friend do, Bumper? Sell the Emporium and come back here to muck out your cow stalls?"

"No," Bumper said. "But what I'm thinking is, it might just be time for our friend to fold up his hand, cash in his chips whilst he's still ahead, and find another game to sit in on further down the line. So, Frank," he said, stubbing out his cigar, "if you'd find a way to let him know he might want to take a gander at greener pastures, I'd appreciate it."

❦

"What church fellas do, Frank Bennett? Sneak round in white bed sheets, pointy white hats, burn cross? Burn Land of Free Emporium? Hang Dr. Rong up from heels on American elm on common, burn him?"

Sam laughed hard over the idea of being hanged from an American elm tree and immolated. But I was worried. "That's not the way these particular people operate. I don't know exactly what they will do. But our mutual friend, the person who warned me, said you should—Sam! You're not even listening."

"Call 'Doctor,'" Sam said as he poured boiling water from his enameled kettle into a flowered teapot, and the acrid fumes of ginseng filled the Emporium. "Show respect."

"Yes, but Dr. Rong, the selectmen—"

"No but. Let Sam deal with selectmen. Wild bee honey in friendship tea tonight, Frank Bennett? Or straight up? You say which."

❦

"Don't understand charges! What means ill alien?"

Judge Forrest Allen closed his eyes for a moment. He sighed. Then, for the third time since the hearing had begun, he tried to explain. "It means that you're not legally a citizen of this country, Dr. Rong. Yes, you've lived here in Kingdom Common for four years. But you've never been naturalized. You've never even applied for American citizenship. You didn't have permission to come here in the first place. That makes you an illegal alien, I'm afraid."

"Nonsense," shouted Dr. Rong, who was representing himself in order to save money and because he didn't trust lawyers. "Aliens green all over. Come from Mars."

From the courtroom balcony, where Bumper Stevens and his rogues' gallery were encamped, came a barrage of guffaws. But the town officials and businessmen who had sent a delegation to report Sam to the U.S. Immigration and Naturalization Service office in Memphremagog the week before sat in the rear of the courtroom as grave and silent as the granite tombstones of their ancestors in the village cemetery.

Judge Allen frowned up at the balcony. Then he positively scowled at the town fathers. In the ensuing silence he looked out the courtroom window in the direction of the tall statue on the green of his great-great-great-grandfather Ethan, as if seeking counsel from his famous forebear. After perhaps thirty seconds he said, "Dr. Rong, in America—"

"Land of the free," Sam interjected. "Maybe so, maybe no."

"Yes. But even in the land of the free, you still need approval from the government to come here. Unless you can prove that you were born in this country."

"Wait. Why Sam got to prove anything? Why not innocent til guilty? How you prove I not born here? Where proof Sam from Mars?"

More laughter from the balcony.

"Sam, Dr. Rong. You need to show cause why you should be allowed to remain in America."

"Here cause." Sam reached into the pocket of his white doctor's coat and produced one of the green figurines of the Statue of Liberty that he sold out of his souvenir barrel. "This cause. Exhibit one. Miss Liberty."

Sam rushed forward and shook the misshapen statuette under the judge's nose. "You listen. Miss Liberty say send tired. Say send poor. Send huddled masses. Okay. That Sam Rong many year ago. No more. Now tired poor come see him. Come borrow money cheap. Buy coffin, bury old dead grandfather, don't cost arm leg. Moo! Cow starving. Farmers come Sam buy feed on credit. Cows eat, farmers eat. Everybody happy."

Sam whirled around and shook the statue again, this time in the direction of the stony-faced businessmen who had come together to betray him. "What Dr. Rong ever do Miss Liberty say not do? Nothing. This land of free. Innocent till proven otherwise. Who here prove otherwise? Where alien? Why cause? Judge got law all backward. Case dismissed!"

To a rousing cheer from the balcony, Sam marched out of the courtroom, waving Miss Liberty over his head. With me at his heels, he repaired in triumph to the Emporium where, half an hour later, Sheriff Mason White served him with a citation stating that if he could not show cause within ten days why he should be allowed to remain in this country, he would face deportation.

Appended to the bottom of the document was a note in Judge Allen's crabbed handwriting imploring Sam to hire a real lawyer and apply for temporary political asylum. The judge himself would call his lawyer son-in-law in Burlington, Editor Kinneson's son Charlie, who had never lost a case.

"Double talk," Sam Rong declared. He wadded the citation up in his fist, tossed it high in the air, caught it in his mouth, and devoured it.

*

"So, Frank Bennett. Land of the free not so free after all, eh? Very fine joke on Dr. Rong."

It was late in the afternoon, a few days after Sam's hearing. He and I were high on the ridge east of town, digging ginseng. Far below us, a mile and more away, the pink granite buildings of the town sparkled in the rays of the lowering sun. A few of the hardwood trees on the ridge had started to turn color early. They too shone brightly in the mild September sunshine.

"Land of the free. Maybe so, maybe no," Sam Rong said as he dropped a root into his wicker gathering basket. "Hope for best, expect worst. Eh, Frank?"

Actually, Sam seemed quite pleased to have his worst expectations of the land of the free confirmed. More than once over the years he had confided to me that being proven right was what people longed for above all else on earth, with the possible exception of being in the know about a great scandalous secret. Now Sam had been proven right about America.

He continued digging with his peacock shard. As always, he was careful to take only every third or fourth root. His face was as placid and ironical as ever, though only three days remained before his scheduled deportation. Judge Allen had set bail at twenty-five dollars—his maximum estimate, the judge had angrily announced, of the total amount Sam had cost the dozen or so businessmen who had turned him in for underselling them.

"Sam, you should have heard Father G's homily in church this morning. He shouted at us for twenty minutes. He said if he ever found out who was responsible for turning you in, he'd horsewhip them from one end of the village to the other."

"Yes, Father G very good man, very good to Sam, other riffraff. Not bad idea, horsewhip town fathers through village. Too bad I not think to draw on scroll, laugh at over jin-chen tea."

"What I don't understand is why *you* aren't mad, Sam. I sure would be."

"Call 'Doctor.' What good getting mad do?" Then, a moment later: "Well, sure. Sam get angry too, sometimes. Not made of china, you know, like bird on digger here. But. Got plan."

Sam stood up. "Come on, Frank. Got plenty jin-chen now. You be good to jin-chen, jin-chen be good to you. Not like land of the free. Sam good to weary refuse, like Miss Liberty says, land of the free sells Sam down river."

"What's your plan, Dr. Rong?"

"Obey law. Law says go away. Sam go."

"Go where?"

"Don't worry. Maybe go college, like you. Get another medical degree. Many friends, Frank Bennett, all over country, many customers of Chinese bank. Speaking of money, listen this. Old red-nose auctioneer try give Sam thousand dollars hire shyster lawyer. You imagine? Sam buy Bumper one hundred time over."

"I doubt Bumper ever had a friend before. Cronies, maybe."

"Ever the best of, eh? Run-out-of-town Chinese doctor has two friend. Red-nose auctioneer, wet-back-of-ear kid named Frank Bennett. How lovely."

"Come on, Dr. Rong," I said, hurrying to keep up. "You've got tons of friends. Look at all the people you've helped."

"Yes, look. Where ton of when government haul Sam into court, ride out of town on rail? Talk sense, Frank. Won't talk sense, at least listen. One: Be good to jun-chen, jin-chen be good to you. Two: After forty, less you eat, better you feel. Three: More you fish, longer you live. Four: Hope for best, expect worst. Five. Grandfather die, father die—"

"Son dies," I said.

San Rong nodded. "Remember."

A few minutes later we came into the village in the early fall dusk. Outside the Land of the Free Sam handed me his ginseng basket. "You wait here."

He was inside the Emporium no more than a minute, returning with his tall black account book and a manila envelope. The envelope he gave to me. Then he held out his hand, pale as ivory in the mountain twilight, dry as old parchment. "So long, Frank. Good luck at college."

"I'm not leaving until tomorrow, Sam. I'll stop here before I go."

"You leaving tomorrow, I leaving tonight."

"Where are your things?"

"What thing? Came here with no thing. Leave same way."

"Leave for where? This doesn't make sense, Dr. Rong."

"No sense at all," Sam agreed. "Like great American pastimes. Like sending back refuse."

"Where's your money? How can you go away without any money?"

"Very much money in here." Sam tapped his black book. "All written down, very safe. Say so long to Bump Steve, Frank. I leave him Emporium, deed and key inside envelope. Good joke, eh? What old auctioneer do with Chinese pagoda? Drive him crazy. You get Orient Express, jin-chen patch. Paper inside envelope tells where to send roots. Bye now."

Sam headed down the dirt lane of Little Quebec, past the mill and the railyard, toward U.S. Route 5. He did not look back. Soon all I could make out was his white coat. Then he vanished.

"There."

Even before I whirled around I knew who had spoken. "There," Bumper said again, and he headed back up the lane toward the commission-sales barn, leaving me standing by myself in front of the Emporium in a tobacco-laden shroud of loneliness.

❧

Bumper never reopened the Land of the Free Emporium, looming up on the edge of Little Quebec, its gaudy colors fading, its sloping roofs and eaves rotting, as anomalous in our tiny Vermont village as a dairy barn in a Chinese rice paddy. The spring after Sam disappeared, Bumper sold most of its contents at auction and began storing hay and farm equipment in the building. Canadian bull thistles and wild cucumber vines ran rampant in Sam's old vegetable beds. Scavenging there, Louvia the Fortuneteller turned up a few hexagonal coins with holes in the middle that Sam had lost or perhaps planted for good luck.

Each fall for the next four years I visited the secret place under the butternut and basswood trees high on the ridge above the village to harvest the roots of the shy and aristocratic ginseng plants, which I dried and mailed to the Hong Kong wholesaler whose address Sam had left me. With the proceeds I paid for my college textbooks and bought gas for the Orient Express, which held up until my last semester at the university.

As for Dr. Rong, even as he became absorbed into the mythology of the Common, rumors of his whereabouts floated back to us. Julia Hefner, visiting her son in San Francisco, was positive that she spotted him wearing a motorman's hat and driving a cable car. Bumper's once and future ring man, Little Shad Shadow, swore that Sam was keeping books for an opium den in Fredericton, New Brunswick, where Shad had a half-brother in an asylum. Even Father George confided to me that on a sightseeing trip to New York City with his Catholic Youth Organization he had spotted Sam drinking tea and disputing with a Wonder Rabbi in an automat on East Fortieth Street; but then Father George had to chase after his charges and haul them out of a peepshow down the block, and by the time he had the kids rounded up, the rabbi, Dr. Rong, and the automat itself all seemed to have disappeared. For my part, I heard nothing at all from my friend until the summer I returned to Kingdom Common to work for Father George, when the postcard arrived directing me to send the Chinese bank to the address on Staten Island.

In White River Junction I changed trains for Hartford. Later I drifted into a restless sleep, full of dreams about the girl with the morning-glory eyes whom I'd met in Little Quebec with Louvia. At dawn I arrived at Grand Central Station, its ornate dome echoing with blaring announcements of the arrivals and departures of trains whose very names—the Empire State Express, the Twentieth Century Limited—made me want to chuck everything—plans for the future, teakwood box, and all—and hop aboard. But no. I had come here to see an old friend, and half an hour later I was riding the ferry to Staten Island.

A faded red and yellow bus with a snub nose delivered me to the address on Liberty Street, a long narrow market with a scarlet dragon emblazoned across the display window. Streaming out of the dragon's mouth was a flaming jet of Chinese characters and below them, in English, the words "Land of the Free Emporium #2 Dr. Sam E. Rong Prop." Several clerks were filling sidewalk bins in front of the store with Chinese vegetables and popeyed fish on ice. Another assistant was cranking down a green awning with red and yellow stripes. Another was preparing to wash the display window. Yet another was hosing off the sidewalk. Inside the window two pretty girls were hanging a young roast pig on an iron hook beside four glazed ducks dangling by their plucked necks. I stepped inside, past a clerk running accounts on a red abacus. The air was full of the scents of dried cuttlefish, freshly washed vegetables, tea, ginger, and twenty different spices I hadn't smelled in four years. Tacked to the walls just above eye level was a scroll on which someone, I was sure I knew who, had begun to draw a tableau of a Chinese coastal city, including a soaring temple in the background shaped startlingly like the Empire State Building and, in the nearby harbor, the colossal statue of a young Chinese woman with a paper lantern held over her head and an unmistakably ironical smile on her face.

No one paid any attention to me as I walked, past barrels of

Chinese candy and shelves lined with porcelain Buddhas and mandarins and watercolor prints of pagodas with hanging gardens, to a high desk at the back of the store. On a stool behind the desk sat Dr. Rong, reading a thick book with a battered red cover. A blue kettle simmered on a hotplate on the desk. Beside it was a teapot decorated with pink and purple periwinkle blossoms. Sam sat perfectly immobile, as still as the porcelain mandarins for sale in his shop. His jacket gleamed as white as ever.

"*Pickwick Paper,*" Sam said by way of greeting, holding up the spine of the red book so I could see its title. "Funny as a crutch, Frank Bennett. You want a job sweeping floor? Shooting rats?"

Already laughing, I set the lacquered teakwood box down on Sam's desk. "I've brought you your Chinese bank, Sam."

"How many times I tell you, call Doctor. Dr. Rong. So. Pull up stool. We brew friendship tea anyway."

I sat down on a tall stool across the desk from Sam and smiled happily at my old friend, who looked just the same as he had four years before. He slid open the lid of the teakwood box, rummaged under the stacks of envelopes, and fished out two or three roots, which he broke into small pieces. He dropped the broken roots into the periwinkle teapot and covered them with boiling water from the blue kettle. Immediately the unmistakable pungency of jin-chen tea, of friendship, drifted out of the steaming pot into the room. Sam reached into a cubbyhole under the desk and brought out two handleless periwinkle teacups.

"Let steep now," he said. He riffled through the envelopes in the box. "Four year ago, Frank Bennett, when I leave Celestial Kingdom, I take address of all banking clients in black account book. Didn't need envelopes in Chinese bank. Then lately I get thinking. What if envelopes up at the end-of-earth Kingdom fall into wrong hands instead of Rong's hands? Cause much bad trouble for clients, eh? Same kind trouble Sam had in Kingdom. Many very respectable Chinese-Americans run out of country. Still. You could have mailed. U.S. mail one thing in land of the free Sam more less trusts."

"I wanted to see you, Dr. Rong."

"So look. What I tell you long time ago? What I write on scroll? 'World change, human bean stay same.' Eh? Eh, Frank Bennett? Ha! Here come first ones already. Early today."

I turned around on my stool to see what Sam was scowling at. In front of the Land of the Free #2 a Gray Line bus was disgorging tourists. Wielding cameras and guidebooks, they came pouring into the shop and began to mill here, there, and everywhere, sniffing the dried octopus, pinching the Chinese cabbage, holding eggshell porcelain teacups up to the light.

"Hey!" Dr. Rong shouted. "You break, you buy. Or go to prison. You want go prison this morning?"

He winked at me and chuckled gleefully over the idea of sending a busload of retired Iowa schoolteachers to jail. Then he filled the two periwinkle cups, and together he and I sipped the hot beverage, flavored like the Vermont woods in the fall, like ancient Chinese villages, like ironical conversation and laughter and friendship.

"Dr. Rong," I said. "I want to ask you a question."

"So ask."

"I'm enrolled to start seminary this coming fall. But recently —I don't know."

"Do what heart tells," Sam said immediately. "Now I ask you a question. Why Sam E. Rong set up Emporium Two here this rundown warehouse? Why I sit up on high stool like Ury Heep, porcelain fortuneteller in old broken-down carnival?"

"Because you're on the tour bus line here?"

"Not on any bus line at all till I open shop. No. Tell you what. You and I change place. You sit behind desk. Then you know why I come here. Get good laugh besides."

From Dr. Rong's stool behind the desk I could see everything that went on in the Land of the Free #2 and on the sidewalk in front. But Sam shook his head. "You looking in wrong direction, Frank, as usual. Look out side window."

I peered out the narrow window to my right. At first I saw only the alleyway, strewn with broken wooden crates, and beyond, a section of bleak cityscape. Then, looming up in a space between two distant rooftops, as sudden and surprising as Dr. Rong's own appearance in Kingdom Common eight years ago, was the crowned head and torch of the Statue of Liberty, magnified by the smog and morning haze.

"So. What think?"

Perched high on Sam's stool in this place far from home, listening to the gabble of the early-morning tourists and staring out at the miragelike statue, I had no idea what to think, about the Land of the Free #2 or exactly why I had come to Staten Island or, for that matter, what my heart told me about my future.

"I don't know, Dr. Rong," I admitted.

"No," Sam agreed, laughing. "I not know, either. Life full of mysteries, eh? All we can say."

Sam returned to his seat. He poured us more hot tea. "Catch

up on news now. How old judge? How Bumper? Louvia find coins I hide in garden? Talk, Frank. Gossip. Enjoy tea. Sam Rong, Frank Bennett, Mr. Charles Dickens. Best of friends, eh? That one thing we know for sure."

I nodded and smiled and lifted my thin teacup in agreement. Sipping the jin-chen tea and inhaling the strong and enduring scent of friendship, which now seemed to fill every corner of the Land of the Free #2 and the entire neighborhood and all Staten Island, I had no notion where my own life might lead me, now or later. But I was glad beyond words to have made this trip to see my old friend Sam E. Rong, whoever he might be. For now, that was enough.

❦6❦
Night School

All citizens of the Kingdom Republic will enjoy complete
personal freedom so long as their actions and beliefs do not
encroach on the freedom of other Republic citizens.

—The Kingdom Republic Constitution,
as quoted in Father George, "A Short History"

A T SIXTY-EIGHT, with chronic angina, Father George
needed more help in the parish than I could give him that summer. From time to time a priest from Memphremagog or Pond
in the Sky would come to Kingdom Common to celebrate Sunday mass when Father George simply didn't feel up to doing it
himself. At other times he seemed much the same as ever. But as
the summer wore on, it was evident that the job was becoming
too much for him.

One of my duties that summer was to drive Father George to
his doctor appointments and, two or three times a week, out
into the country for short rides. While returning from one of
these excursions one afternoon, soon after I'd visited Sam Rong
in Staten Island, he asked me to pull up beside the baseball in-
field at the south end of the common. We got out and walked
over to the unpainted bleachers along the third-base line, where
Father George sat down. Although it was a hot day, I had

brought his lap blanket from the car. I arranged the blanket over his legs and sat down beside him.

Father George leaned over and pulled up a few blades of grass. He tossed them into the air to see which way the breeze was blowing, in or out, an old power hitter's habit. It was something the greatest scholar and third baseman in the history of Kingdom County had done a thousand times while kneeling in the on-deck circle or waiting at third for the surprise bunt, the smashing line drive, the soaring, windblown foul fly ball. But today the grass fell straight back to the field; there was no wind at all.

As we looked out over the diamond in the late-afternoon sunlight, I suddenly began to laugh. I'd remembered an evening here on the ball field, one of many, when I was twelve or thirteen. I was crouched at home plate with my twenty-eight-inch Adirondack while Father George, then in his fifties, stood out on the mound beside a gallon pail of baseballs and threw me one pitch after another, trying to teach me how to hit a curve ball.

"What's funny?" he said.

"You and me. Us. Remember those batting practice sessions? You were pretty tough on me."

"I was tough on all my players."

"You were tougher on me. One evening you were out there with a bucket of balls—I can see us right now—and you told me if I didn't learn to wait on your curve and go with it, I'd never amount to anything."

Father George grinned. Though he'd lost weight recently, his voice was still strong, and as wryly humorous as ever. "Did I say that?"

"You did. It was almost too dark to see the ball, at least until it was right on me. We'd probably been here an hour already, and I was frustrated and mad besides. When you told me that, about not amounting to anything, I'd had it. I shouted out to you that baseball was just a game. You remember what you said?"

Father George shook his head.

"You stared in at me and you said, and I'm quoting you exactly, 'I'm not talking baseball, son. I'm talking life. You don't learn how to hit that dinky little bender of mine, you aren't ever going to amount to anything in *life*.'"

Father George nodded. "I was tough on you. And before you got to high school you learned how to hit a curve ball."

"And amounted to something?"

If he heard, Father George didn't answer. He was looking out over the diamond, his blue eyes focused somewhere beyond deepest center field. Then he turned to me and said, "Your first class meets tonight, Frank. At the courthouse."

"My first what?"

"Your first citizenship class—for immigrants who want to become Americans. I used to call it night school. Right up until this morning I thought I could still teach it. But I can't. I don't have the strength. You'll have to teach it for me."

Something akin to panic came over me. "I never taught a class in my life, Father George. I'm not a teacher. I wouldn't have any idea what to teach. Or how to teach it."

"You're a natural, son," Father George said, gesturing out toward home plate. "You'll do just fine."

🍁

The front doors of the courthouse weren't locked when I arrived. Walking in quickly, so as not to lose courage, I went up the flight of stairs to the courtroom. It was a long room with a very high stamped-tin ceiling and propeller-blade fans hanging down, and it occupied most of the second story. Two rows of tall windows faced each other on the west and east. On the wall behind the judge's bench was a mural, painted decades ago, of Lake Memphremagog and the Canadian mountains to the north. Just to the right of the mural was a plaque inscribed with the one-sentence constitution of the Kingdom Republic, which had declared its independence from both the United States and Vermont in 1810. The room smelled like old legal tomes and oiled wooden floors, like furniture polish and officialdom.

I sat down in the front row of benches. In the dwindling evening light, the empty courtroom with its plain wooden seats and old-fashioned ceiling and wooden paneling looked as disused as the roped-off balcony, recently judged to be unsafe. Someone had wheeled a portable blackboard out in front of the defense attorney's table. This was the only indication that a class would be taught here tonight. Something about the arrangement of the blackboard, attorneys' tables, and empty jury chairs made me think of a stage set, with me as the principal player. A player who had forgotten all his lines, if he'd ever learned them.

"What in blazes are you doing here?"

I whirled around. The man had come in so quietly, and I had been so absorbed in my apprehension of the class to come, that I hadn't heard him. He was standing in the center aisle, just a few feet away, a big man of about forty-five, wearing a blue uniform. He had a gray crew cut and a bullet-shaped head. On the lapel of his uniform jacket was a metal name tag: Inspector P. W. Bull, U.S. Immigration and Naturalization Service.

"I asked what you're doing here," Inspector Bull said. "How did you get in?"

"The same way you did. The doors were unlocked."

"Do you always walk through unlocked doors?"

I couldn't help it. I laughed out loud.

P. W. Bull, in the meantime, jutted his truculent chin even farther forward. I actually thought he might lose his balance and topple over onto his face. "I said, do you always walk through unlocked doors?"

"Always," I said, smiling.

"Then you can walk right back out again. You want to be an American? You'd better learn how to tell American time. Now go on back outside until I officially open the door. I could have you arrested for trespassing."

Suddenly I was sick of Inspector P. W. Bull. I stood up, with the folder Father George had given me in my hands.

Inspector Bull was three or four inches taller than I was and seventy or eighty pounds heavier. But when I took three quick steps toward him, the big man took a step backward.

"I know how to tell time," I said. "And I'm not here to take the citizenship class. I'm here to teach it."

P. W. Bull gave me a long and incredulous look. Finally he said, "What kind of joke is this, anyway? Father George Lecoeur is teaching this class. Who the hell are you?"

"I'm Frank Bennett, and Father George has asked me to teach the class because he's too sick to do it himself. That's number one. Number two, I don't like being sworn at. Don't do it again."

I looked hard at Inspector P. W. Bull for a second or two longer, then turned around and went up to the front of the courtroom and found the switch to the lights. They were old-fashioned globe lights hanging from the ceiling on slender metal rods, and when I flipped them on and looked back, P. W. Bull was still standing in the aisle, bent forward like a bellicose gander, his mouth slightly open. Once again I felt like laughing, but this time I didn't.

As soon as the doors were "officially" opened, students began to arrive. I knew some by name, including, to my considerable surprise, Louvia the Fortuneteller who, I had supposed, was already an American citizen. In all there were eleven. Except for Louvia, who sequestered herself at the rear of the courtroom, they sat scattered on either side of the aisle in the first two rows of spectators' benches. While I greeted them, P. W. Bull visited with the two selectmen who had arranged for the citizenship class to use the courthouse, Roy Quinn and the Reverend Miles Johnstone.

At exactly 7:30 by the courtroom clock, Bull walked up to the judge's dais and turned to face the class. "My name is Inspector P. W. Bull of the Northern Vermont District of the U.S. Immigration and Naturalization Service. This"—jerking his head at me, standing below the dais and in front of the defense table— "is Frank Bennett. In the unfortunate absence of Father Lecoeur, he'll be your instructor. At least until I can find someone better qualified."

Just then a tall young man with long dark hair sauntered into the courtroom. The newcomer came down the center aisle, taking his own sweet time and grinning. He sat down four rows back.

It was Frenchy LaMott, who ran the slaughterhouse on the edge of the village.

"You're late," Bull said. "This class started at seven-thirty."

Frenchy slouched back on the bench. In his heavy French Canadian accent he said, "I thought it started at eight."

"You thought wrong," Bull said.

I wasn't sure, but I thought Frenchy grinned at me.

"It's my understanding," Bull continued, "that in the past the district immigration office has been lenient to the point of laxness. As a result of new laws and my appointment, that's going to change."

Bull paused for this to sink in, then looked at Roy Quinn and Reverend Johnstone. "Would you gentlemen like to add anything?"

Roy cleared his throat. "On behalf of the town, I'd just like to say that it's an honor, as always, to have you aspiring citizens use the courthouse for your classes. All we ask is that you leave our building in the condition you found it."

The minister took a step forward, held up his hand like a bishop, and intoned, "Our dear heavenly Father, we ask Thy blessings upon this most worthwhile enterprise and upon all of these aspiring citizens and their fine young instructor, Frank Bennett, and the fine village where we live. Amen."

Roy Quinn and Reverend Johnstone hurried out of the courtroom as though eager to get away from the class. P. W. Bull, after one more look at the group, steered me down the aisle by my elbow. "I'd like a private word with you, Bennett."

Near the door he stopped with his back to the class. In a lowered voice he said, "Look. You and I got off on the wrong foot. I'm prepared to forget about that and start with a clean slate. Here's my card. Don't hesitate to give me a holler if there's trouble of any kind."

I ignored the card in Bull's hand. "I'm sure there won't be any trouble."

Inspector P. W. Bull sighed. "Listen, Bennett. Don't get the wrong impression. I don't have a thing in the world against any of these people. But frankly"—he glanced over his shoulder, then swiveled his head back to me—"if half of them stick it out for the next three weeks and half of those who do pass the test, I'll be surprised. Nobody, least of all me, expects or even necessarily wants you to work miracles. Understand?"

Staring right into Bull's eyes, I said, loudly enough for the entire class to hear, "I understand that every single one of these students is going to pass that test and become a United States citizen."

P. W. Bull gave me a profoundly skeptical look, as if we both knew better, then marched out the door.

❧

"Well, folks, how many of you have ever done anything like this before?"

No hands went up.

"Me neither," I said, hoping desperately to break the ice. "So we're all in the same boat."

"You ask me, Bennett, it a goddamn leaky boat," Frenchy LaMott piped up. "We don't pass, you in big trouble."

I laughed, but the class looked even gloomier.

A small man with wispy gray hair and dark eyes turned around in his seat. It was Abel Feinstein, the village tailor. "Please," he said. "Mr. French LaMott. Rule number one. Show respect to the teacher."

"Thank you, Mr. Feinstein," I said. I took a deep breath and plunged onward. "For any of you who don't know me, my name's Frank Bennett. I'm helping Father George this summer. And whatever our friend the inspector may think, I'm going to be your instructor for the next three weeks. One more thing. I meant what I said about everyone passing the test."

On the tray of the portable blackboard were a pointer and several broken pieces of chalk, some white, some colored. I picked up a white stick and wrote my first and last name on the blackboard. "We'll be getting to know each other pretty well, so just call me Frank."

Up shot the hand of Abel Feinstein. "Please," he said again. "*Mr.* Frank Bennett. You are our teacher. Rule Number two. A teacher we must call mister."

"Just Frank is fine, Mr. Feinstein."

"Mr. Frank, then," Abel Feinstein said.

"Okay," I said, opening the folder that Father George had given me. "I'm going to hand out a sheet of one hundred questions to each one of you. We'll meet twice a week for the next three weeks to go over them. They deal with basic American history, the Constitution, and the way our government works. At the end of the class, you'll be asked these same questions. To become citizens, you need to get eighty-five percent on the test. Mr. Feinstein, would you please help me pass these out?

"The questions aren't hard," I continued. "You'll have them down pat in a couple of weeks."

Frenchy scowled at his sheet. "Don't count on it," he muttered.

"Mr. Frank will teach, we will pass. Not to worry," Abel Feinstein told the class as he returned the leftover question sheets to me. "Not to worry" was Abel's trademark and refrain, and he meant it. A fixture in Kingdom Common for years, Abel was a tireless local booster. He led the Fourth of July parade around the common with a flag as big as a horse blanket, belonged to the volunteer hook-and-ladder brigade, served faithfully on the village water board and library committee, organized charity drives as if his life depended on it. In addition to tailoring he repaired shoes, hung wallpaper, refinished furniture. Some villagers called him Jack, for jack of all trades, though this name he disliked. Most Commoners called him Mr. Feinstein. "Not to worry," Mr. Feinstein repeated as he sat down.

But many of the other people in the room looked puzzled as they studied their question sheets. A few looked really scared. Probably I did myself. Still, I had to start somewhere.

"Question number one. What are the colors of the flag?"

A group of upturned blank faces.

"The colors of the flag?"

Mr. Feinstein put up his hand. He pointed apologetically at the limp flag behind the judge's bench. "Is red, white, blue?"

"Yes! Thank you, Mr. Feinstein."

"One down, ninety-nine to go," Frenchy said.

"Number two. How many stars on the flag?"

"Forty-eight?" Mr. Feinstein said after a moment.

Soon I found myself all but pleading with the class to help Abel answer the questions. Yet my impression, as I raced through the number of states in the union, the date of Independence Day, who elects the president, and how long he serves, was that most members of the class were only too glad to have Abel answer all the questions himself.

Finally it was nine-thirty. The local train that would take some of the students back to Memphremagog was due in at the station in ten minutes. Somehow, with the help of Abel Feinstein, I had managed to stumble through my first class.

Afterward Abel shook hands with me fervently. On his way out of the courtroom, his head bent over the question sheet, the tailor mumbled questions and answers fast to himself, like a man praying. I, for my part, fought off a strong impulse to collapse with my head on the defense table.

"Frank!"

It was Louvia, still seated in the last row of the courtroom. "Come back here. I have something to show you."

The fortuneteller was impatiently swinging her feet back and forth an inch or two off the floor. In the bright globe lights her rouged cheeks glowed like fire. Her dark eyes shone like a cat's.

"So," she said. "How's your love life?"

"Good God, Louvia. We've been over all that before."

"I wasn't born yesterday. You don't pull the wool over Louvia DeBanville's eyes that easily. I have my sources."

Unaccountably, the thought of the blue-eyed baker's girl crossed my mind. But I said to Louvia, "Your sources know more than I do."

With a knowing smile, she stalked out of the courtroom, down the stairs, and into the night.

❦

"How'd it go, son?"

Father George was sitting at the bird's-eye maple table in the Big House kitchen, reading over his "Short History."

"Great. I met an immigration officer who detests immigrants, was pretty much displaced by Abel Feinstein, got threatened by Frenchy LaMott, and called everything but a whoremaster by Louvia DeBanville."

"Louvia's in your class?"

"Big as life. Or, in her case, little as life."

Father George smiled. "So how do you like teaching? Apart from the minor rain delays you mentioned?"

"It's tiring."

"It is. I guess doing it off and on for fifty years must be what tired me out."

"You want a nightcap?"

"I want a lot of things," Father George said cheerfully. "Youth. A sixteen-ounce porterhouse steak. An evening fishing the Broadhead River in Quebec. I'll settle for half a glass of warm milk with a dollop of blackberry brandy stirred in."

I got myself a cold beer and sat down across from Father George at the table with the manuscript pages of the "Short History" spread out on it. Over our drinks we talked, as we had talked together in the Big House kitchen since I had learned to talk. Or, rather, Father George talked and I listened. He talked about baseball, about teaching in the one-room school in Lost Nation Hollow, about teaching and coaching at the Academy. He talked about the history of the bird's-eye table and about his own family history. Talking was one thing my father could still do without getting tired, and I never tired of listening to him.

Finally a lull settled over the conversation.

"What should I do with my class, Father G? Tonight was a disaster."

He shrugged. "You'll figure it out, son. The same way I did fifty-some years ago when I stepped into that mountain school-house and looked at twenty kids in eight different grades. Five of them couldn't read a word. It took me a while. But I figured it out. You will, too."

"Look. Mr. Frank Bennett. Time flies!"

Mr. Feinstein was smiling and holding up, of all things, an hourglass. He set it on the corner of the defense table, where the entire class could watch the sand pour through. It was a cheap red plastic affair such as one might buy at a five-and-dime store or through a mail-order novelties catalogue. Perched there on the defense table like Exhibit A, it looked absurd. I wanted to tell Abel Feinstein to put the thing away, but I didn't know how.

"Sands of time are running," Mr. Feinstein announced. "Please, Mr. Frank. Teach!"

With one eye on that infernal hourglass, I announced that we'd begin with a quick review of the first twenty questions, then tackle the next batch. I added that tonight I had decided to write the answers on the portable blackboard.

The review started with me asking the questions—Who was the first president? What is the date of Independence Day?—and writing down the answers the class members gave. Tonight I had also decided to direct questions specifically to a few other members of the class besides Mr. Feinstein, people who presumably would know the answers. Even so, they had to answer quickly to head off the indefatigable tailor.

What is the Constitution? Can the Constitution be changed? What do we call a change to the Constitution?

As I wrote the word "Amendment" on the board, Abel was on his feet again.

"Mr. Frank, no offense, please. But your writing is terrible. No one can read. Please, a favor. You ask the question, explain answer, teach. Abel will write for you."

Abel Feinstein stepped forward and plucked the chalk out of my hand. "Next question," he said.

I realized I was losing control of the class. Yet short of seizing Mr. Feinstein by the shoulders and shoving him back into his seat by main force, I didn't know how to get him to sit down. Besides, he was right. Even when I printed, my writing was almost indecipherable. But how would the class take this?

"Question twenty-two. Who wrote the Emancipation Proclamation?"

"Not to worry," announced Mr. Feinstein, and before anyone could answer, he wrote "Abraham Lincoln" on the board in tall elegant script.

The man's earnestness and good will were inexorable. To Abel, learning was joyful, teaching nothing less than rapturous.

❧

"Time flies," Abel was saying, as he pointed at the hourglass. While we watched, the last grains of sand ran through the narrow neck. Sixty minutes had elapsed in what had seemed to me like fifteen.

Abel grabbed the glass and turned it upside down to start the second hour.

"How about a five-minute smoke break?" Frenchy said.

Abel shook his head vehemently. "Please," he cried. "We must study, Mr. French. No break."

"Let's vote about the break," Louvia said. "The way people vote for their congressmen."

"You bet you ass we vote," Frenchy said. "Turn this god-damn outfit into a democracy. How many here in favor of a break?"

Two or three hands went up.

A triumphant expression appeared on Abel Feinstein's face. "How many vote straight through the break to keep on learning?" he asked.

A few more hands.

"Learners have," he said. "Next question."

❧

"So?" Father George said as I came into the kitchen. When I went immediately to the refrigerator, he grinned. "I see."

"On the positive side, nobody's dropped out," I said, opening my beer. "On the other side of the ledger, Abel Feinstein's usurped my job. I don't know what to do about it."

"Where are you with the questions?"

"Up to fifty. Ten ahead of schedule. The questions are going fine. It's Abel I'm worried about. I'm going to have a mutiny on my hands if I don't shut him up."

"Does the class understand what they're learning?"

"They seem to."

Father George shrugged. "Whatever you and Abel Feinstein are doing seems to be working. If it works, stick with it. There aren't any hard and fast rules for teaching."

"Okay. But Feinstein's shouting out the questions like the Grand Inquisitor, Frenchy argues with everything I say, and Louvia glowers at me the whole time. There may not be any rules, but this doesn't seem like the way a teacher should run a class."

"There isn't any single way a teacher should run a class. There's no formula. If they're learning the material, that's all that matters. It sounds pretty lively."

"It's like teaching a class in hell."

Father George laughed. "I think everybody's having a pretty good time but you, son. Loosen up and enjoy it."

❧

The third session, the following Monday evening, got off on exactly the wrong foot when I walked into the courtroom to discover Inspector P. W. Bull, Roy Quinn, and the Reverend Mr. Johnstone waiting for me. They'd come, Bull said, to sit in on my class.

"To see how things are going," Roy added.

So not only was I going to have to compete with Abel Feinstein, Louvia DeBanville, and Frenchy LaMott, I was going to be officially observed!

Everyone showed up on time, and again Abel stationed himself at the blackboard. Tonight Frenchy was wearing on his belt the pistol he used at the slaughterhouse to dispatch cows. Louvia had taken her rose quartz Daughter out of her reticule and was consulting with her and frowning at me.

At first the students seemed cowed by the visiting dignitaries. But well before the review session ended, a class discussion had started up. It was exactly what I'd wanted and what Father George had advised me to encourage. But not necessarily in front of P. W. Bull and the selectmen.

The discussion began about twenty minutes into the class, with dissension over a few paired questions reminiscent of the old Abbott and Costello "Who's on First?" routine. Question twenty-eight, for instance, was "What is the Fourth of July?" Question twenty-nine was "What is the Date of Independence Day?"

"Wait, Mr. Frank," Evie St. Francis said. "You just asked us that."

"It a goddamn trick question, dummy," Frenchy called out.

"Please, Mr. French," Abel said. "Rule number three. Respect one another."

"Thanks, Mr. Feinstein. Question thirty. Independence from whom?"

"From Great Britain," said Evie.

Ed Handsome Lake, an Abenaki Indian from Magog, Quebec, raised his hand. "Fact is, Frank, Great Britain never owned this continent to start out with."

"I guess that's right, Ed. Your ancestors did."

He shook his head. "Hell, no. They didn't, either."

"Please, Mr. Handsome," Mr. Feinstein said. "Don't contradict teacher. Say 'I beg to differ, Mr. Frank.'"

Paying no more attention to Abel than to a black fly during a big rise of trout, Ed stood and walked up to the front wall of the courtroom, behind the judge's bench. He pointed to the mural of the northern range of the Green Mountains, with Lake Memphremagog, stretching off between the peaks.

Ed reached up and touched Jay Peak. "How can a man or a government own a mountain? Don't matter whether those men are red or white." He looked out at the class and the visitors, then turned back to the mural and touched Lake Memphremagog. "Or a beautiful wild lake? You folks really believe any man or government can own a lake? How many of you believe that?"

"I believe that," Roy Quinn said. "What's going on here, Frank? You'd better get your class back on track, don't you think?"

"We're having a class discussion, Roy."

Frenchy laughed out loud. "You tell 'em, Bennett. You tell 'em where old bear shit in the buckwheat."

But Ed Handsome Lake just shook his head. "Tell you what, mister," Ed said, looking at Roy but jerking his thumb over his shoulder at the mural. "You venture up on any of these mountaintops on a January night when the snow's eight foot deep and the temperature's twenty below zero and the north wind's blowing up a thirty-mile-an-hour gale. Or you paddle out on this big lake in a canoe when the waves are four foot high and crawling over the side into your lap at every stroke. Then you tell me whether a man or government can own a wild mountain or a lake."

Ed nodded and went back and sat down. For me, this was the best moment of the evening.

"Question thirty-one. Name three freedoms guaranteed by the Bill of Rights."

"Freedom of speech," someone said.

"Freedom of the press," someone else said.

"Freedom of religion," Louvia said. "Including the freedom not to have any."

Reverend Johnstone turned around. "Louvia! How can you become a citizen if you don't believe in God?"

"Oh, I believe in God," Louvia said. "He's been my mortal enemy for many a long year."

Mr. Feinstein, still writing the answers on the board, called over his shoulder, "Peaceable assembly."

Then came Frenchy LaMott's great moment. Standing up, he marched down the aisle to the front of the class, pulled his slaughterhouse pistol out of his pants, and pointed it straight up in the air over his head like a drunken cowboy. "Right to bear arms!" Frenchy shouted and pulled the trigger three times. Three deafening roars filled the courtroom, followed immediately by the sharp scent of gunpowder.

"Blanks," Frenchy said, doubling over with laughter. But the selectmen were scurrying for the door, P. W. Bull was on his feet with his hand on his holster, and Abel Feinstein was bravely and ineffectually trying to get the revolver away from Frenchy.

Louvia saved the day. Jumping to her feet, she hurried forward, stayed the alarmed immigration inspector's gun hand, and cried out, not without irony, "Please, Inspector. No cruel and unusual punishments!"

*

"Only left one more class after tonight," Mr. Feinstein said exuberantly as I came into the courtroom the following Monday evening. "Tonight all questions we review, studying the Preamble to the Constitution, going over the Independence Declaration and oath of citizenship. Also, for you on the table is a letter, Mr. Frank. Maybe from a student. I don't touch."

I picked up the envelope, which had my name typed on it in capital letters. The letter inside read:

Frank:

   We the Selectmen in charge of the Kingdom County Courthouse have determined that the conduct of the members of your citizenship class is not in keeping with the purposes of the building. The members of the class are inappropriately dressed. Furthermore the class uses inappropriate language. Finally, one member of the class brought firearms into the courtroom and discharged them. Therefore we must regretfully inform you that after tonight the Kingdom Common Courthouse will no longer be available for your class.

   Sincerely,
   Roy Quinn, Chairman
   Kingdom Common Selectmen

At first I was sure the letter was a joke. But who would play a joke like this? Who in the class could type? I looked at it again. It was written on the town's official letterhead.

Other class members were beginning to appear, singly and in twos and threes. The 6:45 local had pulled in while I was reading the letter, and the contingent from Memphremagog was coming through the door.

I reached for the question sheet on the defense table, picked up the letter instead, decided that could wait, and dropped it again.

"What are the colors of...?" Mr. Feinstein said helpfully a minute later.

I took a deep breath. "What are the colors of the flag?" I said. And by degrees, as the sand ran through the hourglass, I taught.

❧

It was my old friend Louvia to whom I decided to show the eviction notice, during a short break I'd insisted the class take between the two hours. And Louvia, after consulting with her Daughter, suggested that I read the letter aloud.

I looked at the fortuneteller, her black eyes full of outrage.

"All right," I said. "I'll read it. But what this class wants to do now is graduate. There's too much at stake here to mount some kind of protest."

"There's too much at stake not to," Louvia said. "Besides, they will graduate."

"You don't know that."

Louvia looked at her rose quartz gazing ball. "I know that."

"How?"

"Because you won't let them not. For some unknown reason my Daughter has faith in you. And she's never wrong."

❧

"...all of which unfortunately boils down to the town fathers ordering us out of the courthouse," I concluded after reading the letter to the class. "I don't really see it as a big deal with only one session left after tonight. I'm sure Father George will let us meet in the social hall at the church. As for this letter, the best way to respond is to pass the test with flying colors. For everyone to become an American citizen."

Frenchy was the first to speak. "What difference it make, Bennett? Whether we citizens or not? Letter like that make one thing clear. Far as this town concerned, we trash anyway."

"That's just their opinion," Louvia said. "We know who the real trash are."

"Examination day, who and what we are we will prove," Mr. Feinstein said.

"Probably they find some way cheat us out of passing test," Frenchy said.

Mr. Feinstein sprang to his feet, the question sheet in his hand. "No, Mr. French. That they cannot do. Mr. Frank is right. Even harder now we must study. We must"—he thought, a frantic expression on his face—"we must all get every question correct. We must all get one hundred percent on the test."

The question sheet shook in his hand. But he glanced at it and all but shouted, "What is the Fourth of July?"

No hands went up. Mr. Feinstein looked at the hourglass. The sand poured through the neck in a thin steady stream. "What is the Fourth of July?"

"Independence Day," Frenchy said. "But only if you got the right last name. LaMott ain't it. Neither Feinstein."

"Last name don't matter," Abel said. But when he asked for three freedoms guaranteed by the Bill of Rights, Frenchy was on his feet again, this time furious. "Listen," he shouted. "When you dummies going to get it into you thick heads? We don't have no freedoms under Bill of Rights. On account of we don't have the right last names. Might better ask how many freedoms the town fathers yank away from us. I say we ought to go on strike!"

Once again, Abel came to the rescue. "Mr. French. Wait. How many are the number of our rights the fathers have violated?"

"Four," Frenchy said immediately. "Free speech, peaceable assembly, bear arms, no fair trial. Maybe five. Getting kicked out of public courthouse pretty goddamn close to cruel punishment."

"Then tell them so we must. We must write them a letter. From our class."

"What the hell good that do, Feinstein?"

"Always it is right to speak out. Right, Mr. Frank?"

"Right," I said. And this time I meant it from the bottom of my heart.

✦

When the last grain of sand had run through the hourglass, the chalkboard read:

Dear Selectmen:

This letter is to express our dismay and anger over being evicted from the courthouse. In our citizenship class we have studied many things. We have studied the Constitution, the Declaration of Independence written by Mr. Thomas Jefferson, and the First Amendment to the Bill of Rights. The First Amendment guarantees the freedoms you want to take away from us. It guarantees one, freedom of speech. Two, freedom to assemble peaceably. Three, freedom to bear arms. Four, the right to have a fair trial. Five, no cruel or unusual punishments. All of these rights you have violated. We have decided not to let this happen. We have decided to exercise our constitutional rights and stay in the courthouse for our last class.

—Respectfully,
Your Soon-To-Be-Fellow-Citizens

One by one, the entire class and I signed our names. Then I wheeled the chalkboard over to the bailiff's desk and faced it outward toward the courtroom, where anyone coming in would be sure to see it immediately.

"What if somebody erases?" Mr. Feinstein said.

"They'll read it first," I said. "And I don't think they'll erase it until everybody reads it. They'll be too mad."

"I don't know, Mr. Frank," Abel said as the class members left for the evening. "That our letter is not erased someone should stay here to make sure."

"It'll be read," I said. "I promise you. I'll tell Roy Quinn to come over and read it first thing in the morning. Unless they lock us out, we'll meet here again Thursday night for our last class."

But Mr. Feinstein still looked doubtful. And when I left, the tailor and jack of all trades of Kingdom Common was still sitting in the front row, staring at the blackboard as if guarding it with his life.

❦

At 9:00 the next morning, just as I was about to visit Roy Quinn, he showed up at the Big House with Sheriff White.

"Jesum Crow, Frank," the sheriff said. "What are you folks over in that night class doing? You got the whole town in an uproar."

"What are you putting those people up to, Frank?" Roy said.

"You got to get over to the courthouse right now," the sheriff said. "Before Judge Allen shows up and blows his stack. Judge A ain't going to be happy with this. You've got some explaining to do."

"I'll explain, all right," I said. But when I walked into the courthouse five minutes later, I discovered that Inspector P. W. Bull and five selectmen were already there, along with the bailiff, a couple of local lawyers, and the usual town ne'er-do-wells waiting to answer charges at that morning's court proceedings—all looking from the blackboard with the letter printed on it to Abel Feinstein, sitting in the front row with a massive padlocked logging chain fastening his right leg to the metal foot of the bench.

Apparently the tailor had been there all night; a gray stubble had appeared on his face, the only time I'd ever seen him in need of a shave. "Here sits Abel, Mr. Frank," he said apologetically. "The chain I borrowed from Mr. French LaMott."

"What's this all about, Bennett?" P. W. Bull said.

I thrust the letter from the selectmen at him just as Farlow Blake, the bailiff, said, "Please rise. The Honorable Judge Forrest Allen."

I helped Abel Feinstein to his feet. P. W. Bull stood on the other side of me, still looking at the letter and frowning. The selectmen were gathered across the aisle.

Entering from his chambers at the rear, Judge Allen barely glanced at the scene in front of him before sitting down and opening the folder containing the day's docket, which he read with attention. When he finished, he looked up again, a man well past seventy with sharp eyes and a commanding presence. Over his dime-store reading glasses he looked at Abel Feinstein and the logging chain, at the knot of town fathers, at me and Inspector P. W. Bull, and finally at the blackboard by the bailiff's desk.

"Farlow, please swing that slate around so I can read what's on it," he said.

The bailiff complied and the judge read the letter carefully. Then he looked past the blackboard and out the window down onto the common.

"That ragtag circus that set up out there on the green a month ago?" he said. "I've always wondered where they went next when they folded their tent and left here. Now I know. They've moved their scene of operations to my courtroom."

Abel Feinstein began to tremble.

"Well?" the judge said. "Perhaps someone can shed some light on this — situation."

I stood up. "Your Honor, I have here a letter that I think —"

I felt a hand, a very strong hand, grasping my arm. Beside me, Mr. Feinstein rose and took the letter.

"Abel Feinstein, tailor, shoemaker, jack of all trades, your honor. Please. I wish to speak."

"By all means," the judge said. "And Abel. I know who you are. I've done business with you for years."

Putting one foot in front of the other, dragging the slack in the chain across the polished hardwood floor, Abel hitched his way forward past the defense table to the two steps leading up to the judge's dais.

"Please," he said, holding out the letter to Farlow Blake. "Take to judge."

As Judge Allen read the letter, he began to scowl. Still scowling, he looked again at the letter on the blackboard, then back at Abel.

"Please, Your Honor," Abel said. "Meaning no disrespect. But rights we have too." He gestured toward our letter on the blackboard. "I ask you, Your Honor. On behalf of our night class. Is true? These rights we have?"

The judge looked out over the courtroom. "Gentlemen," he said, staring at the selectmen. "Mr. Abel Feinstein seems to feel that you want to deprive him and the citizenship class of their basic freedoms under the Bill of Rights. That's a fairly serious charge, wouldn't you say?"

Roy Quinn rose. "Forrest — Your Honor — we don't want to deprive anybody of anything. But these folks in the citizenship class aren't Americans yet, so they don't really have any rights. And the selectmen are in charge of renting out space in the courthouse and keeping it up. We figure we have the right to direct young Frank here to take these people elsewhere."

Outside the window, the elm trees shimmered in the heat of the summer morning. But the judge's voice was as icy as the Kingdom River in January when he said, "Is that all you have to say?"

Roy looked at the other selectmen, then nodded.

"Good," the judge said, "Because I think someone else here has something to say now. George?"

Judge Allen seemed to be looking just over my shoulder. When I whirled around, I was astonished to see my ailing adoptive father standing in the center aisle two rows back.

"Now, goddamn it, Forrest," roared the unorthodox priest and greatest scholar and third baseman in the history of Kingdom Common, "I've just got one question for our estimable town fathers. Have Frank and his class done anything to forfeit their rights under the Constitution of the Kingdom Republic?"

Father George pointed angrily at the framed Constitution behind the judge's bench. Then, with his face as red as I'd ever seen it, he shouted out, "For those of you who have scales over your eyes, it says, 'All citizens of the Kingdom Republic will enjoy complete personal freedom so long as their actions and beliefs do not encroach on the freedom of other Republic citizens.'"

"Thank you, George, you can sit down now," Judge Allen said mildly. "Your face is you-know-what."

He looked at Roy Quinn. "Well, Roy?"

Again Roy glanced around at the other selectmen. Then he repeated, lamely, "It's just that we're in charge of the courthouse, Forrest—"

"Fine," the judge said, quite pleasantly now. "And I assume that perhaps at this time I might secure your permission to say a few short words myself in your courthouse?"

"You're the judge, Forrest."

"That's so," Judge Allen said. "I'd nearly forgotten that for a moment. But yes, Roy, I am the judge. And have been the judge for—" He looked at Farlow Blake.

"Thirty-two years," the bailiff said.

"Thirty-two years. So, presuming on the strength of having been the judge for thirty-two years, I will, with your permission, make one small ruling. While you gentlemen may determine the use of your courthouse, I, thank you kindly, will determine who may use my courtroom. Therefore, it is my ruling that in accordance with the Constitution of the Kingdom Republic, Mr. Abel Feinstein and his classmates may stay here until they graduate and become full-fledged citizens."

To my astonishment, P. W. Bull gave me the thumbs-up sign. But when Judge Allen asked Abel if he felt he could unlock his chain now and go back to his tailor's shop, Abel shifted his feet so that the chain clanked, and shook his head. "Better I stay here, Your Honor. Until next Tuesday. When comes graduation."

The judge sighed and looked out the window. "Well, Abel, that's an unusual decision. But if you can make arrangements with Frank to provide for your—necessities—that's fine with me. After all, it's a free country." He looked at Roy and the flabbergasted town officials. "Isn't it, gentlemen?"

❧

That afternoon after court let out, I brought Abel a few things from his apartment over the tailor's shop. A couple of changes of clothes, a blanket, a wash basin, soap and a razor, a chamber pot. A few tins of sardines and a loaf of bread from the local grocery store, which Abel insisted on paying for. When I promised to bring him a hot supper from the hotel, he shook his head emphatically. "Please, Mr. Frank. No. I will be here only for one week. Class day after tomorrow night, examination Monday, then one night later graduation when we become citizens. Is not long."

"Abel, for God's sake, now that the judge has ruled we can hold class here, why not go home? You can trust Judge Allen."

"Of course. But is time to speak out, Mr. Frank. Abel will stay here and make sure no one erases what we have spoken. When we become citizens next week? Then I will unlock. In front of town."

"You think the whole town's going to come to the ceremony? Come on, Abel. The town doesn't give a damn. That's the point."

"Come they will. Reason number one, curiosity. Never under-estimate. Number two, guilt. Guilt is powerful. More even than curiosity. Attending ceremony is a way for town to get rid of. Come and see new citizens sworn in, make as if nothing has happened, no hard feelings. You must put when, the time and place, in the newspaper. Also would be good a few posters."

What could I say? I agreed to the newspaper notice, even to the posters.

❧

Thursday was the last class of night school. By then all the students had heard about Mr. Feinstein's chain and had arrived early to see the man who had manacled himself to the court-room bench in protest of the way they had been treated. As for Abel, a new confidence seemed to possess him. Though he'd eaten nothing all day but a sardine sandwich and an apple, he was more intense than ever. "Teach, Mr. Frank," he exhorted. "One last time we review. Monday we take and pass test. All with one hundred percent."

Tonight the class sailed through the questions, whose answers Mr. Feinstein wrote on the back side of the blackboard inscribed with the now famous letter, our declaration of independence. Everyone seemed ready. At Father George's suggestion, I had printed up new sample question sheets in the format of the exam, and the class spent the second hour writing out the answers, then correcting one another's sheets. Everyone scored well above 90 percent.

"Well, folks, you're all ready for Monday," I said at the end of the evening. "Just remember. If you come to a question on the test and don't know the answer, go right on to the next one. You can always come back later."

"Remember we will, Mr. Frank. One hundred percent!"

"Yes, Mr. Feinstein. I'm sure. The swearing-in ceremony is Tuesday evening at eight o'clock, here in the courtroom. You can invite all your friends and family."

"I have a question," Louvia said. "Will there be a valedictorian?"

"Speak English, Fortuneteller," Frenchy said. "What you talking about? Val what?"

"A graduation speaker," I said. "To sum up the class's time together in a farewell speech."

"Who gives?" Mr. Feinstein said. "You, Mr. Frank?"

"Usually a student gives it. The student who graduates first in the class. Or the class can vote for valedictorian."

"We're all going to finish first," Ed Handsome Lake said. "So let's vote. I nominate Mr. Abel Feinstein."

I gave the class paper ballots torn from my notebook. There were two votes for Louvia, one for Frenchy (his own, no doubt), and eight for Mr. Feinstein. Louvia exercised her constitutional right to abstain.

But Mr. Feinstein was mortified. "Class is a democracy, Mr. Frank. All equal. How can Abel be first?"

"You'll be giving the speech for the rest of the class," I said.

"That's right, Feinstein," Frenchy said. "You tell 'em for us. Same way you did old judge yesterday."

"Well, then. On behalf of class." Abel thought a moment, then smiled. "Between now and Tuesday plenty of time I will have to prepare, eh? But now in five minutes remaining, we finish preparing for test. Yes? Question seventy-two. Who is the current president of the United States?"

"You ought to be, Feinstein," Frenchy said. "Probably find a way to, before you through."

❧

Monday, the day of the test, was the first fall-like day of the year. Though it was only mid-August, there was a dusting of snow on top of Jay Peak. A few leaves on the village elms had turned yellow, and some of the swamp maples along the river road had started to redden.

I was concerned that not everyone would arrive on time that morning, but they all did. The class took their written test at ten, and that afternoon Bull called me at the Big House with the results. "I can't believe this, Bennett, but your students didn't miss a question. How do you account for it?"

"Mr. Abel Feinstein," I said. "And pride. And spite."

From the other end of the line, silence.

"Listen, Inspector. The class voted for Abel to say a few words at the ceremony tomorrow night. I'm assuming that's okay with you."

"I have no objection. As long as your buddy LaMott leaves his gun home."

I laughed. This was the closest to making a joke I'd heard P. W. Bull come.

"Bennett?"

"I'm still here."

"You want to do it again in the spring?"

"I appreciate that, Inspector. But I don't have any idea where I'll be in the spring. I know somebody who'd take you up on the offer in a minute, though, and do it better than I could. So do you. Abel Feinstein."

"Yeah, well," P. W. Bull said. "I'll see you tomorrow night."

❦

Over the weekend Abel Feinstein had worked frantically on his speech. By Monday afternoon he'd written several long drafts on the lined yellow tablets I'd brought him, then thrown them all away. He ate only enough to keep himself going, nibbling at a few crackers, sipping a little water. He refused to tell me what he was planning to say or to accept any assistance. "This must be Abel's story and the class's story. In ten minutes or less it must all be said. It must be from the heart, yes? And for the whole town to hear. After all, work here and live here we all have to do together."

"One possibility, Mr. Feinstein—"

"Abel will find his voice. For the class. Now I must write. Thank you for taking care of, Mr. Frank. Not to worry. I will make you a new suit, very stylish." He grinned slyly. "To get married in."

"Jesus, Abel! What the hell are you talking about?"

"Please, Mr. Frank. Rule number four. No profanity!"

❦

The cold snap held. Tuesday the sky over the mountains was a sharper blue, Canadian-looking, and on the courthouse cupola, high above the room where Abel Feinstein labored on his speech straight through the morning's hearings, Blackhawk turned his nose straight into the north, signifying more clear, cool weather to come.

That evening the crowd began to arrive around 7:30. Abel had been right. The turnout was astonishing, though whether people were coming from curiosity or guilt or genuine pleasure in seeing their fellow townspeople become citizens, I had no idea. Everyone in the village seemed to be there. Roy Quinn and Reverend Johnstone and the other selectmen, Father George, Editor Kinneson, and Judge Allen, who would administer the citizenship oath. By five of eight the courtroom was packed. To me, the room seemed entirely different from the place where I'd taught classes for the past three weeks.

The ceremony opened with a lengthy invocation from Reverend Johnstone, issuing some firm marching orders to God and the new citizens alike. Then P. W. Bull gave a short talk about the rights and responsibilities of American citizens and the crucial role in the universe played by the U.S. Immigration and Naturalization Service. He ended by announcing that for the first time in his recollection, every member of a citizenship class had scored one hundred percent on the test. The audience, including the selectmen, applauded enthusiastically.

To take the citizenship oath, the class members lined up in front of the judge's bench. When Abel hobbled forward with his chain still attached, everyone craned to see him. Frenchy wore a herringbone jacket from the 1930s, Louvia was arrayed in all her gypsy finery and held her Daughter in her left hand as she raised her right hand to take the oath.

At last I introduced Abel Feinstein, who, chain clanking, stepped up between the defense table and the prosecutor's table and turned to face the town. Outside it was dusk. Inside the courtroom was quiet. Mr. Feinstein wore a brown worsted suit, the fresh shirt I had brought him from his shop, a wide brown tie. His newly shined shoes gleamed in the overhead lights like the polished oak benches and tables. Never a man who carried an extra ounce, he looked more gaunt than ever.

"Greetings," he said, smiling, his voice a little rusty, his lips quivering slightly. "I am Abel Feinstein, tailor of Kingdom Common. But tonight Abel comes before you not as tailor. Comes instead as fellow citizen."

He looked around. "Three weeks ago began night school I and eleven others. Our teacher was Mr. Frank Bennett. Him we thank. Also we thank Judge Forrest Allen. For allowing us to stay. And Inspector P. W. Bull of U.S. Immigration."

Mr. Feinstein took a deep breath. "At first, when decided the night class who would give the valedictory, Abel did not want to speak. What says a man who has been silent for twenty years? I will try.

"Twenty years ago, in Poland, I am a student. Just started at university, sixteen years old, youngest in class. Of a tailor the only child. I am studying to be a teacher. Then comes war. My parents, Abraham and Sarah, say, 'Abel, you must leave. You must go to America. There you will study and teach. In America, everything is possible.' But by then the trains are too dangerous. So Abel begins to walk. He walks west."

Mr. Feinstein pointed out the window toward the afterglow of the sunset behind the mountains. He shook his head. "West is no good. Too many soldiers, taking people to camps. So I turn around and head the other way. East. I walk. Through forests. Through fields. Around small villages. Sometimes the people help Abel, sometimes they drive away with dogs and sticks. Two times soldiers shoot at. Winter comes. Summer again. Then winter. Always I am walking, away from. From soldiers, towns, camps, railroads. I seek empty places. Woods, fields, rivers. When for work or a little food I must ask, I say nothing of my past. I am silent like the woods. I walk.

"Goes by three years this way. I have walked hundreds of miles. Somehow I have come to Russia. There I manage to get on a boat. For Canada, for Vancouver. In Vancouver I work as a tailor, like my father. I save money and go to Montreal. Ten years ago from Montreal I come here. At last, America. I set up as tailor. Here I promise myself: Abel, teach you may never do, but walk away from a place again you also will never do. This place will be your home.

"In Kingdom Common, Abel works as tailor, shoemaker, jack of all trades. This already you know. Yet always he wishes to teach. To teach is his dream. Finally in night school, comes true. He is appointed the helper. Then he and his classmates are told they must leave. This part I make quick. I blame no one. But Abel decides he will not leave." He reached down and picked up the slack in the logging chain. He shook it. "Not if must chain himself to bench. For Abel, no more walking away from."

He dropped the chain. "What means an American? Means free speech, assemble peaceably, fair trial, no cruel punishment. Means no more walking away. Means farewell to old lives, hello to dreams, whatever that they are being."

He fumbled in his suit coat pocket and removed a small key. He bent down and unlocked the padlock fastening the chain to his ankle. He rubbed the ankle, winced, grinned, tossed the chain aside. "Hello, our neighbors," he said. "As Americans we greet you. Together as fellow citizens we will walk out with you tonight."

From the courtroom came polite clapping. The ceremony was over. People were shaking hands with the graduates. Everyone wanted to shake Mr. Feinstein's hand. Roy Quinn and Reverend Johnstone were among the first to congratulate him. I overhead Judge Allen tell Father George that it was gratifying to see that for once democracy had worked in Kingdom Common the way the founding fathers had intended it to.

I needed some air and found myself standing on the common, near the right-field foul line of the baseball diamond.

"Good job, son."

That was all Father George said. But that was enough, as he and I stood on the ball diamond and watched the villagers head home together, among them Abel Feinstein, limping across the green toward his tailor's shop, dark these past seven nights, now soon to be light again.

·7·

The Mind Reader

One of the wonders of Kingdom County in those days was a mural of the village, painted on the backdrop of the town hall stage, which changed subtly with the amount of sunlight falling on it through the tall side windows of the auditorium, so that the time of day actually seemed mirrored in the painting.

— Father George, "A Short History"

THE POSTERS APPEARED in the village at the beginning of the third week of August. About two feet wide by three feet tall, they announced in blazing red, green, yellow, and blue:

Mr. MORIARITY MENTALITY
and
His Ravishing Assistant
THE PETROGRAD PRINCESS
Will Present an Astonishing Exhibition of
MIND READING and ILLUSIONISM
on
Friday August 22nd 7:30 P.M.
at
The Kingdom Common Town Hall

Framing this bold announcement were two figures. On the left was a tall magician in an emerald top hat and a swallowtail coat with a crimson lining. The illusionist was staring over his shiny black mustache and goatee into the golden eyes of a lovely young woman wearing high-heeled silver slippers and a low-cut gold-colored gown.

Under the announcement, in smaller type, the poster said: "The direct stage descendant of the celebrated Messrs. Washington Irving Bishop and Randall Brown, and the erstwhile student and protégé of Mr. Harry Houdini, Moriarity Mentality will perform many astounding and unprecedented feats of mnemonic agility." Then, at the very bottom: "Co-sponsored by the United Church of Kingdom Common and St. Mary's, Queen of the Green Mountains. Adults $2. Children 12 and under $1."

I remembered seeing Mr. Mentality's show once or twice when I was a boy. At the time I'd been mightily impressed by the mind reader, who multiplied large numbers in his head, memorized that week's *Kingdom County Monitor* and several entire pages from the local phone book, and, in a question-and-answer exhibition at the end of the show, repeated private conversations between members of the audience he'd never met, told people where to find lost items, and even divined what they were thinking.

Father George was sure that the mind reader used a stalking horse: a confederate, somebody posing as a salesman or an out-of-state fisherman, say, who drifted around the village a few days before the performance keeping his ears open. The stalking horse didn't call attention to himself, Father George said. But all the while he was soaking up information like a human sponge. At some point before the show, this confederate passed his information along to the mind reader.

"So who's Mr. Moriarity Mentality's stalking horse?" I said.

"I've never been able to figure it out, Frank. Maybe you can. In connection with your next job. I want you to escort Mr. Mentality around town, son. Make sure he gets to the hotel and the town hall all right, look after him while he's here. If you figure out who his stalking horse is, good for you. But I'll make a prediction."

"What is it?"

"You won't," Father George said. "Have fun with Moriarity. He's due in Friday morning on the 7:14."

*

A run of bright warm days and cool mountain nights held all week, and Friday dawned clear as well. Mr. Mentality didn't arrive on either the 7:14 or the 9:28 train. By 10:30, when I walked over to the station to meet the Combination bringing the morning mail up from White River Junction, I was beginning to wonder whether he'd appear at all.

Today, besides the windowless mail car, the Combination was hauling five empty Quebec North Shore and Gaspé newsprint boxcars, two flatbeds, and one dusty Pullman coach. The train stopped just long enough to leave a single sack of mail and take on another. Only at the last moment did two passengers get off: a heavyset middle-aged woman with her hair in pink curlers and an older man in a shabby gray suit.

The travelers looked nothing at all like the dashing figures on Mr. Mentality's posters. The man's suit was rumpled and baggy and hung limply from his emaciated frame. His gray hair was uncombed, his eyes a sickly yellowish hue and sunk far back in his skull. His face was sallow, as if a long illness was now fast gaining the upper hand. He was holding a frayed carpetbag with shiny wooden handles. His shoes looked as though he'd walked to Kingdom Common in them from his last engagement. The woman in hair curlers carried a large battered suitcase, far from new.

As the train pulled away from the station, the strangers peered around. The man blinked rapidly several times, as if wondering whether they'd gotten off at the right stop.

"Mr. Mentality?" I said. "I'm Frank Bennett. Father Lecoeur from the church committee sent me over to welcome you."

The stranger took my outstretched hand and gave it a single slack shake. His fingers were as cold as icicles, and he continued to look everywhere but at me as he said, in what I thought might be a slight Texas accent, "Moriarity Mentality. This would be the Princess. Princess, Bob Bennett, from the local sponsor."

The Petrograd Princess nodded. To Mr. Mentality she said, "It's Frank. Frank Bennett."

The mind reader gazed at me with his amber-colored eyes. "Sorry, son," he said at last. "But the sad fact is, once you commence to get along in years, your memory isn't what it once was. Which, when you're a mentalist by trade, is a crying shame."

Mr. Mentality was looking at me with an unmistakable air of satisfaction. "What can you do about it?" he said.

"About—?"

"Becoming forgetful?"

The Princess rolled her eyes in my direction, an amused and indulgent expression, as if we were old friends who had affectionately relished Mr. Mentality's idiosyncrasies together over the years.

"I guess I don't know," I said.

"Neither do I, Bob. Neither do I. Lodging's this-a-way, right?"

And, handing me his carpetbag, Moriarity Mentality struck off down the street in exactly the opposite direction from the hotel.

❧

Oh, the Common took it all in in a flash. Within scant minutes of the unprepossessing arrival of the vaudevillians, the hundred-eyed village knew exactly how tawdry and vulnerable and confused the little mind reader had become in the seven or eight years since they'd seen him last. And when the Princess and I finally did get Mr. Mentality turned around, as we passed the railway platform again I distinctly heard Harlan Kittredge say to Bumper Stevens, "Pathetic old bastard, ain't he?"

"Part of my trouble," the reader was telling me as we headed back up the cracked slate sidewalk in front of the courthouse and the Academy, "is I have too long a memory for riprap."

"Riprap?"

"That's it. I mought, for instance, misremember to pull on my left stocking in the morning because I'm recollecting riprap. Numbers outen the 1942 Portland, Maine, telephone directory. Answers to multiplication sums set for me by ranchers in Tulsa. Numbers, names, dates from history, whole long columns in fine print from various hefty cyclopedias. No doubt it's a given gift, but it clutters the mind."

Mr. Mentality had forgotten to make reservations at the hotel, but Armand St. Onge had two adjoining rooms on the third floor. Then the mind reader forgot which pocket he carried his money in, necessitating a fairly lengthy search, after which he forgot my name again as he handed me a lone tarnished dime out of his black snap purse.

"Keep it," the Princess whispered. "Makes him happy."

I put the dime in my pocket for a souvenir.

Upstairs in his room, Mr. Mentality said, "Come back at, say, two o'clock, Bob. Right now I need me a little lie-down. Come two, we'll meet in the lobby and go for a walkabout."

The mind reader sat down on the bed and unlaced his dusty shoes. Then he stared at them for some seconds, as if unable to muster the energy to pull them off.

"Are you all right?" I said.

"Fetch along this week's issue of your newspaper when you come back," Mr. Mentality said. He switched on the reading lamp on the bedside table and stretched out on top of the covers with his shoes still on.

"If you want to read, I'll get you a paper right now."

"That water spot on the ceiling up above? It puts me in mind of the state of Idaho." Staring at Idaho, Mr. Mentality said, "I don't want to read. I want a little shuteye. Can't get to sleep with the light off. I'll meet you down in the lobby at two sharp. And Bob? Leave the hall door ajar on your way out. I don't sleep good in a room with the door shut."

❦

At noon the northern Vermont sky was still blue as blue, though the midday forecast predicted that a storm was on its way. An unusually early hurricane, the first of the year, was working its way up the eastern seaboard, and its tail was scheduled to swing inland and arrive in the village sometime the following day. High above the common, atop the courthouse tower, Blackhawk was beginning to shift toward the southeast; a storm was certainly possible.

At two o'clock the hotel lobby was empty. I climbed up to the third floor and tapped on the half-open door. There was no reply. Mr. Moriarity Mentality was right where I'd left him, lying fully dressed on his back on the bed. The reading light shone down on his pallid face, which, with its partly open eyes, looked like the face of a corpse waiting to be embalmed. He had kicked off one shoe, revealing a grayish big toe jutting through a hole in his sock.

"Mr. Mentality?"

Nothing. For a dreadful moment I thought the mind reader might actually have expired in his sleep. But thankfully no — his toe gave just the slightest twitch.

I reached out and tugged it gently. "Mr. Mentality. Wake up."

"Whah!" the mentalist cried out in an astonishingly powerful voice and sat bolt upright, his topaz eyes terror-stricken. "Where am I? Who are you?"

"It's Frank Bennett. You're all right, Mr. Mentality. You're in Kingdom Common. Here's your newspaper."

But Moriarity Mentality just looked at me blankly. "Why would I want a newspaper?" he said. "Let's head out, Bob."

On the walkabout, Mr. Mentality did not seem especially interested in the town and didn't ask many questions. Instead he delivered a running monologue in his querulous southwestern drawl about the indignities of aging and the slings and arrows routinely encountered by a man in his embattled profession. From the hotel we walked up Anderson Hill past Judge Allen's place and the Big House. At the crest of the hill we stood looking down at the back of the long brick shopping block and the courthouse and Academy across the common. Framed by abrupt green hills rising to darker green mountains, Kingdom Common this sunny afternoon looked as free of strife and care as a Currier and Ives lithograph.

"Peaceful, isn't it?" I said.

"Appears peaceful from here," Mr. Mentality said. "It does appear peaceful from here." He pointed past the American Heritage mill, over the steep roofs of the bright row houses of Little Quebec, at the ridge east of town. "Who lives in that shack away up yonder in them piney woods?"

"Louvia DeBanville. The village fortuneteller."

The mind reader reflected for a moment. "Can't say that I ever put a great deal of stock in fortunetellers and all such like that. Gal consults with them now and again. Let's have us a look-see at your town hall, Bob. Then we'll call it quits for the afternoon."

The town hall was a long three-story brick houseboat of a building located at the north end of the village, just past the bank and catty-corner from the hotel. The auditorium took up the entire ground floor. A rickety balcony ran around three sides of the room, and a makeshift projection booth jutted out from the upper rear wall. The wooden floor slanted sharply down toward the stage like the deck of a ship sliding down a steep wave. Some of the thin plywood seats were missing.

Mr. Mentality sat down, looked around and nodded. "Well, Bob," he said, "Carnegie Hall this is not."

I laughed and sat down beside him.

"This hall holds what? Five hundred? So if we half fill her tonight at two dollars a head for grown folks, a buck a throw for kids, say half the audience is kids, split with the church sponsors sixty-forty my way, this old trouper's share of the take would be..." He began to figure on his fingers, got mixed up and started over, derailed himself again, looked up at the ceiling of the hall in exasperation.

In the meantime I did some quick calculations. "Two hundred and twenty-five dollars?"

The mentalist nodded and said, "Wonderment is that I can still work at all. Speaking of which, ain't that painting up there one?"

"One what?"

"A wonderment."

He was pointing at the picture of the village painted on the backdrop of the stage, a mural I had seen so many times over the years that I'd come to take it for granted. Just during the five or so minutes since Mr. Mentality and I had arrived, the sun had gone behind a bank of clouds, and the scene in the mural had faded from mid- to late afternoon.

"Amazing effect, ain't it?" Mr. Mentality said. "Daylight fades, it fades. Interesting as anything you'll find in your big city museums, New York, over across, wherever. One thing we have to give these little one-horse towns, Bob."

"What's that?"

"The wonderments ain't all been leached out of them."

Mr. Mentality stood up. "Coming to the show tonight?"

"I wouldn't miss it."

"Neither would I," the mind reader said, heading up the aisle.

At the door he stopped and gave me the very slightest grin that could still be called a grin. "Unless, of course, it should slip my mind."

✢

Father George and I walked down Anderson Hill to the town hall that evening at quarter after seven. "Mr. Moriarity Mentality, Mind Reader, Tonight Only at 7:30," the announcement on the marquee said. Half of the dim string of silver lights around the border were burned out, and the others flickered as though about to expire at any moment. A disappointingly small crowd was waiting on the sidewalk in front of the hall for Roy Quinn, from the church committee, to open the ticket booth. Father George shook his head, no doubt thinking of former times, when a traveling showman would fill the hall to overflowing.

"Mind reader indeed," said a harsh voice nearby.

Father George whirled around faster than I would have thought he could still move. "Louvia!"

"None other." The fortuneteller, standing in line two places behind us, was so short that I had to peer out around a pair of twelve-year-old girls to see her. She was dressed to the nines for the show. A royal blue shawl, a former tablecloth, I thought, was draped over her shoulders, setting off the same red plush dress she'd worn for the citizenship swearing-in ceremony. Her hair, piled high on her head, was so dark it glinted. Her fingers glittered with rings, her tiny oval ears were adorned with blue glass sequins, and her homemade rouge gave off a macabre glow.

"I'm surprised you're going to let this charlatan impose on us tonight," Louvia said to Father George. "He's no more than a licensed confidence man, and you and I both know it."

The line moved a few steps closer as Roy Quinn opened the ticket booth. "Get back where you belong," Louvia snapped at the two young girls. "Do you want me to cross your eyes and give you each a wart on the end of your nose?"

They shrieked with delight—none of the children in the village were at all afraid of Louvia—but she wasn't through with Father George yet. "You know this imposter works with a confederate, and that makes him a con artist. I work alone."

"Who's his confederate?" I asked.

"Ask me something difficult. It's obviously that fat woman he lugs around with him. 'The Petrograd Princess.' Well, the Petrograd Princess was snooping all over town this afternoon, gathering information for the fraud. She even paraded up to my place and pretended to want her fortune read. I read her something she won't soon forget."

Louvia shot me a look over her gold-rimmed dress spectacles. "This so-called mentalist is nothing but a two-bit scam artist, Frank. Sit near me tonight. I'll have him reduced to tears long before the eggs and tomatoes start."

We selected three seats two rows back from the stage, with me in the middle between Father George and Louvia, who insisted on taking the aisle seat.

A moment later the kids in the balcony began clapping and stomping their feet in unison for the show to begin. Sheriff White came down the aisle and held up his hands for silence. The stomping intensified. At its crescendo, the house lights went off and the Petrograd Princess wheeled a portable blackboard out onto the stage. In the footlights she looked dowdier than ever. Her lime chiffon evening gown was tattered and smudged. One strap had been mended by a safety pin as big as a bass plug. Her slip showed in back. Her hair was a washed-out shade of blond.

"Please, boys and girls," the Princess called out. "Mr. Mentality will be with you momentarily."

When at last the clamor had subsided somewhat, the Princess announced, "And now, ladies and gentlemen, just returned from a triumphal tour of Europe, Asia, and the subcontinent, the world-renowned mentalist, Moriarity Mentality. "

Except for a black frock coat and a green felt stovepipe hat caved in on top, the illusionist looked as seedy as ever. Slight as an underfed waif, his cloak hanging from his frame like an old coat on a scarecrow, his face and eyes positively cadaverous in the footlights, he looked old, out of place, far from well, and close to desperate.

"Here at last, the flimflam man!" Louvia shouted.

"Louvia, hush, or we'll have you removed from the hall," Deacon Roy Quinn hissed from across the aisle.

"Try it, you hypocrite. I'll snatch your eyes out."

For a moment the spotlight wavered on the fortuneteller. Then it jerked to the Princess, now dragging a card table out onto the stage in front of the blackboard. The light swung back onto Mr. Mentality, who stood stock-still in its dusty beam as if consumed by stage fright. "Look at him," Louvia said loudly. "He doesn't even bother to polish his shoes. He looks more like a railroad tramp than a magician."

"I never set myself up as that much of a magic-man," Mr. Mentality said mildly. "More of a mentalist, you could say."

Hurriedly, as though to cut off further dialogue with the audience, the Princess said, "Mr. Moriarity Mentality will begin by amazing the house with rapid arithmetical calculations. He will take any three-digit multiplication problem."

"Eight hundred sixty-two times four hundred and twelve," someone sang out from the rear of the hall.

As the Princess started to write the problem on the blackboard, Mr. Mentality said, "Four hundred and fifty-five thousand, one hundred and forty-four."

For a moment, while the Princess calculated, the hall was silent. The only noise was the tapping of her chalk. Unfortunately, the answer turned out to be *three* hundred and fifty-five thousand, one hundred and forty-four.

The mind reader shrugged. "Missed her by a digit."

"You missed her by a cool hundred thousand digits," Louvia shouted.

Over the laughter, the Princess invited the audience to set Mr. Mentality another problem.

"Square root of six hundred and twenty-five," Father George said, obviously trying to help him out.

Mr. Mentality frowned. He started to say something, hesitated, then stood beside the card table with his mouth slightly open as the Princess waited by the blackboard, chalk poised to write his answer. "Sometimes it's right there on the tip of my tongue but I can't spit it out," he said.

Louvia whirled to face Roy Quinn. "Make the fraud refund our money."

As the audience began to murmur agreement, the Princess swung the portable blackboard around. Scrawled in childish block numbers on the back side was the figure 25.

"Amateur sleight of hand," Louvia shouted. "A cheap carnival trick. The woman scribbled it while we were distracted. If you're such a great mentalist, where's my Daughter? I misplaced her earlier today."

"You misplaced your daughter?" Mr. Mentality said in an incredulous voice.

"See? He doesn't have the faintest clue what I'm talking about. My gazing stone, ninny. Where's my beautiful quartz gazing stone?"

Mr. Mentality peered up the left sleeve of his coat. "In here, maybe?"

To his consternation, instead of Louvia's rose quartz crystal, he produced three live doves, pink, yellow, and blue, which promptly became entangled in the ream of multicolored scarves he'd accidentally unraveled from his sleeve at the same time.

To a gale of laughter the Princess rushed offstage with the fluttering mess. Suddenly, amidst the laughing and catcalling, a fishbowl with a pinkish object suspended in it appeared on the card table beside the flustered mind reader. The Princess, returned from the wings, reached into the bowl and pulled out Louvia's gazing stone. She approached the footlights, made a small palms-up stage gesture, and the ball appeared in Louvia's hands.

"Aiee!" Louvia screamed out. "The fraud's paramour must have stolen it from my house this afternoon. Jail the thieves."

"We purloin nothing," the Princess said in her formal theatrical voice. "Please, fortuneteller. Rejoice in the restoration of your Daughter."

"One affront follows another. Now the trollop patronizes me."

But Mr. Mentality's success with Louvia's gazing stone had earned him a reprieve from the hall's ire. Over the next several minutes he was allowed to proceed with his show, giving, upon request, the exact populations of Brisbane, Amsterdam, and Vladivostok; quoting verbatim from the classified ads in that week's *Monitor*; and accurately reciting a column of names and numbers from the thin local telephone directory. And while anyone might have told him before the show that Ben Currier's best Jersey had given birth to a six-legged monstrosity last Thursday, how did he know that on the same day, Old Lady Winifred Blake's dead grandmother had manifested herself to Winnie while she was picking snap beans and reprimanded her for leaving too many beans on the bushes?

At the Princess's urging, the people scattered through the hall moved down closer to the stage while the reader answered their questions. And for a time the show had the comfortable hominess of a neighborhood get-together with an amateur entertainer.

Now that he had hit his stride, Mr. Mentality concluded the first part of his show by confidently releasing more doves from his hat, drawing a skein of rainbow-colored sashes from the glass fishbowl, and shooting a deck of cards high out over the audience to form a spiral staircase of cards to the hall's ceiling, then pulling them neatly back into a tight pack again.

Next he announced that after a short intermission he'd perform his pièce de résistance: the solving of a murder mystery. "I'll leave the building with the gal and we'll slope down the street for a breath of fresh air. Whilst we're gone, you kind folks invent the murder. Choose a victim, a perpetrator, and a weapon. Hide the weapon here in the hall. I'll come back and have a trusted member of the audience blindfold me and take aholt of my wrist, see to it I don't go to bumping into things. If my luck holds I'll identify the victim and the dastardly killer. Then, by the Great Sam Houston, I'll uncover the murder weapon. All within fifteen minutes."

Mr. Mentality blinked out at the audience for a second or two, started to shuffle offstage, then turned back to say, "I ask only that during the solving of the murder you sit in the same seats you're in now."

He stepped off into the wings, then reappeared instantly. "Oh," he said. "If, in the allotted quarter of an hour, I should fail to identify the victim or the murderer or the weapon, I'll donate my entire share of tonight's take to the sponsoring churches."

❧

When the roaring finally died down, someone in the audience nominated Father George to moderate the selection of victim and murderer. At first he demurred, but the unorthodox priest had never been good at saying no to anyone so, shaking his head and laughing, he climbed slowly up onto the stage and asked for a volunteer victim.

Instantly Louvia was on her feet. "The whole village has wanted to murder me a dozen times over. I'll be the victim."

"That's too obvious," Roy Quinn said. "You've called so much attention to yourself already, he'd guess it in a minute. What we want is a chance at those ticket receipts."

"Fine, then I'll be the murderer," Louvia declared. "Pick a victim. Pick the least likely victim. Someone the opposite of me. Pick the most popular person in town."

"That would be Father George, hands down," Julia Hefner, the town busybody, called out. "We'd never want to kill Father G. Even you wouldn't, Louvia."

Again the hall erupted into laughter.

"I don't much feel like being murdered tonight," Father George said. "Who else has a nomination?"

But Julia was not to be deterred. "All in favor of selecting Father as the victim say aye," she said, to a huge chorus of ayes.

The choice had been made. It remained only to select a weapon.

"Sheriff White's revolver," someone yelled.

"Winnie Blake's cane."

"No, no, I've got it," Louvia said. "My Daughter."

The fortuneteller had her gazing stone out and was waving it over her head. "It's the perfect choice. We'll hide it in the sheriff's uniform jacket. I brained old Lecoeur with it. The charlatan won't ever guess."

"I can't be involved in such antics," Sheriff White said. But everyone urged him on. Finally he agreed to hide the pink quartz rock in his pocket. Even my ailing father seemed to be getting into the mood of the evening. When Julia suggested that he remain on stage to time Mr. Mentality as a means of further throwing the mind reader off the scent, Father George laughed and got out his gold pocket watch. Rarely, except in cases of a natural catastrophe, had there been such unanimity in the village.

Reverend Johnstone hurried out of the hall to fetch back Mr. Mentality; a few minutes later the house lights flickered off and on, and the mind reader and the Petrograd Princess reappeared. This time she was holding a long dark scarf. "Mr. Mentality will need someone from the audience to blindfold him and serve as his medium," she said. "He'd like to invite Frank Bennett to come up onto the stage."

I couldn't believe my ears. From my earliest school days, I'd hated to be the center of attention. But Father George, standing off to the side of Mr. Mentality with his watch in his hand, beckoned to me as though to say that if he could be part of the fun tonight, so could I. To all kinds of laughter and mock applause, I forced myself to go up and wrap the dark scarf several times around the mind reader's head.

The Princess guided Mr. Mentality's left hand to my right wrist. His grip was loose, his hand cold as a corpse's. Looking like nothing so much as a hooded condemned man, the reader stood beside me as if in a trance.

"Ladies and gentlemen," the Princess announced. "Mr. Moriarity Mentality will now solve the murder. Father Lecoeur will time him. If by some chance Mr. Mentality fails within the agreed-upon fifteen minutes to identify the victim or the killer or fails to discover the murder weapon, he will, as promised, forfeit his share of tonight's receipts. First the victim."

Father George opened his watch and grinned at me. "How did you and I get roped into this?" he whispered.

Just at that moment Mr. Mentality bore down on my wrist with the grip of a barroom arm wrestler, did an abrupt about-face, marched straight away from the audience to the rear of the stage, and cracked into the painted backdrop of the village.

"Wrong way," I whispered frantically. "Mr. Mentality. You're going the wrong way."

Paying no attention, the mind reader began to reel up and

down in front of the painted flat, pulling me along beside him. Up close, the village on the backdrop didn't resemble a village at all, just dizzying splotches of color. From the audience came peals of laughter.

Finally I got the blindfolded reader turned around and headed upstage. As we started down the steps toward the audience, Father George announced, "Fourteen minutes." Already we had blundered away sixty precious seconds.

Linked hand to wrist, Moriarity Mentality and I moved up the sloping center aisle. At first there seemed to be no method at all in his short, erratic lurches from one side of the aisle to the other. Twice he barked his shins on chair legs. As Father George ticked off the minutes, sheer panic seemed to govern Mr. Mentality's progress. At the ten-minute mark he put on a sudden burst of speed, veered sharply, and fell into the lap of Julia Hefner, dragging me off my feet after him.

Then he wasted another entire minute standing still and turning his swathed head from side to side like a baffled hunting dog trying to pick up a scent.

"Nine minutes," Father George announced.

Only then did Mr. Mentality begin to edge back down the aisle. Now creeping, now gliding, he was making straight for Louvia, stalking the fortuneteller with his head jutting out and swaying from side to side like a snake slithering toward its prey.

"Mr. Moriarity Mentality is about to reveal the murder victim," the Princess announced. But if the reader misidentified Louvia as the victim rather than the murderer, he would forfeit his entire share of the night's receipts! A breathless silence fell over the audience. Mr. Mentality reached out toward Louvia with his free hand. At the last possible moment he drew back from her as if he'd stepped on a bare electrical wire, staggered the few steps to the foot of the stage stairs, pointed his finger, and announced in a highly agitated voice, "The victim is Father George Lecoeur, the unorthodox priest of Kingdom County."

The Princess looked at Father George, who looked at her, astonished. "Time?" she asked.

"Eight minutes and twelve seconds remaining."

The Princess nodded. "Mr. Moriarity Mentality has successfully discovered the victim. He will now proceed with his investigation and identify the murderer."

Once again the mind reader began to lunge up and down the aisle like a powerful leashed animal struggling to free itself. When he bumped into me, as he did repeatedly, his body was as taut as a bent bow. His hand bore down on my wrist like a pipe wrench. His strength seemed to have doubled as he tacked up and down the aisles in a series of false starts, dead-end sprints, jolting about-faces. Twice he passed Louvia without slowing down. As much as I wanted him to succeed, I was determined not to give away the identity of the murderer.

"Seven minutes," Father George announced.

Mr. Mentality charged back up the center aisle, ascended the stairs to the balcony, staggered toward Farlow Blake, who was operating the spotlight, wheeled, and started down toward the railing. I was afraid he'd pitch over into the crowd below. Or what if he had a heart attack? Such an outcome seemed far from impossible. He was dragging me along behind him like a puppet, all but yanking me off my feet.

Once again the reader stopped in his tracks, a foot or so from the balcony rail. Below in the hall, every head was turned upward. Backlit by the spotlight, his head inclined forward, he began to sway from side to side in that serpentine rhythm. Pointing out at the crowd below, he roared, "J'accuse! The murderess, Louvia DeBanville."

This time, after a brief stunned silence, the crowd cheered loudly, no doubt partly in appreciation of the mind reader's histrionic timing. But immediately Father George called out, "Three minutes," and again the reader and I embarked on our strange linked peregrination, back down the balcony steps and up and down the aisles of the hall. Now we proceeded to rhythmic clapping from the audience. Sweat ran down the sides of the reader's face, and he seemed to give off a faint metallic scent, something like the sulfurous scent of the paper mill at Memphremagog when the wind was out of the north. I wanted desperately for him to find Louvia's rose quartz gazing stone in Sheriff White's jacket pocket, but I was more determined than ever not to divulge any clues.

"Sixty seconds," Father George said just as we stopped in front of Sheriff White at the rear of the hall. I could see the bulge in the sheriff's pocket. The mind reader began to make a high-pitched noise. His hand glided toward the sheriff's pocket. His keening intensified. The clapping and stomping reached a thunderous peak. The reader's hand stole closer.

"Thirty seconds."

Mr. Mentality jerked back his empty hand and started down the aisle, dragging me behind him in a grip of iron.

"Fifteen seconds ... ten, nine, eight..."

Now the hall was counting with Father George. "Seven, six, five..."

In front of the stage the reader whirled again to face the audience. He dropped my wrist and whipped off the blindfold.

"Three, two, one...," chanted the crowd, now on its feet.

"Behold!" croaked Mr. Mentality, shooting his right hand high above his head. "The weapon of destruction."

Sparkling in the spotlight like the Star of India was the fortuneteller's Daughter, which Mr. Mentality immediately dropped into Louvia's lap.

To the prolonged applause of the standing crowd, the exhausted reader mounted the steps of the stage, bowed once, and half collapsed into the arms of the Princess, who helped him into the wings. The show was over.

※

Father George and I found Mr. Mentality backstage, peering into the envelope that Roy Quinn had just handed to him. He shut it up, then looked in again. He frowned.

"Divvy-up agreement was sixty-forty my way or a flat one hundred dollars, whichever was the greater," Mr. Mentality said.

"Yes, but the turnout was disappointing," Roy said. "So, frankly, were parts of the show."

"Parts of the show," the mind reader repeated in an inflectionless voice.

"That's right. You'll have to admit you got off to a pretty shaky start. Even so, we're willing to pay you fifty dollars. I'd call that handsome compensation for an hour and a half's worth of work."

"Out in West Texas, where I hail from, a man's word is—"

"This isn't West Texas," said Zack Barrows, the former local prosecutor and also a deacon in the United Church. "Take it or leave it."

"See here, goddamn it," Father George said, his face getting red. "This is disgraceful. This man earned his money and, by God, I intend to see to it that he gets it."

But Mr. Mentality shook his head at Father George. He got out his round dollar watch, which had stopped at 6:23. For a while he stared at it as if he had never learned how to tell time. Then he shook it half-heartedly, the way a person might shake a pair of dice he had every good reason to believe had been loaded against him. As he did so, the hour hand fell off. And for the first time that evening, the mind reader smiled.

"Well, folks," he told the church committee, putting the watch in his pocket and handing the envelope with the fifty dollars in it back to Roy Quinn, "in this old world, a fella has to know when to fold up his hand."

"Wait a minute," Father George said, reaching for his wallet. "What about your money? I'll make up the difference myself."

"Put it toward the hall rental," Mr. Mentality said.

"The hall rental?"

"For when I come back again," Mr. Mentality said.

"You'd actually come back here?" Father George said, astonished. "When?"

"Soon," Mr. Mentality said, and headed out the stage door with the Princess.

❧

TONIGHT ONLY
Town Hall
at 7:30
Mr. Moriarity Mentality Will Reveal the
INTIMATE SECRETS OF KINGDOM COMMON
$10 per Head
No One Under Eighteen Admitted

Nobody knew how the posters had been printed up and distributed. The following morning they were simply there, on the elm trees on the common, on the hotel and courthouse doors, on the sides of the commission-sales barn and the railway station, plastered to telephone poles along the county road and Route 5. The day had dawned gray and chilly, and there was something unsettling about the garish posters under the overcast sky, though no one thought Mr. Mentality would have much of a crowd at ten dollars a head.

By seven o'clock that evening the hurricane had blown in. The wind howled through the elms, and rain was pelting against the tall windows of the town hall, which, contrary to expectations and despite the weather, was filling up fast. I noticed that some of the men buying tickets had pulled their hats down over their faces, and some of the commission-sales crowd and barbershop gang had sacks and parcels under their arms. A few reeked of liquor. A number of the women wore shawls, which they left up over their heads inside the hall, as if attending a funeral. Father George was played out from the night before and had elected to stay home tonight. Once again I sat beside Louvia.

At exactly 7:30, with no fanfare at all, Mr. Mentality walked onto the stage and approached the footlights. While the Princess wheeled out the portable blackboard, he surveyed the audience nearsightedly. Tonight the mind reader looked more wan and jaded than ever. His yellow eyes were bloodshot. His frock coat was tattered and threadbare. His shiny, bottle-green top hat sat on his head at a cockeyed slant. A mossy gray fuzz had sprouted on his jaw, and his hair stuck out from under his hat in all directions. The Princess, in a little girl's pink party dress, seemed to have gained another ten pounds overnight. Mr. Mentality's carpetbag, which she placed on the card table, had a new rent in one end, through which a flat, reptilian head flicked out and then back in again.

There was something vaguely malignant in the air of the old hall tonight. There was no bantering from the gallery, only a muttering audible between blasts of the wind. The town seemed outraged that the old showman had the sheer gall to return the night after he'd been cheated. It was as if, having mistreated him, the Common was now determined to despise him as well. A low growl spread through the packed rows of seats. There was no doubt in my mind that the audience of semidisguised villagers could easily become a mob. Sheriff White stood near the dimly lighted exit door just left of the stage. But what could he do by himself?

"Mr. Mentality will now unlock the intimate secrets of Kingdom Common," the Princess announced. "I'll circulate through the audience and take your written questions. Please ask anything you wish."

The glass fishbowl that had contained Louvia's rose quartz gazing stone the night before appeared in the Princess's hand. She descended from the stage, and as she started up the center aisle the magic bowl floated down the first row of seats and up the second. Members of the audience scribbled questions on the backs of old check stubs, sales slips, whatever they could find. It did not appear that the bowl was being passed from hand to hand; it levitated right past Louvia and me of its own accord. The Princess continued to keep pace as the bowl worked its way back through the hall. When she reached the commission-sales gang, Harlan Kittredge reached out to grab her breast. Writhing in his hand instead was a short black viper, which he flung away with a shout, whereupon the serpent turned into a green and crimson butterfly, fluttered up to Mr. Mentality, and landed on his hat, its six-inch swallowtails iridescent in the footlights.

As the Princess followed the progress of the bowl up to the balcony, Mr. Mentality released more butterflies from his carpetbag. Suddenly Hook LaMott stood up and heaved a dead cat onto the stage. But when Mr. Mentality nudged it with his toe, it sprang up, arched its back, gave a great yowl, and leaped into his arms, where it transformed itself into something inert. He gave it a puzzled look, then smiled. "I believe this belongs to you, Mr. Barrows," he said, and sailed the dark, furry object out over the audience. As all eyes followed, it landed on Zack Barrows's gleaming bald dome—the old prosecutor's hairpiece. But even as the hall filled with laughter, the Princess withdrew from the bowl, in rapid succession, Bumper Stevens's truss, Julia Hefner's voluminous girdle, and Sunday School Superintendent Lily Broom's pointed falsies—all of which the prestidigitator nonchalantly restored to their rightful owners.

From the balcony a tomato came flying, striking Mr. Mentality just above the breast pocket of his frock coat, where it instantly turned into a scarlet Floribunda rose. A lone brown egg hit the card table beside the glass bowl. Instead of splattering, it opened slowly and a yellow chick emerged, flew to the blackboard, picked up a stick of red chalk in its tiny claw, then vanished while the chalk, as if held by an invisible hand, wrote on the slate in fiery letters large enough to be read from the rear of the hall:

What Goes Around Comes Around

Another sleight-of-hand trick? The Princess was standing near the blackboard; no doubt she was manipulating the chalk, the way she had somehow caused the glass fishbowl to float through the audience.

The storm roared louder. Inside the drafty hall, the stage curtains swayed to and fro. The summery sky above the painted village at the rear of the stage turned a steely gray; the painted elms on the common seemed to stir in the wind.

The Princess selected a slip of paper from the goldfish bowl and read it out. "Topic: Child geniuses and savants. Question: Who persecuted Foster Boy Dufresne?"

Instantly a terrific booming voice that seemed to emanate from the turbulent sky on the backdrop filled the hall. "THE ENTIRE VILLAGE OF KINGDOM COMMON, SAVE ONLY A FEW."

The Princess plucked out another slip. "Who tried to help him?"

"NO ONE!" thundered the voice, which, to my horror, did not resemble that of Mr. Moriarity Mentality or of any other living being.

The footlights flickered. Outside the windows a bolt of lightning, more red than yellow, raced across the sky. At the same instant a flash of lurid red light flared above the painted village on the tableau.

Mr. Moriarity looked at the Princess, who selected another slip from the bowl and read: "Topic: Biblical scholarship. Question: What did the adult Bible study class tell Foster Boy?"

"ANSWER," boomed the terrifying voice. "NEVER TO DARKEN THEIR DOORWAY AGAIN."

"Topic," said the Princess. "An examination of the personal conduct of the members of the Bible group. Question: Where was Julia Hefner last Thursday evening when Mrs. Zachariah Barrows was calling overnight on her daughter in Burlington?"

"ANSWER: FROLICKING WITH OLD ZACK IN THE BARROWS'S FEATHERBED, NAKED AS TWO JAY-BIRDS."

A gasp of laughter went up from the audience. Zack struggled to his feet. "See here. Objection. That material is ir—"

"Hush, you old fool," Julia hissed, yanking him back down into his seat.

On stage the Petrograd Princess had already selected another slip of paper. "Question: Who embezzled five hundred and twenty-three dollars from the Church Fair fund fifteen years ago?"

"DEACON ROY QUINN," came the reply, echoing through the hall like a voice of judgment.

"Question: How does Mrs. Twyla Quinn amuse herself every third Saturday night of the month when the Deacon attends his Masonic Lodge meeting?"

"ANSWER: SHE TAKES THE 6:45 LOCAL TO MEM-PHREMAGOG AND DRESSES UP IN MEN'S CLOTH-ING WITH MRS. EVELYN SIMON."

"Question: Who traveled to Montreal last leap-year day to have an abortion?"

"SUNDAY SCHOOL SUPERINTENDENT LILY BROOM," came the reply.

"Who was the proud father?"

"THE REVEREND MR. MILES JOHNSTONE," rumbled the great voice of doom.

I was sure that the audience would begin to stampede from the hall or perhaps rise up in a body and charge the mind reader and the Princess. Astonishingly, everyone remained seated. Perhaps the questions and answers were coming so fast that we were stunned into immobility. Or perhaps we were willing to run the risk of hearing our own most shameful secrets unveiled in order to learn those of our neighbors. Or perhaps we simply couldn't bear the thought of not knowing what was said about us if we left. Whatever the reasons, we sat as though bewitched and listened greedily to Mr. Mentality's revelations, which, as the tempest outside the windows gathered force, became stranger still—more penetrating and savage and enunciated in that merciless resounding voice that now seemed to emanate from the wild stormy sky on the undulating backdrop.

"What does the Reverend Johnstone long for most?"

"HIS WIFE'S DEMISE."

"And Choirmistress Hefner?"

"TO COUPLE WITH AUCTIONEER STEVENS'S PRIZE BULL, SAMSON."

At this, the painted sky in the tableau turned into a roiling sea of flames. Simultaneously, both the Princess and Moriarity Mentality seemed to undergo a metamorphosis of their own. Before everyone's eyes the Princess became slimmer and younger. Her stained dress transformed into a shimmering evening gown. Her hair fell over her slender bare shoulders in a golden cascade. On her feet was a pair of high-heeled silver shoes. As for the mind reader, his shabby frock coat had been replaced by a brand-new cloak with a crimson satin lining. His suit fit like a glove, his frilled shirt front gleamed like fresh mountain snow. The nap of his tall green top hat shone in the spotlight. The slicked-back hair on the sides of his head glistened like black ice. And, like the imposing Svengali on his posters, he now sported a commanding dark goatee that enhanced his Mephistophelean presence.

"QUESTION," thundered the voice from the burning sky. "WHERE DID ZACK BARROWS RECEIVE HIS LAW DEGREE?"

"NOWHERE," boomed the same voice of brass. "IT'S AS FALSIFIED AS HIS HAIR."

Clutching his chest, the ancient prosecutor sank back in his seat. Outside, the wind screamed like the voices of the damned. The hall shook with its force. Fire shot across the wildly swaying backdrop. On the blackboard beside the Princess the invisible hand was writing again:

Sow the Wind and
Reap the Whirlwind

The illusionist seemed to have grown a foot taller. He looked nothing at all like the confused little man who'd gotten off the train the day before. In an amazingly loud voice he roared, "Who clapped his elderly father in the state lunatic asylum and made over ten thousand dollars from the sale of the old man's house into his own name?"

"SHERIFF MASON WHITE," replied the even louder answer from the burning sky.

From the ceiling of the hall came a chorus of guttural laughter. Etched in flames, the words

Mene Mene Tekel

manifested themselves on the blackboard.

"Eat, drink, and be merry, for tomorrow you die," translated Sal the Berry Picker from the back of the hall, to the astonishment of no one more than herself.

There was more bestial laughter, over which Sal's shrill, cracked voice shouted, "Who drove Dr. Sam Rong out of town?"

Several of the town fathers sprang to their feet. "We churchmen. God-fearing gentlemen all!"

One by one, the long-buried secrets of the village were uttered by the demonic voice, sometimes issuing from Mr. Mentality, sometimes from the fiery sky: secrets heretofore disclosed only in deathbed confessions, whispered into the darkness by couples clinging to each other late at night, or inscribed in coded diaries meant for the author's eyes alone.

Louvia jumped to her feet. "Just what I've been telling them all for years."

But the mind reader pointed at her, and a rivulet of yellow sparks sprang from his fingertip to her breast, driving her back down into her seat like a stunning electrical shock. "BE WARNED, FORTUNETELLER," intoned the encompassing voice. "THE SECRET THAT YOU AND YOUR DAUGHTER HAVE CHERISHED SO LONG WILL BE DIVULGED BEFORE THIS YEAR IS OUT. ITS REVELATION, WHETHER RUINOUS OR OTHERWISE, RESTS IN YOUR HANDS ALONE."

Some of the villagers whose transgressions had not yet been disclosed began to clamor, "Me, me. Tell mine!"

At the height of the hysteria, the footlights came on again. The card table and blackboard disappeared. So did the Princess herself, leaving only a filmy pink haze. In the place of the towering satanic figure that had dominated the stage stood the aging Moriarity Mentality in his worn suit and scuffed shoes, with that rather aggrieved and slighted bemused expression on his sunken face. Outside the windows, the tempest seemed to have let up.

"Hark," he said, cocking his head.

Over the diminished wind came the faraway moaning of the 10:06 Montreal Flyer, five miles to the south in Kingdom Landing. The mind reader shrugged and grinned his feckless small grin. He jerked his thumb over his shoulder at the backdrop. "Then again," he said, letting his voice trail off into silence like the train whistle.

Now on the tableau, instead of high summer it was late fall. The hills and mountains rising above the village were bare and gray. Instead of midafternoon on a sunny day, it was an overcast evening; the sky was as gray as the hills. The village was different, too. The elms on the common were not only leafless but dead. The green was sere and brown, as though no rain had fallen in many weeks, the baseball diamond grown up to weeds. The village houses were dingy and peeling. The rail yard was empty, no smoke rose from the tall mill stack. Not a sign of life appeared anywhere.

The countryside beyond the village was abandoned as well. Farmhouses and barns had collapsed into the overgrown fields around them. Once-cleared pastures had been overrun with wild redtop grass, barberry, juniper, and thorn apples. The painting was a study in desuetude. What it depicted was nothing less than the eradication of a way of life.

And of all the mind reader's revelations and prophecies and shifting sleights of legerdemain, this somber scene of utter emptiness hit me hardest.

The train whistle hooted again at the crossing three miles south of town. Mr. Mentality respectfully tipped his hat. Then he vanished.

❧

I hurried across the dark, wet green toward the railroad station. In the rainy darkness the wind whipped the invisible tops of the elms back and forth like something alive. Even so, I was relieved to find the trees still standing, the ball diamond still intact — that was how unsettling and real the ghost town on the backdrop had been to me. Here and there I encountered a few other townspeople, hastening home wordlessly in shared human frailty.

I arrived at the station just as the brilliant light of the Flyer came into sight. Moriarity Mentality and the Princess stood alone on the platform. The mind reader looked more tawdry than ever. One handle had fallen off his carpetbag, his shoes and trouser cuffs were sopping wet and splashed with mud, his overcoat was missing two buttons. His goatee was gone, and in the searching headlamp of the braking Flyer, he looked a hundred years old. The Petrograd Princess seemed to have regained twenty years and thirty pounds.

"Sorry to rush off without saying so long, Bob. Thought I'd best skedaddle while the skedaddling was good."

"Frank," the Princess said. "It's Frank."

The reader looked at her blankly, then mumbled something about making a tight connection in Montreal for a kiddie matinee the next day in North Bay.

"Try not to get old, Bob," he said as he ascended the steps of the Flyer's single passenger coach ahead of the Princess. "Old age is a hard pull."

From the deep shadows at the corner of the station a familiar voice hissed, "A philosopher, no less."

I spun around. "Louvia!"

But the fortuneteller was already slinking off through the night, and when I looked up at the coach, the Flyer was gathering momentum for its journey north through the mountains to Canada. Mr. Mentality and the Princess sat opposite each other at a window. At the last possible minute the mind reader looked back and raised his top hat an inch or two. Then he and the Princess passed out of sight forever.

❧

"No doubt it was all an illusion," Father George said to me a few days later.

"I suppose it was," I said. "But you weren't there for the second show. You didn't see that painting change in front of our eyes."

Father George shrugged. "Sleight of hand, mirrors. He and his helper spent half the day over at the hall getting their props ready. He's a pro, Frank. The best of the best and the last of the best. As for his revelations, I'm more certain than ever that he uses a stalking horse."

Reflecting on the matter later, I too was quite sure that the mind reader had employed a confederate, very probably someone who lived in the village. Incredible as it seemed, the likeliest candidate in my estimation was Mr. Mentality's great adversary, Louvia DeBanville. Who else but my friend the fortuneteller could have supplied him with such unsettling details about the village, true or not? Nor, I suspected, was it any coincidence that along with the few people in town who had had sense enough to stay away from the reader's second performance, Louvia herself had been spared the worst mortifications of Mr. Mentality's revelations. Surely, after her attack on him the night before, he would have gone for her throat before anyone else's had they not been in league; and even at that, he had warned her about her great secret, whatever that might be.

Still, I had no idea how even Louvia could have known some of the horrors the mind reader had disclosed. And what was her motivation? Revenge? Retribution because the village had laughed up its sleeve at her for thirty years? This seemed unlikely. Louvia had long ago cultivated a moral ascendancy over her detractors in the Common because of her very lack of hypocrisy.

Other mysteries bewildered me. What was Mr. Moriarity

Mentality's connection to Foster Boy Dufresne? Could he conceivably have been the boy's father? I wondered but had no idea. And wasn't the mind reader's terrorization of the village on the night of the hurricane cruelly out of proportion to our crime against him? What lesson could be extracted from such an act of pure vengeance? "Do unto others as you would have done to you." No one anywhere can deny the wisdom of those words. They were the entire basis of Father George's own faith, the way he had always explained the concept of faith to his parishioners and to me. But wasn't everything we had witnessed on that fateful night in the town hall in complete contradiction of the golden rule, not to mention all that we knew of the forgetful, deeply hypochondriacal, mildly irascible yet essentially kindly old magician?

And what of the transformed painting on the stage backdrop? While few of the mind reader's catastrophic prophecies came to pass, at least in exactly the way he'd forecast them, the tableau of the village never did regain its bold and vivid summer colors. Rather, it has continued to fade into a somber reminder of its original splendor, while the town itself has come to resemble that faded image of its former self. One by one, the elms on the common have succumbed to disease. The railroad and the mill have shut down. The parti-colored houses in Little Quebec have fallen into disrepair. The farms in the surrounding hills have continued to go under until today there are only a handful left. If you visit the village, look at the tableau. Yes, it's still there. Then step back outside the hall and look at the Common. Doesn't it seem as though life here has come to imitate art?

A few days after the show, I asked Louvia point-blank whether she'd had any private traffic with Mr. Mentality. She frowned and replied that she and her Daughter knew ten times as much as the reader did about the village and one hundred times more about humanity in general.

I laughed. "You didn't answer my question."

"I've told you before, Frank. You ask too many questions. Ask fewer, you'll learn more. The man was the worst kind of mountebank. He was right about the ravages of age. I say nothing more."

"Louvia, I have to know. Were you his stalking horse?"

"Louvia DeBanville says nothing."

And she never did. The mysteries surrounding what happened in our town hall on that stormy night long ago remain mysteries to this day.

❦8❦
A Short
Local History

It is worth bearing in mind, before undertaking any enterprise in Kingdom County, that much of the region was settled by a Connecticut Tory fleeing the American Revolution, who homesteaded here on the false assumption that he had reached Canada and safety. In other words, we should not forget that from the start Kingdom County was, essentially, a mistake.

—Father George, "A Short History"

THE FULL TITLE of the manuscript was "A Short History of Kingdom Common," and it was one of the wonders of the village. The book contained chapters on local lumbering and log driving, farming and hunting, woodworking and the American Heritage furniture factory, railroading, even railroad tramps. There were lively portraits of local characters and heroes, such as the log driver Noël Lord and the fabled whiskey runners Henry Coville and Quebec Bill Bonhomme, all three of whom Father George had known personally. The greatest scholar and third baseman in the history of the county had even written a long chapter on town-team baseball in northern Vermont.

If Father George felt inspired, during the course of a chapter on brook trout fishing in the Kingdom, to digress with a thousand-word treatise on the effectiveness of the red-and-yellow grasshopper fly, he did so without hesitation. The "Short History" also contained many unpredictable and delightful vignettes, such as the story of Sylvie LaPlante, who was deserted by her husband as a young bride and kept a candle burning in her window for him for thirty-five years. There were tales of authentic Kingdom Common witches, of beekeepers and wild-honey hunters, footloose spruce gum gatherers and half-crazed barn burners. There were scholarly chapters on the history of French Canadian immigrants, including Father George's own ancestors, complete with the genealogies of each of the families in Little Quebec and Irishtown. There was a chapter on the history of the international border between Kingdom County and Quebec. There were exhaustive chapters on the plants, animals, and fish of the Kingdom. What's more, every page of the "Short History" read like an entertaining story.

What I liked best about Father George himself was that for as long as I could remember, he had treated me like a man. He talked to me exactly the way he talked to Editor Kinneson or Doc Harrison or Judge Allen. For this reason we were not just acolyte and priest, athlete and coach, a young man and his mentor, a boy and his adoptive father. We were friends. And each fall we celebrated our friendship and the traditions Father George was passing on to me by going to his hunting camp, far up in Lord Hollow.

The hunting camp, which had originally been a lumber camp, was made of logs chinked with moss. Its cracked old stove had once heated the Lost Nation school, where Father George had gone to teach when he was fifteen. A dozen deer and moose antlers were nailed to the outside front wall. Inside, a six-pound mounted brook trout, a brilliantly colored male with a hooked jaw that Father George had caught in the beaver bog north of camp, hung over the door. On shelves and tables were odd rocks and tree fungi and animal skulls that he had picked up in his ramblings. The shelves were strewn with his favorite books. Thoreau's *Maine Woods*, Keats's poems, John Burroughs's nature essays, and all kinds of guidebooks to the birds and animals, fish, plants, flowers, shrubs, and trees of northern New England. Especially trees, for which Father George had an abiding love.

When I was ten years old, my adoptive father took me by canoe through the great bog beyond his camp to the remnants of the stand of bird's-eye maples that he had long ago made into furniture for the Big House. "What I like best about these trees," he told me, "is the mystery of them. Nobody knows exactly what makes the maple sap rise in the spring or the leaves turn yellow in the fall. It's like religion, son. Or falling in love. Nobody really knows why we worship God or fall in love."

At ten I was far more interested in maple trees and partridges and brook trout and deer than in falling in love. But love was a subject that Father George often came back to; the story of Sylvie LaPlante and the candle in the window was just one of several local love stories included in the "Short History."

❧

The year I turned twelve, Father George took me up to the ridge behind the hunting camp to cut down a large paper birch tree.

From its bark we made a canoe, which from then on we used to fish and explore the bog. For my thirteenth birthday, he made me a two-piece, seven-foot bamboo fly rod. With it, and the brightly colored old-fashioned trout flies that Father George tied each year by the score, I caught hundreds, perhaps thousands, of brook trout, in Lord Hollow and elsewhere in the Kingdom.

Father George had other unusual skills. Frequently he flew me into remote lakes and ponds across the border with the birch canoe lashed to the wing of his float plane. And I never tired of hearing how he had bought the Big House with money earned from smuggling whiskey into Vermont from Canada before World War I or of how once, with a large load of booze, the plane had been forced down by cloud cover on the bog north of his camp. When the ceiling lifted and he discovered there wasn't enough taxiing room to take off, he promptly disassembled the plane, moved it piecemeal by horse-drawn dray over the height of land to Lake Memphremagog, welded it back together again, and continued the whiskey run. Lately, I'd started writing a story about Father G's smuggling days, which was fast turning into the first draft of a novel about him.

Father George knew a great many things that I very much wanted to know. He knew where the last big brook trout spawning bed in Kingdom County was, up on the flow north of his hunting camp. He knew how to find a bee tree, full of wild dark honey; where the hidden springs in the bog and the big surrounding woods were; where the best spots were to wait in November for a buck to come down to the flow to drink. He showed me where, nearly two hundred years before, Robert Rogers and his fabled Rangers had passed through the bog.

At the hunting camp, Father George was the first man into the woods in the morning and the last man out at night even in his late sixties, when at last his angina began to wear him down. He could outwalk me well into my teens. When he first came back to Kingdom Common from the university, he continued to box at come-one, come-all Saturday night matches all over northern New England. On the wall of his camp were two faded photos clipped out of the *Kingdom County Monitor,* both taken after he had entered the priesthood. One showed him accepting the heavyweight boxing championship trophy at Kingdom Fair after winning six consecutive fights in one day by knockouts. In the other, taken when he was in his fifties, he was wearing his Outlaws baseball uniform and charging the mound with fists flying after being brushed back from the plate by an opposing pitcher!

Father George was appealingly human in any number of ways. While delivering a blistering sermon from his pulpit on the cardinal sins of swearing and anger, he might become so angry that he would enjoin us, at the top of his lungs, "And don't you good people forget it, goddamn it!" After his angina set in, he would station me in the first row at St. Mary's to alert him, by raising my hand to my cheek, that his face was getting red during these interesting jeremiads. This private signal was supposed to remind him to calm down lest he sustain a stroke—but in fact he rarely noticed my frantic gestures or was too worked up by then to care if he did. Though he feared little else, Father George had a dread fear of a common cold. And while he liked most animals, cats made his skin crawl, and he'd cross the street to avoid one. He never wore a clerical collar outside of church but was famously fastidious about his dress and appearance. At home he wore a white shirt and necktie even when he was working in his extensive flower beds, transplanting an old-fashioned apple tree, or just raking leaves. At the hunting camp he always looked as though he'd stepped out of an L. L. Bean catalog.

✻

Recently, since Father George's health had started to fail, I'd begun thinking seriously about postponing my matriculation at seminary, at least for a semester. But one night in mid-August, as he and I were sitting in the kitchen of the Big House visiting over a few beers, he confided something to me that, in its way, astonished me more than anything that had happened that summer.

"Frank," he said, "I want you to be the executor of my will."

I had known for years that I had been well provided for in Father George's will and that with the balance of his estate he had established a scholarship fund for graduates of the Kingdom County Academy. And, as much as I hated to contemplate Father George's death, I immediately agreed to act as his executor. But I was amazed when he went into his study off the kitchen and returned with a special bankbook for the scholarship fund, showing a balance of slightly more than $750,000, which he told me he'd amassed over the years as a result of careful investments and reinvestments of the original small fortune he'd made smuggling bootleg whiskey—not to mention interest on loans he'd made to the diocese for various charitable endeavors, which to me shed some illumination on why the monsignors he'd served under had allowed him to lead such an unorthodox life.

"Well, there's no point dwelling on this, then, son," Father George said, returning the bank book. "But knowing that you'll take care of things for me when the time comes is a relief."

"I'm sure you'll live another twenty years," I said hurriedly. He just smiled and shrugged.

Over the next couple of weeks, I was further alarmed by the rapid deterioration of Father George's health. By the last week of August he'd stopped work on his "Short History" and in his extensive flower gardens and had begun going to bed right after supper. His spirits were flagging along with his energy. Some days he didn't shave. Until that summer Father G had been known as the champion walker of Kingdom County, out tramping the roads at all hours of the day, but recently he hadn't gone outside at all. He had missed the last two Sunday masses. Clearly he would soon have to retire altogether, though the thought of that was terribly discouraging to him.

To my surprise, it was Louvia DeBanville who finally summoned me up to her place and demanded to know what long-range provisions I'd made for my adoptive father. She insisted that at the very least I should use my influence to persuade him to hire a live-in companion to stay at the Big House. She added with vehemence that neither I nor the parish was doing right to let the stubborn old fool disintegrate from ill health and old age.

The fortuneteller was also right in predicting that Father George would not put up much of a fuss when I suggested he hire a companion. "You've been working too hard on all fronts yourself lately," he said when I broached the subject. "Go ahead and advertise, son."

One evening in early September, when it was just chilly enough for a wood fire, I was working late painting the inside of the basement social hall at St. Mary's when suddenly Father George appeared at the door looking ten years younger. He'd had a haircut, was freshly shaven, wore a neat white shirt, a tie, twill slacks, and a new pair of walking shoes.

"Frank," he said, his voice stronger than it had been all summer. "You aren't going to believe what I'm about to tell you."

"I don't imagine I could," I said. "But you look like a million bucks."

"I ought to look like a million bucks. I just let out the room you got me to advertise to a very special person. Her name's Chantal and she's from Montreal. She looks like a movie star, Frank. But the surprising thing is, she's like you. She's interested, I mean really interested, in this town and its history. She sat at the kitchen table and we visited for two hours this evening. You're going to like this girl a lot, son."

I laughed. "She seems to have done wonders for you already."

"You're right. She makes me feel alive again. And there's something else I want to tell you. Chantal knows amazing things about me. Things that she wouldn't have had any way of learning. She just knows."

"Like what?"

"Like the fact that I played ball in Canada when I was in college. And flew for the RCAF. I don't know if she's some kind of seer, but she knows things."

"Come on, Father G. You don't believe in seers any more than I do."

"Well, maybe not, but I believe in this girl. You will, too. We made a deal. She's going to drive me to the doctor's and so forth, do a half hour or so a day of light housekeeping, sort of keep track of me, in exchange for the room."

"In exchange for which room?"

Father George hesitated. Then he grinned. "She wanted the cupola."

"My room."

Father George stood up and rubbed his hands over the stove. "You won't mind when you meet her. You can move into the bedroom off the kitchen. I'm telling you, son. You're really going to like this girl. She's moving in this coming Sunday."

And he was on his way out the door, walking with more spring in his step than he had in a year.

I thought for a minute, then shrugged. A beauty queen who claimed to be clairvoyant wasn't exactly what I'd had in mind when I'd advertised for a live-in companion for Father George. But if having an attractive young woman hang on his every word and drive him around in his Roadmaster made my father happy, that was fine with me.

❦

I divided Sunday afternoon between working on my whiskey-running novel and plugging away at the painting job at the social hall. Late in the afternoon, Father George came by to notify me that he'd be serving tea at the Big House in fifteen minutes.

"Tea?" I laughed. "Since when has the beer-drinking unorthodox priest of Kingdom County started serving tea? Are we talking about high tea here or low tea?"

"This is definitely high tea," Father George said. "You'll see why when you get there. Chantal wants very much for you to come right over. We'll have dinner later."

"Chantal what? You haven't told me her last name."

Father George chuckled. "Just Chantal. It's like a stage name, I guess. It turns out she's a professional astrologer."

"I'll be there in ten minutes. Maybe she can read my future in tea leaves. Like Louvia."

But the girl sitting at the bird's-eye table in the Big House kitchen when I walked in bore little resemblance to Louvia. She wore a deep blue dress, the color of the late summer sky; her long hair was dark and shiny and fell below her shoulders; and her wide-set eyes were the same blue as her dress. She was already smiling at me as I came through the door, and I was so surprised that I reached out for the edge of the table to steady myself.

It was those eyes and the smile, the unmistakable delighted irony in them, that made me positive. Chantal was the baker's girl from the patisserie in Little Quebec, who had kissed me earlier that summer.

And it seemed to me that she was fully aware of the effect her presence had on me and delighted by that, too, because she covered her mouth with her hand as if to conceal laughter.

"Chantal, I'd like you to meet Frank Bennett," Father George said.

"Hello, Frank Bennett." Chantal smiled her ironical smile. "How nice to see you again."

To Father George, who was pouring our tea, she said, "Frank Bennett and I are old friends, you might say. Isn't that so, Frank?"

I looked around the kitchen, but the bird's-eye table, the blue porcelain stove, the worn yellow linoleum I'd grown up with, all seemed unfamiliar.

"Why are you holding the table down?" she said. "It isn't going to fly away."

I looked at my hands, still gripping the edge of the table, and slowly let go.

"So. You didn't know I intended to visit Vermont for a time," Chantal said. "When I saw the ad in the newspaper, I came to see Father George immediately. Here I am. It's all settled. But what about that prying old woman you were squiring around last summer? Your ancient grandmother, the self-declared witch? Did she ever get her recipe?"

I laughed. "No. And she's no witch. She's a good friend of mine."

"I'm not surprised," Chantal said. "You should see the ancient gypsy woman he consorts with, Father. A born trouble-maker if one ever existed."

"You've got that right," Father George said. "I know all about her."

"Frank was very forward with me," Chantal said. "I think the old woman put him up to it."

Father George laughed out loud. Everything about Chantal seemed to please him. "I don't quite know what's going on here," he said. "But you two obviously don't need me around to carry on a conversation. I'm going to put three big steaks on the grill."

❧

"Chantal," I said. "What are you doing here?"

"That's for me to know and you to find out."

"You said the same thing to me in Little Quebec. How can I find out if you won't tell me?"

"I did some research before applying for this job. It has interesting possibilities. You're a very suspicious young man, Frank Bennett. You don't seem to trust anyone."

"I trust Father George. Do you know that he's sick?"

"What are you endeavoring to say? That having a young woman flitting about will be too exciting for him?"

"I'm endeavoring to say that I'd like to know why you came here."

At Chantal's suggestion we went out to the porch and sat down on the glider where, on that long-ago snowy night, Thérèse LaCourse and Peter Gambini had waited for Father George to make a decision that would change their lives forever. "You and I have important things to discuss, Frank. I haven't forgotten how you lured me out to the old stone oven. Then, before I knew what was happening, you were making unwelcome advances. I'm certain now that the old matchmaker put you up to it."

"That's not quite how I remember it. And how do you know Louvia's a matchmaker?"

"I know a great deal. Not like the aged female impostor who merely pretends to know things. Your consort."

"Let's leave Louvia out of this. Why were you smiling at me that way in the kitchen?"

"What way?"

"The way you are right now."

Chantal made her dismissive, blowing-out-a-candle noise. "That's for me to know," she said, and stood up. "I'm going to my room now. The room that used to be yours. I have a great deal of important business to take care of up there. Call me when dinner's ready."

During the next week it became clear that Father George's life had been transformed. He went for long morning walks, usually with Chantal. Often, on the way back to the Big House, he stopped in at the social hall to show her off to me. In the afternoons Chantal drove him out into the hills, to Lost Nation Hollow, Lord Hollow, Pond in the Sky. Chantal, he told me, was a marvelous driver, a wonderful listener, a spellbinding storyteller in her own right. When I returned home to the Big House in the evenings, I found the pair laughing together like old friends.

The village seemed divided in its assessment of this new development in their priest's life. Some Commoners said flatly that Father George was infatuated by the attentions of an extraordinarily attractive and intriguing young woman and that it was inappropriate for her to be staying in the Big House with us. Others felt there was nothing wrong with the situation. I had no idea what to think. Of one thing I was sure, however. I was becoming more attached to this beautiful young woman than I had ever been to a girl before. To make a peculiar situation more so, Louvia had stopped me on the street soon after Chantal arrived and accused me of deliberately establishing her at the Big House so I could see her regularly. Of course I was quick to remind the fortuneteller that finding a live-in companion for Father George had been her idea in the first place. In fact, I suspected that she was jealous of Chantal, who had set up her astrology practice in the Big House cupola and was already draining off some of Louvia's customers, as well as conducting a lively business by mail with clients as far away as California and even Alaska.

My interest in Chantal seemed to delight Father George almost as much as she herself did. One rainy evening when we all sat talking in the kitchen, with the manuscript of the "Short History" stacked up two feet high on the table next to the large green cardboard box Father George kept it in, Chantal picked up a sheet of typescript. "Page three thousand eighty-four," she said. "Your 'Short History' isn't so short after all, Father. But what does it say about your own history? Nothing. Somewhere in all these pages you should have written your story."

I grinned to see my father grilled the way Chantal usually grilled me.

"Not really, Chantal. It's meant to be the story of the village."

She thought for a moment. "Well, your story is part of the story of the village. An important part at that. You should write about how you taught school at fifteen. About your experiences in the war. You have a whole chapter on baseball in the village but nothing about you as a baseball player. I myself find the game extraordinarily tedious," she added. "But to complete the book, you must tell your own story."

"Frank can tell my story." Father George laughed. "He's always liked to write stories. I could tell you a few on him, for that matter. About his wild young days."

"Do tell me a story about Frank's wild young days," Chantal said with great delight. "Did he spirit lively young women from

230 · THE FALL OF THE YEAR

Little Quebec up to the cupola when you went off on retreat?"

Father George laughed. "How'd you know? But it began even earlier. When Frank was about thirteen, his English teacher hailed me down to the Academy and showed me a whole notebook full of Old Testament satires he'd written. I had to pretend to get mad at him."

"Pretend, hell," I said. "You threatened to give me a horsewhipping."

"In the stories God was a lot like me," Father George said. "He read Moses the riot act for swearing, and every third word He used was profane. Then when Frank was in his first year of college, he wrote a short story about Kingdom Common that made *Peyton Place* read like the Doxology."

Soon afterward, Father George went to bed, and Chantal and I went out to the porch and sat on the glider. The scent of wood fires hung in the cool air, and Chantal pulled a throw rug over our laps. She told me about her travels in Europe during breaks at the University of Montreal, where she had majored in psychology. An astrologer and psychic with a degree in psychology! She indicated that she had had many boyfriends, all of whom had proven highly unsatisfactory in one way or another. From across town in Little Quebec, a dog howled. Chantal shivered. "You never know," she said. "The werewolf that roams the forests of French Canada, the wicked loup-garou, might have slipped down over the border tonight."

I reached out and took her hand.

Without pausing a beat she said, "What is it that the old priest is trying to conceal about himself? Thousands of pages about this town and not a word about his own life."

"He isn't trying to conceal anything."

"Why didn't he get married and have half a dozen children?"

"Jesus, Chantal. What sort of question is that?"

"No doubt he's impotent, like most writers. I suppose that's why he adopted you. Another would-be scribbler, very probably with the same deficiency. Oh, yes. Don't feign surprise, Frank Bennett. I've seen you scrawling away late at night. Well, better a storyteller than a priest. Not that there's that much difference."

"Chantal, when you get up on your high horse, even Louvia couldn't hold a candle to you."

"Never mind your inamorata, she's the strangest person I've ever known. You, however, are a connoisseur of strange people. Don't try to deny it."

I laughed. "You're right."

"No doubt that's why you like me so exceedingly much."

"Is that a question? If so, it's a double-edged one."

"Why try to hide it? Don't you think I'm strange?"

"I think you're incredibly beautiful and that you have a heart of gold that you try to hide with your sharp tongue."

Chantal blew out an imaginary candle. "What nonsense. You don't know the first thing about me. Can you honestly deny that your priest-father with his encyclopedia of many thousands of pages is strange? I'm terribly worried about his health, Frank."

"So am I, though I don't see how you can call Father George strange."

"I know a great deal more about both of you than you suppose. I know, for instance, that you're dying to kiss me again."

"As a matter of fact, I am."

"Go ahead and see what happens. You must realize that I have powers."

I couldn't help laughing. "Chantal, when I'm with you I feel like I'm with about three different people."

Then I kissed her, and this time there was no doubt at all in my mind how I felt about Chantal and how she felt about me. Until, that is, she jumped up and exclaimed, "This house would be a nice place for me to live with my husband. Perhaps I'll marry Father George!"

Then she laughed and ran inside, leaving me more baffled than ever.

❦

What did I know about Chantal? That she'd been raised by a maiden aunt in Canada, had a degree from the University of Montreal, had also studied in Paris, and had traveled widely in Europe. She took her work seriously, casting horoscopes and developing elaborate astrological charts late into the night, and seemed to have all the clients she could handle. Exactly what her interest in Father George was and whether her coming to the Big House was a coincidence, I had no idea.

In the meantime, she and Father George went out to lunch together four or five times a week and continued their afternoon drives to places of local historical interest. One afternoon they drove north to Canada to get the rest of her possessions, returning with a large black tomcat, which quartered itself in the Big House as though it had lived there all its life. Father George, despite his feline phobia, actually seemed rather fond of the animal.

"Chantal wants to see you," he said when I came in the following evening. "Go right on up."

Since Chantal had moved in, the cupola resembled nothing so much as a wizard's aerie. A powerful telescope jutting out one window pointed up toward the heavens. Pasted to the walls and ceiling were all sorts of astrological symbols: individual planets, half and quarter moons, entire constellations. Along with a compass, a protractor, and a plumb bob, arcane books were strewn over the writing table—medieval treatises on astrology, biographies in French of Nostradamus, Spenser's *The Fairie Queene*, works of Jung and Freud, all kinds of guidebooks on birds, minerals, butterflies, plants, and trees, about which Chantal seemed to know all there was to know. Archaic instruments, including an astrolabe and a box compass, lay on the desk. Atlases and maps were heaped on the floor.

"What's the telescope for?" I asked. "Astrological inquiries?"

"Hardly. I like to look at the stars. There are a good many up there, you know. Someone needs to keep tabs on them."

"A present from Father George, no doubt."

"Yes. As far as he's concerned, the best is good enough for me."

"As far as some people in this town are concerned, you're bilking him out of house and home."

"Some people in this town should mind their own affairs or they'll soon wish they had. Give me your hand."

She led me over to the single bed in the middle of the room, and we sat down on a blue quilt appliquéd with more bright stars and moons.

Abruptly she turned my hand palm up. After a quick glance she dropped it, and her hand shot to her mouth. "Oh! Mal!"

"What do you mean? I don't believe in any of that nonsense."

"It's as well that you don't. You'd never have another moment of peace. Far from becoming a priest, you're destined to marry a veritable shrew. Ask me a question."

"Why did you come to Kingdom Common?"

"You'll learn in good time. Ask another."

"What's your last name?"

"Last names are a great inconvenience. I have just the one. I'm sorry that it doesn't suit you. Ask one more."

"All right. Will Father George get better?"

Chantal took my hand again, her marvelous eyes the same deep blue as the bed quilt and very serious. "Frank Bennett, you must ask the right questions. How, otherwise, can I give you the right answers?"

We sat on the edge of her bed, looking at each other.

"It's a sincere question, Chantal."

"I know. But I can't answer it. It isn't given to us to know the future."

"Then what good is it being a psychic?"

Chantal frowned, bit her lower lip. She pointed outside the east window where the moon was rising. "What do you know about the moon, Frank?"

"It's a quarter of a million miles away and exerts a gravitational pull on the oceans."

"What an odd reply. I was hoping for something more poetic. Still, it exerts a pull on people as well. When it's full like this, we astrologers don't get a minute's rest. People are after us night and day to bail them out of all kinds of difficulties. You wouldn't believe the mischief they get themselves into."

"What do you tell them? If you can't predict the future?"

Chantal shrugged. Her perfume smelled like the lavender in Father George's gardens. Sitting on the bed this close to her, far and away the most beautiful and desirable woman I'd ever known, was driving me crazy. What's more, I was certain that she knew it.

"What do you tell your clients?" I said again.

"I listen carefully. Which, frankly, you must learn to do if you have any hope of becoming either a priest or a story writer. Then I tell them to ask me the right questions. If they do, I answer them. Or, more frequently, they answer their own questions. When you ask the right question, the answer usually becomes apparent."

"All right, then. What is it that you want from Father George?"

"Everything."

"I was afraid of that."

Chantal's tomcat came into the room and jumped up on her lap.

I scratched the animal's ears and it purred loudly. "Is this customer your familiar?"

She laughed. "He's a stray barn cat I picked up on the road. I like cats, it's as simple as that. They're so comfortable with themselves, they make a room like this one comfortable. For a would-be story writer, you have a great gift for missing the obvious. Perhaps you should become a critic instead."

I laughed. "All right, let's get to the obvious. What are all these old maps for?"

"I love to look at them. Occasionally I use them to locate missing objects."

"Can you locate Foster Boy Dufresne?"

"The bottle picker?"

"How did you know he was a bottle picker?"

Chantal smiled. She set the cat down on the bed, went to the writing table, and opened an old atlas to a 1900 map of North America. She held the plumb bob over the map by its string. It described several narrowing circles, finally coming to a standstill over Niagara Falls. "Honeymoon capital of the world, Friend Frank," she said.

A chill went up my back. But I was determined to see exactly how prescient the astrologer was.

"Where did the two old Bonhomme sisters Louvia was looking for, Sylvie and Marie, go to after they disappeared from Father George's church?"

"I don't know," Chantal admitted. "No one knows such things as that. They're unfathomable, like the future." There was a new urgency in her voice this time when she said, "You *must* ask the right question."

"Should I enroll at St. Paul's or not? It starts at the end of this month."

She laughed, and now her perfume smelled like lilacs. "Ah! That, Frank Bennett, is the right question. But only you can answer it."

Before I could reply, she spun away like a dancer and ran downstairs to see how Father George was doing, leaving me standing in the cupola with the cat rubbing against my legs, and far more questions than answers.

❦

Two mornings after my conversation with Chantal in the cupola, Father George awoke with numbness in his left side. Chantal and I rushed him to the hospital in Memphremagog, where the doctors couldn't find anything more than his chronic angina; they speculated that he might have sustained a small stroke in the night and sent him home under Doc Harrison's care, with strict orders to rest.

At the end of that week Chantal had to return to Canada for a day to see a client, and Father George asked me to take him up to his hunting camp. While he napped, with his throw rug over his knees, I drove out along the county road beside the river, up into Lord Hollow, past one abandoned farm after another, and over Anderson Mountain to Lord's Pond. There we launched the birch canoe and paddled across to the camp.

After checking inside to make sure everything was in order, Father George and I sat out on the porch steps in the afternoon sunshine. "Tell me a story," I said. "About your whiskey-running days."

Father George laughed. "You've always loved stories, haven't you, son. Hearing them, reading them, writing them. Maybe that's what you ought to do for a living. Write."

"Chantal told me the same thing."

Father George smiled. "When it comes to your profession, son, you were looking for a fast ball down the middle. Something straightforward. But God tripped you up and threw you a curve on the outside corner instead."

"So what should I do?"

"What I taught you to do a long time ago. Go with the pitch."

"What if someone had told you to consider writing full-time instead of becoming a priest?"

"I was me and you're you," Father George said. "After I was shot down and the Benedictines found me, I felt that I personally owed God a life. A vocation. And I did. God, not a sense of duty, will guide you toward the life you should live. If you want to write stories, that's what you ought to do. That's what God wants you to do. Jesus, Frank. You're getting me worked up. Is my face red?"

"Yes, as a matter of fact, it is. You've got to calm down, Father G."

"I am calm," he said. Then he began to laugh. "I'm *never* calm, and you know it. Now listen to me, son. I'm a local historian and a priest, not a fiction writer. But there's a novel in Kingdom County if you can find it. Hell, there are ten novels. Someday you'll write them, if you go with the pitch God threw you. I'm going down to the pond to see if the trout are rising."

When I joined Father George on the shore of the pond a minute later, however, he was no longer thinking about my vocation or his.

"Son," he said, "I want you to do something for me when I'm gone. I want you to bring Chantal up here. Show her the brook trout spawning bed on the flow in the bog. Show her the big trout there. And take her to the top of Anderson Mountain and show her the view of the Kingdom and Canada. And there's one more thing I want you to do. After I'm gone, I want you to make sure she's all right. To — take care of her."

"That won't be for a long time, Father George. And believe me, Chantal can take care of herself. She'll no doubt be long gone from these parts herself by then. You and I'll fish the spawning bed together this fall. All you'll have to do is sit in the canoe."

Father George thought for a minute. "You and I will go there once more together. But it's important that you come here with Chantal. First with me. Then with her. Then you'll understand."

"Understand what?"

"You'll see. I want to ask you a question, son. Just one. I want you to think about it and then answer it carefully. Will you do that?"

"Of course."

"I want to know your opinion about an important matter," Father George said. "Does Chantal really care for me? Or does she just feel sorry for a sick old man? What do you think?"

I didn't hesitate for a second. "She cares for you, Father. When she and I are alone together, you're nearly all she talks about. She thinks the world of you."

He nodded. "That's good, son. That's really good. Now let's go home, son. It's getting toward suppertime."

On the way back to the Common, past the grown-over farms, past the fallen-in sawmills on the river, over the disused railroad tracks from Pond in the Sky, Father George stayed awake, but he was quiet. Just as we reached the outskirts of the village, he turned to look at me, his eyes astonishingly blue and clear, and said again, quietly and with absolute certainty, "You'll understand."

Then he closed his eyes, and when we passed the ball diamond a moment later and I looked over at him, I knew instantly that my father had left his beloved village for the last time.

❧

"You'll understand." So Father George had assured me. But I did not. I did not understand at all.

When I rushed him to Doc Harrison's and Doc ran out of his office and took his wrist and almost immediately shook his head, I did not understand, or want to understand, the finality of Father George's death. I simply couldn't accept the fact that a man so full of life could leave it so suddenly.

I thought that I might continue to feel Father George's presence on the baseball diamond, in the Big House, in the woods around the village. But I didn't. I had no sense at all of his lingering spirit. Rather, for days after his death the Common seemed unfamiliar. To me, and, I think, to everyone in Kingdom Common, it was as if, so far from leaving some part of himself behind, Father George, in dying, had taken the essence of the village with him. Chantal, for her part, was as grief-stricken as I was. She kept to her room and could not even talk about Father George's death.

My impression of finality was enhanced by the astonishing instructions in his will that there be no religious service of any kind, no calling hours, and no stone in the cemetery. His ashes were to be placed in a bird's-eye maple box he'd made fifty years before; as executor of his will, I was then to bury them. The will did not indicate where.

What I understood least of all was the call I received the day after Father George died, from the office of his longtime personal attorney in Montpelier. Mr. Moulton's secretary informed me that the major provision of Father George's will had been invalidated by the legal transfer of nearly all his property, including the $750,000 trust fund for the Academy, two days before his death.

"Hold it," I said. "What is this you're telling me? That trust fund was intended for the kids' educations."

"There isn't any trust fund, Mr. Bennett," the secretary said. "But you don't need to worry about your own inheritance. That part of the will remains unchanged — ten thousand dollars. Also Father Lecoeur's hunting camp and his car, books, guns, and fly rods."

"I'm not worried about my inheritance, damn it. I'm worried about the trust fund. And what about his house and property?"

"That, too. All his assets, except what was earmarked for you, were transferred, in Mr. Moulton's presence, last Thursday. It was perfectly legal."

"Who was it transferred to?"

"You'll have to discuss that with Mr. Moulton."

"Then you put Mr. Moulton on the phone right this second."

"I'm sorry, Mr. Bennett. He's out of the office."

Moulton called me that afternoon and verified that the trust fund for the Academy students, along with the Big House, had all been transferred; that the transaction had indeed taken place in his presence, with two local persons as witnesses; and that Father George had been in full command of his faculties and these were clearly his wishes.

"Full command of his faculties? For God's sake, Mr. Moulton. He'd had a stroke just days before. I ought to know. I spent the afternoon of the day he died with him."

"Did he seem impaired to you that afternoon?"

I hesitated. "He seemed tired."

"There's a vast difference between being tired and being mentally impaired, Mr. Bennett. Check with your doctor, Doctor Harrison."

"He wasn't the attending physician at the hospital when Father George had his stroke."

"No. But he was one of the witnesses to the property transfer."

"Just tell me," I said angrily. "Who or what did Father George transfer his property to?"

There was a slight pause on the other end of the line. Then Moulton said in a dry, uninterested voice, "To a young woman named Chantal, from Quebec."

* * *

"I know this must come as a shock to you, Frank," Doc Harrison was saying. "But it's true that George did make the transfer, and as nearly as I could tell, professionally and from a personal viewpoint, he was entirely competent to do so. Not that it wasn't a damned fool decision, of course. I'm very sorry about it."

"You know what that money was intended for, Doc. How could you let him do it?"

Doc loaded his pipe. He looked out his office window at the ball diamond on the common, at the yellowing elms. "I argued with him for the better part of two hours. Right up to the point where I commenced to fear that he might have another stroke. But he wasn't to be swayed. What's more, he told me that you'd understand."

"He told me the same thing two days later, without saying what I was supposed to understand. And I don't. Not at all."

"Neither do I, Frank. Not completely, at least. But at the risk of telling you how to conduct your business, I'm going to give you a small piece of advice: Put yourself in George Lecoeur's place and try to understand. Because I'm afraid that's about all we can do now."

"Goddamn it, Doc! I'm going right up to the Big House this minute to have a long talk with our beautiful young heiress. That's one thing I can do."

"Fine. But see Louvia DeBanville first."

"What the hell has Louvia got to do with all this?"

"I don't know for sure," Doc said. "But she was the other witness to the property transfer."

❧

"Understand?" Louvia handed me a cup of catnip tea so strong I could only pretend to sip it. "You young folks think you have to understand everything. Very little that people do is in any way understandable."

"There has to be a reason for all this."

"Is there a reason for love? Of course not. It's a mystery. Old Lecoeur, fool that he was, loved her. There's your explanation."

"Louvia, listen to me. Just before he died, Father George hinted to me that something was up. He asked me to trust him, and he said I'd understand when the time came. Okay. I understand he loved Chantal. But he loved the Academy, too, and the kids. He could have left Chantal something substantial, and for years to come every single graduate of the Academy would still have had a free college education. Ask your Daughter. Assuming that somehow, somewhere, Father George is aware of all this, what does he want?"

Louvia glanced at her rose quartz gazing stone on the table, then looked away.

"What does she say?"

"Nothing. Nobody knows what the dead want. Not even my Daughter."

"Then ask her what I should do about all this."

Once again, Louvia cut her eyes sideways at the rose quartz. After a long minute she looked back at me. "Talk to the astrologer," she said.

❦

It was evening now. The sun had dropped behind Anderson Hill half an hour earlier, though the uppermost section of the courthouse tower still sparkled pink in its last rays. It seemed like years ago that I had stood with my heart in my mouth and watched Molly Murphy scale that tower, eons since the foggy morning that past May when I'd come back to the village to go to work for Father George.

As I hurried up the crushed gravel drive to the Big House, I spotted Chantal on the porch glider. She wore a dark shawl over her shoulders, and her long hair was as black as the shawl. She sat very straight, watching me approach.

I sat down on the glider beside her. When she turned to look at me, I could see that she had been crying again; at exactly that moment all of my anger vanished.

For a while we sat silently, side by side, looking down at the village.

Chantal brushed her eyes. I took her hand in both of mine. "I'm sorry for your loss, Chantal."

"You know very little about my loss. But I'm sorry for your loss, too, Frank Bennett. Still. We can't hold hands, you know. Not now that we're enemies."

"We aren't enemies."

"Certainly we are. I know very well that you're going to drag me into court over Father George's money."

"I want to make a proposal to you, not drag you into court. First I have to ask you a question. Were you in love with George Lecoeur?"

"In love with Father George?" Chantal seemed startled. "No. No, of course not. I loved him very much, and he felt the same about me. But not *in* love."

"Did you know he was giving everything to you?"

"Certainly. As indeed he should have. But what is your proposal, Frank Bennett?"

"Chantal, I know Father George wanted you to have the money. But for years, for decades, he also wanted the school kids to have scholarships."

"That was before he met me."

"Yes. And it can't work both ways. Unless—"

"Unless what?"

"Unless you'd be willing to give half of the trust fund back to the school."

"What trust fund?"

"You know what trust fund. We're talking about three quarters of a million dollars that was supposed to go to the Academy. Half of that would still be a fortune. You could live in Paris for the next ten years."

"There isn't any trust fund to divide, Frank. I've put it where it can't be touched. In a place Father George would have approved of, moreover. As for Paris, I have no interest in living in Paris, though it's a fine place to visit. I intend to live here, in this handsome big house."

"Chantal, Father George thought you were in love with him."

"He did not. He understood the situation perfectly. I have a lover of my own, if you must know. A scholar, and passionate, too. A young man I met just this past year."

I was stunned. "You met someone in Paris?"

"In Quebec, if it's any of your concern."

"And that's why you wouldn't get involved with me? It wasn't Father George."

"No, it wasn't Father George. I told you. I loved him much the way you did, as a son or daughter loves a father. How dare you oppose what your father wished? Do you have any doubt that he wished me to have my legacy?"

"No. I just don't understand why."

"Because he trusted me. You must learn that lesson."

"And you think this experience is going to teach me that? First you take all Father G's money, and his house in the bargain. Then you tell me you love someone you met in Quebec. That's supposed to teach me trust?"

"Absolutely."

"How?"

"You'll understand. No doubt by then it'll be too late. Still, we should part friends."

Chantal stood up.

"You're leaving?"

"For a time. But we will part friends? Despite these unfortunate misunderstandings?"

I stood and looked at Chantal in the twilight.

"Chantal—"

"What is it now?"

She made no move to leave, and once more I thought her eyes seemed amused. "I don't think this is funny," I said.

"You will," Chantal said, and she threw her arms around me and kissed me hard on the mouth, then fled into the house.

✦

The next several days passed, as even bad days do, but that was easily the worst week of my life. Tears would come to my eyes before I knew it, early in the morning when I stood on the red iron bridge over the pool in the Kingdom River where Father George had taught me how to catch my first trout on a fly, when I cut across the ball diamond where I'd played so many games for him, in the evening when I picked up a copy of *The Country of the Pointed Firs* he'd given me or sat alone out on the porch of the Big House, where Chantal might soon be living with her Canadian lover. I had no idea what to do about my plans to enter St. Paul's, which I'd already deferred until January. In view of the arrangements Father George had made, or rather not made, for a funeral, it now seemed quite clear that his own faith had been in this world rather than another. I supposed that I shouldn't be surprised. He had always been intensely a man of this world. But this reflection did little to reinforce my own faith. I was leaning toward putting off my decision for at least a year.

On the last Monday of September I met with the Academy trustees to inform them officially that the scholarship money was gone. The front doors of the school were unlocked, and as I walked into the foyer and saw the trophies in the glass display case, the ancient bronzed baseball gloves and the basketball state championship cups, the sense of desolation hit me again. It was all I could do to make myself go through with the meeting when I read the plaque over the trophy case: "Upon His Retirement from Coaching, Presented to Father George Lecoeur. Priest, Teacher, Coach, Friend."

The three trustees, Roy Quinn, Ben Currier, and Julia Hefner, were sitting at a table near a window overlooking the common when I walked into the library. To my astonishment, they were talking about the cool fall weather, as if this were all that was on their minds.

"Well, folks, let's get started," Roy said. "We'll hold off on the minutes of last month's meeting until we take care of Frank's little business. At this point that's just a formality, I guess."

I looked at the trustees. "I'm sorry Father George's lawyer, Attorney Moulton, couldn't come tonight," I said. "And I'm sorrier still to be the bearer of bad news."

Ben Currier tapped the folder in front of him on the table. "If what's in here is bad news, Frank, I'd like to hear some good news. The Academy just fell into $750,000 for its scholarship fund. We can send every graduate on to the college of their choice for the foreseeable future."

I shook my head. "I wish that were the case, Ben."

The trustees looked at me uncomprehendingly. Ben Currier opened his folder and frowned at its contents.

"I don't understand," Roy said.

"It's no secret," I said, "that a few weeks before Father George died, a young woman, an astrologer named Chantal, from Canada, moved into the Big House. This is a copy of a legal document, executed a few days before Father George's death. In it he transferred most of his estate, including the scholarship fund, to Chantal."

I handed a copy of the property transferral to Roy.

"We know all about the astrologer, Frank," Julia Hefner said. "And we don't approve of Father G letting her move in with him any more than you do. But we assumed from the check that you and she were co-executors of the estate."

"What check?"

Ben Currier turned his file around and shoved it across the table. Inside was a copy of Father George's will. Clipped to the top was a green invoice for a cashier's check dated three days before, from the First Farmers' and Lumberers' Bank of Kingdom Common. It was made out to the Scholarship Fund of the Kingdom Common Academy for the amount of $750,000; and it had been signed by Chantal, in ink as deep blue as her eyes.

❧

My head was still whirling twenty minutes later when I left the Academy. Ben had explained that he had been present at the bank, along with the bank president, when Chantal signed the legacy over to the Academy. He assumed that it was just a formality and had no idea that Father George had actually given his entire estate to Chantal to do with as she wished. But the money was safely in the scholarship fund, which was the trustees' main concern, and though Roy Quinn expressed surprise that I hadn't inherited the Big House, and Julia Hefner was still clucking her tongue over Father George's liaison with Chantal, their business with me and mine with them was concluded.

It was twilight now. Hardly aware of my surroundings, I cut through the cemetery on my way back to the Big House. To my surprise, I discovered Louvia sitting on the iron bench near Peter Gambini's great sculpture of the two life-size embracing figures. She had a blue handkerchief in her hands, and her shoulders were shaking. At first I thought she was cold, but then I realized that she was crying. I'd almost managed to slip by unnoticed when she looked up and caught a glimpse of me.

Instantly she said in her sharp voice, "Why are you spying on me, Frank? Come here this minute."

Louvia dabbed at her eyes with the handkerchief. "Smoke from burning leaves. I've always been extremely sensitive to it."

I sat down beside the old gypsy and took her hand. "I think you miss Father George," I said. "Me too. The Common doesn't seem like the Common without him."

"I suppose it seems like Times Square."

"Come on, Louvia. I know you miss him. Who's left for you to fight with?"

"Miss him? He was a fountain of overbearing authority. Look. Someone put fresh flowers on the memorial here, if you can believe it. No doubt the astrologer did that before she skipped town. In memory of the old fool she seduced."

On the stone bed beside the lovers lay a small bouquet of wild New England asters.

"Father George was no fool, Louvia, and Chantal didn't seduce him. She has a fiancé of her own. From Quebec. Besides, those flowers are fresh. Somebody put them there today."

"A fiancé. Worse yet. Then she was only trifling with the old man's affections."

"It wasn't that way at all."

"Go ahead and defend her. If there's a fiancé in it, she used you just as badly, and you and I both know it. Don't tell me she didn't string you along. You should go instantly to Montreal and avenge yourself on the lover. A true man would exact bloody retribution. Maybe we can manage it from here. My Daughter and I could give you a certain elixir—"

"Louvia, for God's sake, if Chantal has a lover, she has a lover. That's that."

"Why not win her back?"

"You just said she used me."

"You don't think she's worth it?"

"I know she's worth it. But she was never mine to win back. As for Father George, I don't even know where to bury his ashes."

"You can throw them in the river for all I care. But here, the old man gave me this. At the famous transfer of property ceremony. It's for you. I meant to drop it off sooner, but I got to reading it myself. Why I can't imagine—it's full of the most extravagant lies."

Louvia reached under the bench and pulled out the big green cardboard box containing Father George's "Short History." There was no letter with the manuscript, and I was disappointed by that, but it appeared to be intact. I opened it up and read the first sentence. Then I read on until it was too dark to read any longer.

Sitting alone on the stone bench by the monument—Louvia had slipped away at some point—I could hear Father George's voice in my head, hear its slightly speculative, wry resonance. And at that moment, whatever else I still did not understand about the events of the past summer, I realized that long after the passing of the hill farms and the big woods and Kingdom Common as we had known it, these stories would remain: a golden legacy, to me and to the village, from Father George.

❦9❦

The Fortuneteller's Daughter

In the village in those years there dwelt an old, old woman, who had kept a candle burning in her window for over fifty years, to light home the husband who'd deserted her long ago as a young bride. Her husband never reappeared, but she was as much in love with him on the day she died as on her wedding day.

—Father George, "A Short History"

•

THE FOLLOWING DAY I moved out of the Big House and into a room at the Common Hotel. Though I'd begun working on my whiskey-smuggling novel again that morning, I had little idea where I would go or what I'd do next.

That evening Louvia sent word that she wanted to see me immediately. I suspended my unpacking and cut across the green and down the dirt lane between the houses of Little Quebec, wondering what the old fortuneteller wanted now.

The bright pastel homes of the French Canadian mill workers glowed in the twilight. Splashes of scarlet and gold had appeared overnight on the side of Little Quebec Mountain, set off handsomely by the dark green of the spruces and firs. The river between the mill and the railroad tracks was up and slightly cloudy from a recent rain. A year ago on an evening like this one, Father George and I might have gone trout fishing.

As usual after a fall rain, some big German brown trout had run up Little Quebec Brook to feed, and Louvia was out netting them in the pool behind her herb garden. A quilt depicting a French Canadian maple sugaring scene was airing on a sagging clothesline strung between her house and a leaning hemlock tree. The fortuneteller was dressed in a wide-sleeved green blouse and a voluminous crimson skirt. A few yellow birch and maple leaves drifted down the brook. Late-blooming phlox, hot pink and deep red, and a dozen multicolored daylilies, all recently transplanted, grew near Louvia's house.

"My God, Louvia. You've poached these flowers from the Big House," I said.

"Nonsense. I'm perpetuating an old man's dream," Louvia said. "Once that so-called astrologer ensconces herself for good up there, I've no doubt she'll post the property. She'll probably charge us to walk by and admire the flowers. Look here if you want to talk about poaching." From the tall grass beside the brook she picked up a brown trout at least twenty-five inches long, with a bright yellow belly and red spots the size of dimes. "I intend to invite this gentleman to supper tonight. As the guest of honor and main course."

Louvia reset her net, then filleted the big trout expertly on a homemade fish table covered with scales. "What do you want, Frank? I'm very busy, as you can plainly see."

"You're the one who called me up here," I said. "But the fact is, I've been meaning to drop by anyway. I want you to help me find Chantal."

"Aiee! The usurper. However. Now that you're here you'd better come inside. I can't eat this entire fish by myself."

On Louvia's listing porch several dozen butternuts lay drying, still jacketed in their green husks. A cat with one emerald eye and one gold eye surveyed me from the windowsill. As we went up the steps, Louvia had to shoo away her hissing geese to keep them from pecking my shins.

A smoky wood fire was burning in the kitchen range. Louvia opened up the damper and set a large skillet on the stove. She motioned toward a rickety kitchen chair missing part of its back. "So. How old are you, Frank? Twenty, twenty-one?"

"You know how old I am."

It was true. In order to stay one-up on her neighbors, Louvia made it her business to know the exact age of everyone in the Common. Yet tonight she herself seemed much older. Her dark face was tired and sad, and I suspected that she was lonely. Ordinarily I'd have been glad to hear her stories of traveling with the gypsies, working the carnival circuit. But now that I'd confided in Louvia, I was determined to persuade her to help me find Chantal.

From her reticule, Louvia produced her rose quartz Daughter and set it on the table in front of me, atop a stack of paperback romance novels. I looked into the stone's milky pink interior and saw exactly what I was certain Louvia saw there: nothing. Yet something told me that the fortuneteller could help me locate Chantal if she wanted to.

"What does your Daughter have to say tonight, Louvia?"

"She wants to know what you're going to do now that you've ruled out St. Paul's."

"I don't know that I've entirely ruled out St. Paul's. But I've begun writing a story, if she must know. About Father George's early days."

"Another storyteller! Well, well. I suppose that's harmless enough. My Daughter wants to know when you're going to get married."

"Maybe never. For the time being, I'm going to do whatever I have to do to find Chantal."

"Chantal again." Louvia leered at me, her wax bridgework gleaming. "Listen, Frank. I know you miss the astrologer. I suspect that she broke your heart. Well, I'm sorry. I understand something about that from personal experience, as you'll recall. In your case, it's mainly yourself you have to blame, but my Daughter and I intend to help you anyway. We can shake you out of this holding pattern if you'll stop repining for two minutes and listen to us."

"I am listening to you. You're the fortuneteller."

"Who's talking about fortunetelling?" Louvia said, looking right at me. "I'm offering you my services as a matchmaker. Now that you've given up those foolish notions about joining the priesthood, it's time we found you a wife."

❦

"Stop laughing and pay attention," she continued. "My Daughter recommends a girl from Sherbrooke, over the line in Quebec. Brown hair, striking brown eyes with gold flecks in them, an extraordinarily provocative combination. A real head for business besides; she keeps the books for her father's sawmill. She'll make you rich beyond your wildest dreams."

"Louvia, I don't need to have anybody else arrange my dates for me."

"This isn't a date, it's a match. The woman my Daughter and I have in mind is a year or two older than you and deeply experienced in the ways of the world, if you take my meaning."

"What's her name?" I said despite myself.

"Marie. Marie Thibodeau. She plays in a little band with her family. She's a lively one. You'll fall in love with her at first sight."

I groaned. "I don't think so."

"With a wife like her you'll be a millionaire by forty. Also, she's musically gifted, she writes her own songs. I'll arrange for her to be expecting you at seven day after tomorrow evening. She'll take you to a barn dance, then who knows what afterward. You'll never regret it. Marie already has six thousand dollars in a savings bank. My Daughter assures me that this will be your making."

"I'm glad she thinks so."

"Don't mock my Daughter. Do you want to end up like me? Alone and bitter? This Chantal woman has been bad for you, Frank. Look at you, a shadow of your former self. If you don't believe me, you can ask my Daughter."

"I'm not going to ask a stone anything."

"I'll have her materialize for a moment."

"That I'd like to see."

Louvia gestured toward a transparent blue shower curtain that hung across the doorway to her bedroom off the kitchen. It was rumored that as part of her fortunetelling, she sometimes sat behind this sheet of plastic, which she called the Eternity

Curtain, and pretended to be a spirit. Through the Eternity Curtain tonight I saw a candle burning on her bedside table. Suspended in the air above it was an old-fashioned speaking trumpet.

"Isn't the astrologer in league with the forces of darkness to destroy this unsuspecting young man?" Louvia said to the floating trumpet.

"Yes, mother," replied the instrument in a faraway hollow voice. Then the candle flickered out and the trumpet vanished. It was all I could do not to laugh.

Louvia looked into her gazing stone again, as though nothing out of the ordinary had happened. "My Daughter and I might have made a miscalculation with Marie," she conceded. "I know a widower, a pinch-fisted old farmer, who'd love to get his hooks into that six thousand dollars. What we actually intended was for you to see a girl from Pond in the Sky. This one will knock your socks off."

I glanced toward the Eternity Curtain, but the bedroom beyond was dark. "I'm glad to know it. Tell your Daughter thanks, but no thanks. Ask her where Chantal is."

"The new girl will be waiting for you tomorrow night at six-thirty by the old Pond in the Sky roundhouse," Louvia said. "Her name's Gloryanne. She's not a day over sixteen. You can take her to the drive-in in Memphremagog. For that matter, if you give her the money for the drive-in, she'll let you take her to the local gravel pit for the evening instead. She reminds me of myself when I was her age. A real hot ticket."

"Just because I've put off my plans to enter St. Paul's this fall doesn't mean I want to spend the next year in jail," I said. "Thank Gloryanne anyway for me."

Behind the blue shower curtain the candle flame appeared again, and the illuminated speaking trumpet gave a wild laugh. Now it appeared to be drifting around the room at about eye level.

Louvia jerked her thumb at the laughing trumpet. "My Daughter thinks you should let Gloryanne have her way with you. Sex is a sovereign antidote for despair, you know. If nothing else, it would take your mind off the astrologer usurper."

"Chantal's not a usurper and I'm not in a state of despair!"

"She'd only drive you to an early grave, Frank. Look what she did to the old priest."

"I honestly think she loved Father G as much as I did. Louvia, listen to me for once. I know you're trying to help. I don't want you to suppose I don't appreciate it. But these matches you want to arrange. They aren't going to help me find Chantal."

From behind the curtain the spirit-trumpet blared out a great blast of derisive laughter.

"What's the matter?" Louvia said to me, pretending not to have heard anything.

"That idiotic trumpet. How do you get it to do that?"

"Do what?"

"Who's back there, Louvia? With the megaphone? Give me a straight answer for once."

"No one," Louvia said. "No one alive at least. It's the spirit of a dead relative. I had a little daughter once, now long lost to me. Still, it's a comfort to know that even on the other side infants do grow up."

"I didn't know you ever had any children."

"This is between you and me and the lamppost. The child was the result of an indiscretion. A one-night stand. I could never acknowledge her. It was probably fortunate for all involved that she died. As you can see, she visits me now and then from behind the curtain. I must say that she's grown up to be a beautiful young woman and smart as a whip, if rather on the willful side. No doubt she gets that from me."

"I'd like to meet her face to face."

"That's impossible. However. She's taken an interest in your welfare. She has someone very special in mind for you, if you want the truth. She was just testing you with the others. Now we'll get down to business."

I held up my hand. "No, thanks. Not unless her name's Chantal."

Behind the curtain, the candle went out. "There," Louvia said. "You've hurt my Daughter's feelings. I hope you're satisfied. We won't see her again now for who knows how long. See how sensitive she is. And what a temper."

"Where's she gone?"

"Back across. But I can handle matters from here. The new girl is a prize, Frank. I guarantee it on my reputation as a matchmaker. She's a teacher up at Memphremagog and shares any number of interests with you — fishing, book reading, sports of all kinds. A true companion. She's cute as a button into the bargain. You'll adore her."

"Thanks just the same. I can find my own companion to adore."

"She has a boat and wants to take you fishing on Lake Memphremagog."

"I'm a stream fisherman."

"Sunday afternoon at two. She'll be at the boat ramp."

"So you've got it all arranged?"

"I'm just trying to give you a choice, Frank. I still don't see why you don't whisk Gloryanne up to the gravel pit, you'd feel like a million dollars afterward. But not to worry. The new one teaches biology. She can show you a thing or two along those lines herself."

"For God's sake, Louvia, I'm still considering the priesthood."

"Then why are you in such a white heat to find the astrologer?"

"To apologize to her. For supposing she was after Father George's money."

"Never mind all that. You never heard me apologize to anyone, did you?"

"No one could accuse you of that."

"Or the old priest you claim to have thought so much of. I don't recall that he was much given to apologies."

"He used to apologize to God quite frequently. For getting mad at Him."

"How foolish!"

For a minute neither of us spoke. Then Louvia nodded toward the Eternity Curtain. "I might be able to coax my Daughter into making a quick reappearance. Just for a moment. If you once laid eyes on her, you'd trust her. She's a famous beauty over there, you know."

Louvia thought for a moment, then sighed. "You have no idea how hard raising a deceased daughter has been. When she was a teenager, she wouldn't listen to a thing I said. We fought like cats and dogs, and for nights on end she'd stay away. Now she appreciates my advice. She's actually thinking about getting married herself—oh, yes, Frank, they marry over there, too. I talked to her for a solid hour the other night about certain intimate matters. I can assure you, her husband will go to sleep on his wedding night a happy man. If he goes to sleep at all."

I laughed. "I'd like to talk with this Daughter of yours myself. Maybe she'd go out with me."

Once again the candle flame flared on in Louvia's bedroom and the levitating trumpet boomed out, "Marry the schoolteacher and be done with it!"

This time I couldn't help it—I laughed out loud.

"I could talk to the teacher for you, the way I talked to my Daughter," Louvia offered. "She's a long-legged young number. With the right instruction, she'd give you a run for your money."

"I want to know right now, Louvia. Who's behind that curtain?"

"Nobody," Louvia said, and the candle went out.

❧

Louvia picked up an open copy of *Gone with the Wind* that was lying face down on the table and pretended to read for a while. Outside, it was completely dark.

"How many times have you read that book?" I said. "One hundred?"

"Probably more. I'll tell you what, Frank. I'll give you an address in Montreal. You can go there this weekend with fifty dollars in your pocket. I'll even float you a loan. That will put all thoughts of the priesthood out of your head forever. You'll thank me for the rest of your life."

"Louvia, I don't intend to spend the weekend in a Montreal whorehouse. I thought you were going to introduce me to your Daughter."

Louvia thought for a minute, then shook her head. "That's not a good idea. My Daughter thinks people are basically well-meaning, if you can believe a child of mine capable of such a delusion. At heart she's hopelessly romantic. A dangerous outlook at best."

"I think she and I might hit it off."

"Don't be absurd. You need a much more down-to-earth woman. Besides, you can't go to bed with a specter, you know."

"Go to bed with her! I just want to meet her."

Louvia thought for a full minute. Then she sighed again. "All right, Frank. But don't say I didn't warn you."

"I'll take my chances. Especially if she can help me get Chantal back."

"I'm going to leave now, and I have no idea whether my Daughter will show up or not. But if she does, don't, whatever you do, mention Chantal. The girl is murderously jealous. I'll leave the lantern on for you. Good luck!"

❧

Across the river in the village someone was burning leaves in the darkness. Crickets sang in the dooryard. Beyond Louvia's shack, the brook murmured. I had no idea what to expect next. Did Louvia have a confederate? Or was the fortuneteller even now creeping around to the back of the house to sneak in and light the candle herself? If so, who had lighted it before? I knew very well that the Eternity Curtain and the talking deceased Daughter were part of the elaborate gypsy confidence game Louvia had played on credulous villagers for years. Even so, I was excited.

I sat at the table, waiting. From the crossing in the village the Northland hooted. The door was ajar, and on the warm breeze the scent of burning leaves was very strong.

"Turn out the lantern," said a sad-sounding voice from the bedroom.

I turned out the lantern on the table and sat in the darkness, my heart beating fast. After some minutes I thought I heard a noise outside—no doubt Louvia slipping into the house with the speaking trumpet. But when I looked toward the bedroom, the candle on the bedside table was lit, and the spirit-trumpet sat on the table beside it.

"Where's ma mère?" said the same sad and distant voice.

"She left for a while."

"I told her not to do that. But no. Ever the matchmaker."

"I thought I was going to meet you in person," I said. "How can I do that with the curtain between us? This is like talking to a shadow."

"I am a shadow," the trumpet-apparition said in its sorrowful voice. "This is a poor thing that my mother has done, Frank. Arranging this meeting between us. You and I both know that nothing can ever come of it."

"Pull back the curtain and we'll see for ourselves."

"That I can't do."

"How about if I pull it back?"

"Then you'll never lay eyes on me. Tell me. What is it you truly want? Perhaps I can help, as long as you don't ask for the impossible."

"You know what I want. And who. You and your mother both know."

The supposed apparition was silent for a time. Then it said, "What did the old man tell you to do? What did the priest say to you at his camp?"

After a pause to collect my thoughts, I said, "He said we'd go to the woods one last time. And then I'd understand."

"Then why haven't you gone there? Isn't that the least you could do, for him if not for yourself?"

"He said we'd go together. Then he died."

"So?"

"So I can't go with him."

The candle started to flicker. This time I was ready. I jumped up and yanked back the curtain. The room was empty, but on the table next to the extinguished candle, where the spirit-trumpet had been, was the bird's-eye maple box containing Father George's ashes.

❦

"Do as she said and take them to the woods."

I whirled around. Louvia was sitting at the kitchen table by the lantern, now lighted again.

"Where in the woods?"

She shrugged. "You'll figure it out," she said. "Take your old friend to the woods one last time, Frank. There you'll find the answers to all the questions that can be answered."

"What about Chantal?"

"How many times do I have to tell you? No one can predict the future. It's the second greatest mystery there is."

"What's the first?"

"Love," said the fortuneteller. "Love is the greatest mystery and most powerful force in the universe."

❧ 10 ❧
The Fall of the Year

In the fall of the year Lord's Bog is the most beautiful place
on the face of the earth, so beautiful that if you go there
alone, it hurts your heart not to have someone to share it
with. To me, it has always been emblematic of the funda-
mental goodness of Creation.

—Father George, "A Short History"

TWO DAYS LATER I rose in the dark before dawn, took my
fly rod and shotgun, and went alone to the woods at the head of
Lord Hollow. I took Father George's "Short History" and, in
the bird's-eye maple box, his ashes.

In the pale early light I drove Father George's Buick out the
county road, thinking of the changes the Kingdom was under-
going, beginning with the death of my adoptive father and mentor. But everywhere I looked, things were changing. Along the
river east of the village, where within my memory there had
been a score of working farms, fewer than half a dozen barn
lights now glimmered through the mist. A few chalets, second
homes of city people, were already going up here and there in
the woods. A ski resort was being planned for Jay Peak. A four-
lane superhighway connecting Boston and Montreal was
snaking its way up from southern Vermont, though it hadn't yet
reached Kingdom County.

I passed the junction with Lost Nation Road, leading up to the long-abandoned Lecoeur family homestead and one-room school. I continued east along the Upper Kingdom River, steaming in the cold dawn, sending its crystalline breath twenty feet high to delineate its course through the coloring hills. I turned north up Lord Hollow, as Father George and I had done together so many times: in the spring when the hardwoods were just leafing out and the hills were a pale gold; in high leafy summer; and in foliage time, the fall of the year, days like today, when our mountains seemed to glow with an inner incandescence. The road grew steeper and narrower as I entered the woods.

The lumbering trace I drove over was covered with fallen leaves. The woods smelled ripe with decaying leaves and were bright with the red leaves of soft maples, toast-colored beech leaves, golden-yellow birch, purple ash, and the polished yellow leaves of sugar maples, the trees Father George had loved best of all. Red squirrels and blue jays announced the Buick's approach. On another morning I would have stopped at one of the log landings along the trace and hunted partridges for an hour or two in the beech groves. Not today.

As the trace became steeper, bright hardwoods began to give way to firs and spruces. I was climbing Anderson Mountain, with the rushing flume of the Upper Kingdom River on my right and Lord Mountain looming high just across the gorge. At the crest of the ridge, I left the car and hiked the short distance up above the treeline to the summit, taking the bird's-eye box with me. I did not hurry. At the summit I drank from a spring of cold water that emerged from beneath the huge glacial boulder known as Jesus Saves and looked out over the woods and farms of the county to the courthouse tower and church spire of the Common, visible miles away across the multicolored hills.

Beyond the village to the west the Green Mountains ran due north and south in a long jagged line. To the east, the peaks of the northern White Mountains gleamed white with September snow. This would be a good place to be buried, I thought. A good place for a man who had spent his life writing about the Kingdom, spread out before me now in all its autumn colors, with the great boulder for a monument and the spring that ran year-round for music. From here, too, you could look far to the north into Canada, from whence had come Father George's beloved whiskey runners and smugglers, the French Canadian immigrants he'd written about so passionately, not to mention his own ancestors and Chantal herself. Near the spring at the base of the boulder was a fissure, a deep natural sepulcher where the ashes would remain undisturbed. But I decided to wait before making a final decision. I returned to the Roadmaster and drove down the back side of Anderson Mountain to the pond at the head of the notch.

Father George's birch-bark canoe, our canoe, sat upside down in the cedars near the water, untouched since he and I had made our last trip to the camp. As I canoed across the pond through the mist, the sun lifted over the shoulder of Lord Mountain. A few bright red leaves floated on the surface of the water. At the head of the pond, where the current came in over a gravel bar, a trout rose. "See if you can interest him in your grasshopper fly, son," Father George would have said. But Father George was gone, like the water that passed out of the pond into the river below. And today I had more important things on my mind than fishing. Perhaps the camp would be the right place to leave the ashes.

The cabin sat in a stand of second-growth pines just above the east shore, its chinked logs weathered the same dark color as the pond water. I had half expected to see smoke curling out of the chimney, to smell the sweet sharp scent of wood smoke. Its absence reminded me of the absence of Father George.

For some minutes I sat on the camp steps, watching the mist on the pond disperse in the climbing sun. Then I opened up the green cardboard box containing the "Short History" and riffled through the pages to Chapter VII, on Lord's Bog. In the morning sunlight I read again how the bog and the notch below it had been carved out 10,000 years ago by the glacier, how the bog was feared by the Indians, how it was discovered in 1759 by Rogers' Rangers, and, ultimately, how it was preserved from obliteration by the horse-logger Noël Lord, who had used the big flood of 1927 to take out the Kingdom Power Dam being built at the foot of the flume. That, too, I thought, would be a good story to write someday.

When I finished the chapter, I went inside and started a small fire in the stove to take the chill off the air. Then I sat down at the table and continued to read. It occurred to me, reading on into the warming morning, that Father George, with his love of the seasons and trees, the birds and animals, the past and its stories, had been both a romantic and, when he wrote about the dangers of the mill and the dark old tragedies of the Common, a realist as well. His "Short History" told the stories of the village simply and beautifully. Yet as Chantal had pointed out, it revealed little of its teller. His decision to leave his estate in the hands of a girl he'd known less than a month suggested that he was far more romantic than I had supposed. What in Father George's life would lead anyone to suspect that a pretty girl with a beguiling personality could steal his heart so completely that he would give all he had for her love?

Later in the morning, after reading nearly two hundred pages, I came to the wonderful chapter on the secret stand of bird's-eye maples north of the bog. Once more I read how Father George had felled the giant maple and built the furniture for the Big House. The chapter ended: "What I liked best about the furniture when it was completed was that it retained the mysteries of the maple trees themselves."

As I finished the chapter I realized that my hand was resting on the bird's-eye box. And at that moment I knew what I would do with Father George's ashes.

🍁

I walked down the slope to the birch canoe, put the maple box under the stern seat, and started paddling north. The sky was clouding over; it was becoming colder, cold enough for my hunting jacket. By the time I was a mile into the flow, a region of black water and naked dead cedar trees, with the tall Canadian mountains dark in the distance, it was misting. The only noise was the drip of water off my cedar paddle each time I brought it forward. Ahead, within easy range, two black ducks rose off the flow, but I did not reach for my shotgun.

Two miles above the camp I came to the first big beaver dam, audible well before I reached it from the steady murmur of water running out around its edges. I stepped onto the neatly woven sticks of the dam, pulled the canoe up behind me, slid it into the dark flat water above, and continued.

Three more miles and two dams farther north, the flow narrowed into a dark corridor between fir and spruce trees, reflected upside down in the water when the sun abruptly came back out. I looked for a rainbow. There wasn't one, but the entire woods exhaled a rosy golden mist. The fir trees smelled fresh and green, more like spring than fall. On a rise to my right was a stand of double-topped pines. Schoolmarm pines, Father George had called them, in reference to bowlegged spinster schoolteachers.

This was the heart of the bog. Here there were no roads, no logging traces, no sign that any human being had ever passed this way before. No one, not even Father George, knew for sure whether this region was in the United States or Canada.

Above the fourth dam I pulled the canoe out onto the bank. I put the maple box into my jacket pocket, left my shotgun and fly rod in the bottom of the canoe, and walked through the woods over a hidden moose path Father George had shown me long ago. The rosy mist continued to rise all around me. Beside the trail, white caribou moss grew thick on the floor of the forest.

I came out of the woods by the spawning pool, where the bog changed character once again. Here, where the stream emerged from the Canadian mountains, it was a meandering channel of icy pools and riffles, with the clean sand-and-gravel bottom that brook trout seek out to lay their eggs on. Near the bank was a lone, topless, partly hollow maple tree, four feet in diameter and less than twenty feet tall. Decades earlier the tree had been struck by lightning. Yet year after year its few remaining branches still put out leaves, which had turned an umber-orange for fall, a bright lone flag in the bog, shimmering in the watery sunlight. This was the last remaining tree from Father George's secret stand of bird's-eye maples. Below the bank on which the shattered tree grew ran the long pool where the biggest brook trout in the Kingdom still came to spawn.

I set the maple box down on the caribou moss and lay on the bank to look into the spawning pool. There they were, a dozen or so big squaretails, finning slowly on the streambed below. Their backs were as green as the firs on the opposite bank. One of the trout turned, flashing pink. I flicked a bit of stiff white caribou moss into the pool. Instantly two males, each about twenty inches long, swirled at it. Downriver a young moose, as dark as the forest he emerged from, waded into the flow and crossed to the other side. Overhead an osprey cried out.

Of all the places Father George had loved—the long-abandoned farm where he'd grown up, the caved-in schoolhouse where he'd first taught, the Academy, the ball diamond on the Common, the Big House, the Church of St. Mary's—the spawning pool deep in the bog had been his favorite.

I stood up, spooking the trout, and slid the bird's-eye box into the deep hollow of the maple tree. I covered it with a few handfuls of fresh leaves and moss. Here, in what was left of the great maple, what was left of George Lecoeur would be safe. And when this last tree toppled and crumbled, the ashes and it together would join the forest floor and the bog and Father George's Kingdom.

On my way back to the camp it turned colder. Storm clouds over the Canadian mountains were descending fast toward the bog, settling in to conceal Anderson and Lord Mountains. Within an hour the season seemed to have jumped ahead two months to November.

It began to snow. At first the flakes were big and sparse, then smaller and thicker. In the snow I felt utterly alone, yet at peace in the knowledge that, whatever lay ahead, at last I understood what Father George had wanted me to do.

But I did not understand yet, not entirely. Not until I pulled the canoe onto the shore of the pond and went up to the camp through the snow to get the "Short History" and saw the candlelight in the window and found the girl sitting at the table, waiting for me.

She was wearing a dark blue dress that matched her eyes, which were dark blue in the twilight, and white fur boots and a white fur jacket. I took her in my arms and kissed her, and when we stepped apart, it was snowing much harder outside and almost full dark.

"I thought you were in Canada," I said.

Chantal laughed. "How strange. Why would I go back to Canada when all I want is right here? Here I have my house, my work, my lover and husband-to-be, whom I met in Quebec — Little Quebec!" And she kissed me again, more passionately than before.

"Look," Chantal said. "I even have the old woman's foolish stone. She made a great to-do about giving it to me as an early wedding present."

She set Louvia's rose quartz on the table beside the "History" and said, "You were wrong about other things as well, Frank

Bennett, besides my comings and goings. For instance, you thought Father George left no word behind for you. But of course he did. He told me I'd understand when to give this to you. Now's the time."

She handed me a manila envelope with the words "Final Chapter" printed across the front. Inside, in Father George's clear handwriting, was a sheaf of pages on lined yellow tablet paper. I sat down at the camp table to read them by candlelight while Chantal sat across the table and watched me intently.

The final chapter of the "Short History" was an account of Father George's own life, beginning with his boyhood on the farm in Lost Nation, his teaching at the one-room school, and his trek to the Common, at seventeen, with his shoes in a paper bag, to attend the Academy. With increasing excitement, I read the stories that Father George had told me over the course of my life but had never recorded in his "History." Even now there was a certain reticence in the memoir, reflected by his use of the second person to refer to himself in the account of working his way through college, joining the RCAF, living with the Benedictines in France, and coming home to Vermont to take orders. Then, near the end of the chapter, a story that I had never heard before:

To return, now, to those halcyon days of teaching and bootlegging and playing ball before the war. In those summers, the young people of the area sometimes gathered to dance to big-name bands in a pavilion on the common. There they would dance on into the night under colored lanterns strung above the pavilion like Christmas lights, and on the warm summer nights it was easy to fall in love. Those were summer romances, as evanescent as the brief northern summer; and at the end of the summer, when the fall of the year brought the colors and the pavilion on the village green closed and looked all the more desolate by contrast with your summer memories of it, and the Canadian winds and snowfalls came, the romances died like the summer but were not forgotten. For sometimes, years later, when you were walking back up the hill to the house you never, as a boy, could have imagined you would live in, you would think back to those years and wonder what your life might have been like if the war had never come and you'd married a girl you met at the pavilion in your youth.

Now suppose that late one night, many years later, the woman from that long-ago summer appeared at your hunting camp when you were there alone, and it seemed that night as if the war had never been and the intervening years themselves had been mere days, and that from this encounter came the single greatest regret of your life: a regret you could never acknowledge to anyone because of your position in the village and your vocation. But suppose that in the end, miraculously, the secret regret of your life became the greatest joy you had ever known, so much so that illness and impending death meant nothing

Here the last chapter stopped abruptly in the middle of the page. I looked up at Chantal. I was still not entirely sure what I had read.

"So," she said. "Do you understand at last? What he said you would understand?"

My heart racing, I looked across the table at Chantal, her eyes shining in the candlelight.

"And yet," she said, laughing, "you seemed only too ready to abandon me for the imaginary daughter behind the old woman's curtain. How fickle! I can see I'll have to watch you like a hawk, Frank Bennett. When it became apparent to me that you were beginning to show romantic interest in the apparition, it made me a little jealous. I decided I had to take measures."

"I'm glad you did."

She made that sibilant sound I loved, as I loved everything about her. "No doubt you'd rather be courting the make-believe apparition," Chantal said. "Do you think she'd give you a kiss like the ones I just granted you? Or anything more besides?"

I laughed and stood up and went around the table and kissed her again. "Marry me," I said.

"Ask the Fortuneteller's Daughter."

I glanced at Louvia's gazing stone beside Father George's "Short History" on the table. "I'm not going to propose to a rock."

"Listen to me," Chantal said. "Ask the Fortuneteller's Daughter."

Her eyes were as full of laughter and delighted irony now as they had been on the day I had first met her, in the patisserie in Little Quebec. And finally, as I looked deep into those laughing eyes, as blue and wise as Father George's, I recognized her beyond any doubt, and I understood at last all that I had been meant to understand.

The Fortuneteller's Daughter kissed me again, tenderly and fiercely and triumphantly, and said, "Yes, Frank Bennett. I have my father's eyes. And my mother's tongue."

"And your own heart."

"No," she said. "That belongs to you. Now and forever."

Then I blew out the candle and took Chantal by the hand and led her outside into the snow to return to our home in the Common and see what sort of match the fortuneteller and the unorthodox priest, the greatest scholar and third baseman in the history of Kingdom County, had made for us.